SEASONS OF HEAVEN

Nico Augusto

Based on a true story...

SEASONS OF HEAVEN

Title: Seasons of Heaven

SEASONS OF HEAVEN

Cover by Austin Farris
Preface by Grant Wilson

SEASONS OF HEAVEN

Life to death...

When I was fifteen, ghosts were just for Halloween and campfire stories. Then I had an experience that forever changed my perception of reality. All of a sudden, stories from my childhood that were supposed to just be stories, were now a real possibility.

This is the beauty of the paranormal. We, as humankind are always looking for a new frontier to explore, and there it was lying right in front of me. We have explored the world and the depths of the oceans. We know a lot about it, but we don't know everything. We spend immeasurable time and resources to learn about space, and to dive deeper into our own chemical make up. But for some reason, science ignores the call of the afterlife. It's the next frontier. We are inexplicably drawn to it. Why then, is it so stigmatized that we don't dare study it seriously?

SEASONS OF HEAVEN

The great mystery of what I had experienced quite literally haunted me. I continued to have experiences almost daily. What was I experiencing? Was I losing my mind? Fortunately, I had good friends to help me prove that I wasn't insane. Why did I have to prove I wasn't insane? If I had experiences like this, surely others had. So I began my research. I found that the research that had been done was sparse and riddled with theory and speculation. Clearly this wasn't happening to many people on the level I had experienced or else there would be more solid information on the subject. I decided to step out of my comfort zone and start talking to people. Once they had gained a certain comfort level with me, almost everyone or someone they knew had experienced something odd. With approximately ninety percent of the people telling me this, why wasn't the scientific world taking this seriously?

SEASONS OF HEAVEN

I learned over the years that it was due to how science is funded. It is all based on reputation. You don't risk your reputation for something as silly as the paranormal. If you did, then you would lose respect and then funding. Great.

But then I had an epiphany; honestly, I hope we never learn the secrets of the afterlife. I wonder what would happen to society if we knew with perfect assurance what happens when we die. This isn't a frontier to explore fully. But the people I had spoken with were truly troubled by their experiences and the lack of answers. They felt alone and afraid because people couldn't talk openly about this subject. I decided that in order to truly learn about the paranormal I needed to put myself in more paranormal situations, talk to more people, and see what happens.

This is where I realized what the paranormal is about. It's not about monsters, or scary otherworldly beings. It's about people, plain and simple. Sure, some are dead, but they are people. Living people need comfort and help. The dead need comfort and help. It's inter-dimensional customer support.

Everything started to open up quickly and lock into place. If I treated these entities as the people, they are then they would cooperate with me as much as they could. It's true, not all people are nice, so you get your difficult ones, but once they see that you truly care, progress is made quickly. I was able to help them leave, or stay based on what they wanted. I was able to convince entities to agree to special arrangements that benefited the residents of the home as well as the entities living there. I was able to help find out what the entities needed and satisfy that need.

Once I understood how to approach the field psychologically, I began employing the aid of technology, cannibalizing devices meant for other fields to work in paranormal research. Through one disembodied voice caught on tape I was able to help solve a sixty-year-old missing person case. Through knowledge of electromagnetic fields, I was able to keep a boy from being institutionalized by showing him he was hypersensitive to electromagnetic fields and not haunted by terrible entities. Black and white was all I wanted; ghost or not. I didn't personally care what the answer was, I was just happy to have one. To this date, my interaction with the paranormal has allowed me to help millions of people. I couldn't be happier.

But what are we really interacting with? There is definitely some weird stuff happening, and dead people makes the most sense. But what is it all, really? Are they spirits? Inter dimensional beings? Thought forms created by our own minds? Someone from the future or past caught in some fold in space-time? Aliens? We may never know, but that doesn't change the fact that the paranormal is fascinating, and disturbing, and we need to know just enough about it to help bring comfort to those who are troubled by it without killing the beautiful mystery that fuels it all.

This is the wonder of the paranormal for so many; the draw of the unknown. It is fun to speculate on what causes these odd events. This story plays with the idea of what the paranormal is in such a way as I have never seen before. It's a beautiful and terrifying idea that I hope you enjoy.

Grant Wilson

SEASONS OF HEAVEN

One final word before we go.

I began writing this novel two years ago and I've since come to discover that writing one's first novel is a huge event in a person's life that will always be looked back upon as a turning point. It's been said that writing a novel is like giving birth and releasing it is like turning your precious child out into the world to fend for itself. It's all at once exciting and nerve wracking. I've always wanted to write about the things I've been privileged to experience in my life, my obsession with things that are unseen in this world, yet impact us at almost every turn.

I started working in the field of paranormal research ten years ago as a lonely investigator. I've spent many nights alone, deep in the woods. I've stayed in ruins and "haunted" places all across Europe, and although I can't say without a doubt that ghosts do exist, I have to give credence to the fact that there is something there, possibly something that has yet to be identified. I've met many people who have witnessed strange and unusual events and were so affected by them that my own life was changed by their testimony. It caused me to begin asking a lot of questions about the world we live in, questions that have tugged at the souls of man for centuries. Questions like who and what we are, and why are we here? The age old question of what is the meaning of this life we're living really hit home for me on April 8, 2012 and sent me out on a journey of self-discovery.

I've always believed that the animals that inhabit this earth alongside of us are equal to us as spiritual beings. They need us, but we need them as well. I also found out that suffering the loss of a beloved pet can be as heart-wrenching and devastating as the loss of a human loved one.

SEASONS OF HEAVEN

My wife and I adopted a puppy. He was a French bulldog and his name was Ani. When the original owner told us that he was having trouble finding a good family to adopt him because he was sick with a disease known as pulmonary stenosis we decided to adopt him right away. We took care of him and watched over him and we also developed a deep, strong bond with him. When I worked from home, he would lay on my knees and as he was drawing comfort from me, I was drawing it from him as well. We loved him as any person might love a child or their best friend.

One morning Ani was no longer able to walk. We rushed him to the animal hospital and while he was under anesthesia, because of his breathing problems, he passed away. The gamut of emotions that we went through following that is almost indescribable. Life is so unfair, and the good ones always seem to go first. I was angry and sad. I started having bad thoughts about myself and I had such a hard time getting past the unfairness of it all. I would have done anything to have him back, and I know that I'm not the first person to experience a loss like this, one that leaves its imprint on your life forever. I couldn't bring him back; I'm not Dr. Frankenstein although at the time, I wished that I were. I don't believe in zombies although I do believe there are many things in this world not apparent to the eyes alone. As I grieved, and my mind considered the solutions, I came up with only three options.

There was suicide with the hopes of being reunited in another place. There was acceptance and there was moving forward with life. I chose the last one finally and in doing so it allowed me to begin a story where I could channel my grief and preserve my memories. My little buddy would be the center of it, and the things that I learned in my quest for answers would surround him.

SEASONS OF HEAVEN

You'll discover in this huge story that everything in it was inspired by true facts, places and events. You'll hopefully begin to open your mind to the fact that this world we live in is not as quiet as you may have believed. As you read my story, I'd like to ask you to believe that there is nothing in this world more beautiful than respect and love.

SEASONS OF HEAVEN

I am dedicating this book to Ani, Leia and Obi.

To my wife who is always there.

To my family Mama, Dad, Anthon and Laura.

To Julien and his dearly departed mother.

And to all of the people on this planet who have lost someone.

SEASONS OF HEAVEN

Prologue

New world
2047

As the new day dawned the rays of the sun cut through the early morning mist and lit up the tenebrific land. The beginnings of new, green foliage peeked out from amidst the concrete and steel and the deeply rooted trees struggled to survive. The rest of the world that had stood for centuries now lay in ruins. Pieces of structures still stood here and there, a testament to their construction...but the roofs are rotting and the glass is long gone from the windows. Doors are missing or hanging by rusty and rotted hinges. Molded, festering piles of rubble litter what is left of crumbling sidewalks and the smell of putrid rot hangs thickly in the air. Brittle bones left over from those who used to live here are strewn about the dusty ground, effectively turning what used

SEASONS OF HEAVEN

to be a busy, main boulevard into a virtual graveyard for the unburied dead. They lay still now, whereas before they had shuffled like zombies from place to place giving no heed to the very things they needed to survive. As the bones turned to ash, those responsible for this devastation are returned to the very soil that their kind had trampled and disrespected for centuries.

Handfuls of survivors still live scattered throughout the universe. They do not mourn for civilization because that would be akin to mourning the very thing that caused the ruination. For centuries humanity lived as though they were the higher power. They plundered the valuable resources of the earth as if they were infinite. They stripped and polluted it as they took more than they needed and threw the rest away. There was little to no thought of the future and the horrors that

SEASONS OF HEAVEN

would come once their vital resources were depleted.

The strongest animals still roamed the desolate planet, seeking food and struggling to survive. Much of the bright new foliage brought in on the wings of the wind had already been crushed by the constantly crumbling concrete that still stands. But, although the task of surviving has become a daunting one, it's not impossible thanks to the omnipotence of nature. Now that the earth is shed of what wreaked havoc upon it, she will continue to replenish herself until once again she stands strong in her center of the universe because nature will always survive.

The red brick and mortar tip of a cathedral with dark gray smoke curling up above it and blending with the azure blue of the sky is visible to the east, as if to prove that the colors of nature do not need the artificial

SEASONS OF HEAVEN

colors of humanity for emphasis. The sky has a surreal quality to it and it is more beautiful than the canvas of the most brilliant artist. [margin note: Because of no more air pollution, or not as much?] If one didn't know the year they might look around and think they were visiting earth during the seventeenth century before modern civilization took hold. Across from the cathedral where busy buildings once stood was now a make-shift camp for survivors. It's a well-organized camp thanks to one of the stronger survivors who was willing to take charge. Tired and ragged humans gathered around the constantly burning campfire and warmed themselves in between the business of surviving. Seven people sat there now discussing not for the first time the atrocities of what has become of their lives. They do this often, occasionally bickering amongst themselves about who is to blame, but most often ending up agreeing that it could have all been avoided if only people hadn't realized their greed too late.

The man who was courageous and kind enough to take charge of the group speaks gently to the others and offers as much motivation as he can to keep their morale up.

"I need a group of you to go out and forage for food," he told them. "Bring back whatever you can find that might be edible and we'll go through it together. We'll need fresh water too. You four will be in group one," he indicated one side of the group with a wave of his arm and went on to say, "Go now so you can be back before nightfall." He looked towards the other side of the ragtag group and said, "Group two I'll need you to scavenge for useful objects for camp. We need supplies to build more appropriate structures to protect us from the weather."

SEASONS OF HEAVEN

As the adults readied themselves to leave the camp and take on their assignments, two small girls played in the background. One of them had on a blue jacket that is much too long in the sleeves and it is coated with dust. Her face is grimy and her hair dull...but the bright blue of her eyes is like looking directly into the ocean. The other little girl is about five and her face still clings to the baby fat that forms her chubby cheeks. She's clutching what looks like a small bow and arrow set.

While the girl with the blue eyes played with the remnants of toys and chattered to her friend about the hopes of finding a doll to play with, the other child looked off into the distance with a focused gaze. The wind was blowing through the fine hairs that surrounded her cherubic face and if anyone was watching it might appear as if time had stood still for a moment. As the earth stirred around these two children, it seemed to struggle against further collapse.

The small child saw something that intrigued her off in the distance. It's an animal of some sort but she wasn't sure of its name. She vaguely recalled seeing a photo of one in a book...before the world collapsed. They used to populate the forests but like everything else, humanity had depleted them one by one. She raised the bow and laid one of her arrows against the string. Standing very still and quiet she began to draw back with her arm and time world went silent around her. She was on the verge of launching the arrow when she was suddenly startled by the sound of the leader's voice,

"Stop! Don't do that!" She slowly lowered her weapon and pointed it at the ground before turning toward him. "Why would you want to kill her? She's the first one we've seen in a very long time." he asked.

SEASONS OF HEAVEN

Confused the little girl said, "We have to eat, right?"

"We don't eat animals any longer. It's been years since we have. Killing them will bring harm to those of us left here trying to survive."

Still torn, the girl said, "I'm sorry. I just thought, maybe…"

The man noticed how upset she was and putting his arm on her small back he said, "It's okay honey, don't be upset. But please remember that we can't eat them anymore. We don't kill them. We were never supposed to."

"I'm so ashamed to even think about it…Dad. How was it then…really? Will you tell me? Nobody will talk about it. Please tell me what it was like…and how my mother died."

The man looked uncomfortable, but the eyes of his little girl pled with him.

"Okay honey, we'll talk tonight. I'll tell you everything I can. Deal?"

SEASONS OF HEAVEN

The little girl smiled up at her father. "Deal. Thank you Dad, I love you." He smiled back at her and then she looked around and said, "Hey, where's Nina?"

"Don't worry; she's around somewhere," her father said, "Look there."

The little girl followed her father's outstretched arm with her eyes. He was pointing towards the animal...the deer. Nina was standing next to it and gently stroking her tiny fingers through its dark brown fur. He was regal looking with a massive six-point rack and his size dwarfed the blue-eyed child...but he stood calmly and gave her nothing to fear.

"Nina? Let him go. Don't mess with him..." the other little girl was suddenly afraid the massive deer had seen her aiming her arrow at him. *What if he wanted to get revenge by hurting Nina?* She'd heard many stories about the animals seeking their revenge on the human survivors for what was done to them in the past.

SEASONS OF HEAVEN

"He's so sweet. I love him," Nina said. "He's talking to me, Ana! Do you know what he's saying?" Ana watched the dark brown deer walk away from Nina and disappear back into the forest. A small pool of almost invisible pollen floated in the air behind him and the man watched it thinking that nature was always at work. The small girl walked back over towards the camp. She looked like she wanted to follow the deer, but the forest around them is dense and dangerous and the girls know not to enter it.

"Girls, come on," their father called to them. "Do me a favor and go grab some wood. It's time to make some food and get camp ready for the night. Later I'll tell you a story, I guess..."

****

SEASONS OF HEAVEN

As night began to fall the brilliance of the sun and blue sky was replaced by a matte charcoal black sky covered in thousands of bright, silver specks. Star after star danced across the moon and the flickering flames of the fire fought to cut through the darkness the moon and stars were unable to reach.

The sounds of singing floated across the expanse of the campsite. The words the man was singing were designed for the purpose of incanting souls from another dimension. After the extinction the brains of the survivors had begun to evolve. The rationalism and speciesism began to disappear and human kind began to rely heavily on their instincts as their ancestors had. Looking back in history as far as Descartes, the skeptical rationalism of the brain was introduced and encouraged. Science advanced daily and the humans began to believe they were growing ever closer to being as powerful as God.

[margin note: Since this is supernatural they might be ghosts?]

SEASONS OF HEAVEN

The result of that was forgetting their place amongst the other living creatures that roamed the earth. For four centuries civilization continued to push forward and humans concentrated on building a world only for themselves. Today, things were different. The survivors learned from the demise of the others. The singer is the leader of the group and he is now the equivalent of what used to be known as a Shaman.

The man and his two girls sat down around the fire pit. He called them in close and said, "Today was a special day, my girls."

"Why pap?" Nina asked.

"I'm so sorry I aimed at the deer today," Ana said.

"It's okay," he told her. "You've done well. You've both done well with what we have had to endure and I think you're ready. I'm going to tell you a story about how everything changed, and why. Now everything we do must be with them."

The three of them stared into the dancing flames and the memories began to flood his brain. He grasped at them and tried to separate the real from the irrational before he began to speak....

CHAPTER ONE
"Wót'ááh"

Yann felt as if he had just woken up from a long sleep. Confused, he quietly listened to the noises around him. He could hear the sounds of an engine and a soft chugging sound in the background. They were familiar sounds, yet they were not. He knew that simple statement made no sense, but that was how he felt. It was like he knew he was on a train, yet he didn't. He looked around him. There was a window to his left and rows and rows of empty tan seats in front of and behind him. His own seat rocked gently back and forth as the train slid along the tracks, and as he took all of this in he wondered,

"How did I get here, and where am I going?"

He looked out the window to his left, onto the landscape that was passing by pane by pane. There were trees in the forefront of the picture that looked to be in the process of transforming their leaves from green into fiery fall colors of orange and deep and intense reds. The greens were not completely gone he noticed, most of them had just faded into yellow. Yann had no memories...yet he did. The colors reminded him of fire, yet it was a fire without smoke or flame. There was no rage like the one that normally came with fire either. Instead, the day was shrouded in a calm, tranquil shroud and the flamboyant leaves lay still in their trees and scattered about covering the ground.

[marginalia: Is Yann the father?]

Further in the background of the picture out his window the sun poked its warm head over the mountains that lined the pink and purple sky. Winter was trying to come, summer didn't want to go and the result was a battle of vibrant colors left splashed across the countryside.

A little farther down the track, Yann spied a lake that sat so calmly it almost appeared to be painted onto the deep green grass that surrounded it. The only indication that it was real was the reflection of the sizzling colors of the trees off of its mirrored surface.

Yann looked around him and confirmed that he was all alone. He wasn't supposed to be alone. He wasn't sure why he knew that thing in particular when he didn't seem to know anything else. But he had a feeling, one that seemed to be deeply ingrained in him that said he should always be with someone else, someone older, and someone to watch out for him.

He felt confused, yet there was a strange feeling of peace and calmness that surrounded him still. He glanced out the window again, still trying to figure out where he was and where he was going. In the light on the window from the sun that seemed reluctant to completely rise up from behind the mountains was a reflection of his little boy eyes. They were dark pools in the window, surrounded by a thick cover of lashes and it almost seemed to Yann like the little boy was looking in the window at him, rather than him looking out. The boy looked as confused as Yann felt. He didn't know where he was coming from or where he was going either. Yann could hear the train whistling and somehow he knew that meant they were either entering a crossing, or a tunnel. Yann braced himself for the tunnel. Somehow, thinking about the dark replaced his sense of calm with one of fear or anxiety. It was just a flutter and it was gone as quickly as it came. The shroud of peace once again blanketed him in its warmth.

After several minutes he realized that it must have been a crossing. The sunlight continued to splash rays of light and warmth across his face. He glanced around again, still wondering, about everything. As his eyes once again scanned his environment, he spotted a blue backpack sitting on the armchair in front of him. It had two small wings on each side of it and it seemed familiar to him, so much so that he leaned forward in the seat and took it into his lap. Letting his face rest onto the side of it, he inhaled deeply. He recognized the smell of it, and he instinctively knew that it was his backpack. He unzipped it and looked inside. He could see a leather bound book, tied closed with an old and frayed shoestring. He reached in and took it out, recognizing it at once as his scuffed up old journal.

Yann brought that to his face like he did the backpack. Smells were suddenly important to him, comforting somehow. He inhaled the fragrance of the old leather...and something else...a former life perhaps? He must have had a life before the train, but try as he might he couldn't recall it. He knew that was strange and that he should be afraid, but still he only felt harmony and tranquility in his heart.

He slipped open the journal, hoping to find a clue as to where he came from, where he was, and where he might be going. As the pages fell open a photograph slipped out. Yann leaned forward to retrieve it and the sight of it was like a magic portal into a sliver of his closed off memories. The photograph was of Yann, he recognized it as himself right away. His companion in the picture was a cute, black French bulldog. Yann smiled as he looked at it. He felt his heart swell and he knew at once that the dog was Ani. He also knew beyond a doubt that Ani was his best friend in the whole world, and his number one adventure companion. Why he remembered that and nothing else he didn't know. Maybe that was what was happening here. Maybe he and Ani had gone on an adventure…. but then where was the dog?

No matter how hard he tried, he still couldn't grasp any other memories. They were there but they were like the reflections on the lake, floating past too quickly for him to grasp them. When he reached out for one it caused the surface to ripple and the image to dissipate. He had the deep impression of having lived a life that was far from ordinary, the feeling that there was something very special about it. He frowned then but not because he was sad. The sun had gone higher in the sky and its powerful rays were assailing his eyes. His eyelids fought to protect them, half closing and trying to block them out.

He looked back out on the landscape. The train had taken him further now and the air was no longer silent. The breeze forced a path through the green fields they passed and caused them to shape-shift into an edgy deep green sea that went on for miles. He looked back at the picture in his hand. It was the only thing familiar here, and the only thing that made sense.

"Where am I going, Ani? I feel like I just woke up from a deep sleep and I don't know where I am, or what I'm traveling towards. Should I be afraid? I wish you were here with me, it would be nice to rub my hand across your short, soft coat while I figure this all out."

SEASONS OF HEAVEN

Yann leaned back against the big seat and closed his eyes. Like a movie, playing against the wall of a dusty old building he saw dim flashes of life. They were pictures of colors and lights and shadows and shapes of people, but everything was out of focus. There was nothing tangible there, except Ani. He could see Ani over and over as if the dog was embedded into each reel of film. Opening his eyes, he said aloud again to the empty car,

"Where are you, Ani?" He turned his head this way and that, but there was no sign of his friend. Finally, with a detachment that he didn't comprehend he stood up and slid the blue pack over his shoulder. Maybe the answers he was seeking were here, on this train.

He started towards the back of the car, where the door was and he was startled suddenly by the loud whistle. It was different this time, so loud that it sent a quiver through Yann's small body. He could feel the train slowing down and he wondered if they were going to stop. Maybe they had reached their destination, wherever that may be. He went again to the window and this time instead of a lovely slice of nature, he saw an empty platform. It was lit eerily by a single streetlight and adorned only with an old clock that didn't seem to be working. There was no one on the platform, just as there was no one with Yann on the train.

Nervously, he moved towards the door. He pushed it open and looked around…still there was nothing. He stepped down onto the weathered wood of the platform. The heavy door of the train closed behind him and he heard the loud whistle once more just before it began to move again, slowly dragging its heavy cars behind it. He turned and watched it go, wondering why he'd been left here, and feeling confused again. As the train cars slipped past him, he thought he saw the images of people inside, shadows of strangers looking out the windows, seeking the same answers that he was. That couldn't be possible though, since he had been the only voyager on board. His eyes must be playing tricks on him. *(Ghosts?)*

He turned his attention back to the empty platform and train station before him. It was definitely deserted. Yann was the only one here. He walked across the platform hearing the lonely echo of his own footsteps. He came to the end of it and looked out to see that the platform sat alone on top of a hill and miles of breathtaking landscape stretched out before him. He stood there for a while, enjoying the gorgeous views in spite of the strange situation. His senses seemed more alive somehow like each color, smell and feeling touched him in a deeper place than it had in his former life, wherever that life may have been. When he was able to tear himself away from the spectacular art of Mother Nature laid out before him for miles, he turned again in a wide circle, scanning his surroundings once more, looking for a clue as to which way he should go from here.

"Yann," he heard the voice calling out his name and looked around. It was soft and soothing; almost melodic, and it was distinctly female.

"Who's there?" he asked, clutching his backpack close to his body. "I can't see you," he said. Yann was startled by the voice that came from nowhere, but still not afraid.

"Follow me," the voice said. "Yann! Follow me!"

"Okay," he said, instinctually knowing that she meant him no harm. Her voice only served to solidify his feelings of peace and security. "But I can't see you," he said, unsure how to follow her.

"That's okay," she said. "Just follow the sound of my voice," she sang out. Whoever "She" was, she must be familiar with him and his situation because she said, "Be patient, Yann. Soon you'll get the answers you seek."

SEASONS OF HEAVEN

Yann believed her and he did as she asked. He stepped off of the platform onto a cobblestone path. He walked along at a steady pace until he came to a huge meadow that had grown tall with soft, green grass and a splash of pink brought about by the stunning round flowers growing wild across it. Yann was overcome by a desire to run through the grass and roll around in its soft shoots, so he did. He danced and flipped and ran, the way that children should, breathing in the rich aroma of the flowers and all the glory of nature that surrounded him. This was a magical place; he could feel it.

He sat down into a deep patch of the grass and then laid back and spread his arms and legs swinging them back and forth tamping the grass down and making the outline of an angel. He had his eyes closed, intensifying the experience of it all when he heard a sudden roaring sound. It was a sound foreign to his ears and he whipped his eyes open and stood up just in time to see a majestic herd of tigers coming towards him. He stood watching in reverence as their orange fur and black stripes cut a path through the green grass and pink flowers. His breath was literally taken from him by the sight and he once again knew that he should be afraid. He should worry they were coming to maul him. But he knew that somehow he was blessed to be a part of something so grand that it was rarely, if ever witnessed by human eyes. Yann smiled because in his head he could see what the tigers were trying to tell him clearly...they were happy now. He may have stood there watching them all day but he was reluctantly pulled from the sight by another sound. It was a loud whirring and flapping sound, like that of a hundred helicopters firing up for flight all at once. He looked towards it, above and behind the tigers and his eyes were treated to yet another spectacular sight. A huge flock of flamingos flapped their long wings and flew over the heads of the majestic tigers. Their pink wings and bodies were a sharp contrast to the pale blue of the sky and Yann found himself mesmerized by the scene as it played out before him.

CHAPTER TWO
"NIGHTMARES"
NEW YORK CITY, HOSPITAL

[handwritten: Perspectives change?]

The operating room was cool, as always. They kept it that way on purpose because germs loved a warm environment and had a much harder time living and multiplying in the cold. The small patient lay on the operating table swathed in sterile drapes. The large lights that hung above the table illuminated him; helping the surgeons to do their job and also reminding them that this patient was currently center stage. Shadows weren't allowed in the operating room. Everything had to be bright and clear...one mistake could result in the ultimate cost...someone's life.

There was a big machine and a cart that resembled a tool chest at the head of the table. The anesthesiologist stood there next to them, monitoring each breath and each beat of the patient's heart. Next to the operating table was another small, stainless steel table that held the instruments necessary for the doctors to do their jobs. They'd all been sterilized and chosen for this specific operation. Behind the anesthesiologist was a heart/lung machine whose very presence signified the severity of the issue the doctors and nurses were here to tackle.

The patient had a probe attached to one of his tiny little fingers called a pulse oximeter. Its purpose was to continuously monitor the oxygen in his blood. Another was attached to his chest with sticky pads and colored wires, that one monitored his heart and breathing rate, and an automatic blood pressure cuff that was wrapped around his skinny right arm inflated at regular intervals to measure his blood pressure. All of these safety measures had been put into place before the surgery had even begun. The highly dedicated and professionally trained team had scrubbed their hands up to their elbows and donned gowns, gloves and masks before entering the sterile room. In hindsight, there had really been no reason for anything to go wrong.... But it had...so terribly wrong....

The vascular surgeon wore light blue scrubs. He was easily distinguished from the other five members of the team, their scrubs were green. The surgery had been going on for a long time already. The nurse that stood next to the surgeon wiped away the sweat from his brow, not just for his comfort, but the patient's safety as well. If anything, even a drop of sweat disturbed the sterile field; it could cause a chain reaction that could end in tragedy. Ultimately, the dangers of contamination were going to be the least of their worries.

The lead O.R. nurse could see in the surgeon's eyes that something was dreadfully wrong. She whipped her head quickly towards the monitors and then her eyes landed on the face of the anesthesiologist at the head of the table. She wouldn't have had to see the monitors after she saw his face to know they were in trouble. She looked from face to face at the rest of the team and she could see the sheer panic in each of their eyes. They had all spent years training not only to save lives, but to remain calm under pressure that sometimes pressed so hard they felt like they were being crushed underneath it. No one said a word and the medical staff acted as if it were business as usual. The only sign that this moment was going to ruin or change any number of lives was the looks in each of their eyes. The gentle beeps of the monitors and the rasping of their own breaths were the only sounds in the cold room.

****

That light is so bright. Why are they shining it in my face, and why is it so cold in here? All I can hear are sounds of metal clinking against metal and something is beeping and clicking. There's a man standing over me in a white and blue paper shirt with a blue mask covering his face. He looks familiar, but I can't seem to place where I've seen him before. It's strange, but I don't know if I'm asleep, or awake. I feel like I'm floating and for a few seconds, I feel like I'm actually suspended in air above the table. I'm above all of the people who are still gathered around the table, looking at the body lying there unmoving...I realize all at once that it's not just any body, it's my body. I begin to ask why I'm here and my body is there when swiftly and without warning, I am sucked back into it.

While I was up there, away from the table and floating above the five people who still stood around it, I was able to quickly figure out where I am. I'm in an operating room and these people around me are doctors and nurses. I had figured out where I was, but I had no idea what I was doing here and I don't know what they're doing to me. I want them to stop and leave me alone, and I tried to tell *them but I can't seem to form a sound. Or am I forming sound and they just can't hear me? That light is so bright, so intense.... why are they shining it in my face? I can't keep my eyes open...it hurts. I tried blinking rapidly but that didn't help. I was busy fighting the light, trying to shut it out when I felt myself lifting off the table once more. I looked down and I could see me there, still on that table, surrounded by doctors and machines. I'm just above the doctor's heads now, I think. I reached out and try to touch one of them but it seemed like I misjudged the distance. I felt like I was ten stories high, yet I was still in the room.*

The metallic clink of their instruments was beginning to sound like torture to my ears and I tried once more to yell out. In my head, I heard my voice say,

"Hey! Listen to me, I'm here. For God's sakes, listen to me," but in the room, there was still not a sound other than clank, clank, beep, beep, swoosh, swoosh...

SEASONS OF HEAVEN

I began screaming, but still no one could hear me, and then suddenly there was no one to hear. The landscape around me morphed into an empty, gloomy one and then just as quickly as that had happened, I was standing on a precipice watching from above as giant waves crashed and stirred against the crumbling cliff that I stood on the edge of. I watched with a mixture of terror and awe as the waves gained height and speed, gathering more and more water until the peaks rose high enough to engulf the doctors who were sucked into it. They were tossed and turned in every direction their bodies being beaten and battered by the watery fists of the ocean. Just before the waves grew high enough to engulf me I saw them being drawn under. And then I was consumed...

The next place I went had a path. At the end of the path I saw a light...another bright light. I fear it, but at the same time I am drawn towards it. I took my first step and I was set

[handwritten margin note: Heaven? Death of the patient?]

off balance by the contrasts between white and black, light and dark...I stumbled and fell.

****

The surgeon in blue stood next to the table looking down at the body. He was trying not to feel. Surgeons were supposed to be detached, unemotional. He knew this was bad, very, very bad. This had gone very wrong. He could hear gloves being snapped off and instruments being collected around him. Next to him stood the other doctor, the one who had brought the surgeon in blue in on the case. She had her hands on her hips and she was staring at a spot on the wall.

The machines were still beeping and alarming and the surgeon found himself wondering why no one had turned them off. He heard the sound of a female voice, the lead nurse say,

"We've lost him," and that was what snapped him back into action. He was a doctor, patients died. He couldn't allow himself to wallow in it.

"Time of death: 2223. Please clean the block, I will go inform the parents," he said.

The male nurse who had been cleaning up the instruments stopped what he was doing, looked at the doctor and said,

"I...I can take care of it! Really, I think it would be better."

The doctor didn't look as alert as he should, whether it was fatigue or inebriation was a question on all of their minds. He led them towards the correct answer by saying,

"Don't take it so hard; I'll buy everyone a round of drinks when we get off work and we'll relax..."

"I'll pass..." the male nurse said, not bothering to try and hide the disgust he was feeling, "We are really not in the mood for that; we've just lost a patient."

SEASONS OF HEAVEN

The surgeon pulled down his mask and snapped off his gloves before saying in a matter-of-fact tone,

"Well, people come and go..." The nurse's mouth fell open in surprise, but that was nothing compared to what his face looked like after the surgeon's next statement, "Actually they just go, since they never make it back, except as ghosts..."

"OK, that's enough," the lead nurse said before the angry male nurse could respond. "I've heard enough for tonight, I'm wrung out, we'll talk about that another day."

****

Everyone who walked out of the operating room that night had the exhausted, aggrieved look of a team who had just lost the championship title. The Cardio-vascular surgeon, the one in the blue scrubs made it a few steps down the hall before he had to stop and put his hands out towards the wall to hold himself up. He could hear people talking as they passed him. He didn't look up; he didn't want to invite their conversation. He'd been crass towards that nurse in the O.R., but that had only been to mask what he was feeling at the time.

He waited until the others passed him and then he looked up. He could still see a few profiles, everyone looked dazed and their bodies looked weak and weary.

The surgeon, James watched them until they're out of sight. He then forced himself upright, teetering just a bit before he got his balance back. He was exhausted and defeated and drunk.

"What a nightmare," he thought, as he made his way down the hall to find the boy's parents.

****

Before he made it to speak to the parents, a bright flash of light followed by a sudden darkness consumed James suddenly transporting him to another place and time, into a nightmare. He found himself wandering through the empty corridors of the hospital. It was completely empty. Each room that he paused to look into was shrouded in darkness and shadows. The usually bright lights were dim and twinkling. He came to the end of the first corridor and turned towards the second one. As he made his way down that one he saw a door at the very end. It was shaking and vibrating. It looked like someone or something was trying to get out.

    He approached it with caution...his heart was hammering in his chest. He somehow knew he should turn back the way he'd come, but he was inexplicably drawn to the end of the long hallway. He approached the rattling door and placed his hand on the knob...Another bright flash of light transported him once again to another place and time.

    James was a child now, suddenly back in his family home and in his childhood bed. It was comforting at first as his eyes adjusted to the dark and he looked around at all of his old things, things that he hadn't seen in over thirty-years. He suddenly wondered what the reality was, lying in bed as a boy or growing up to become a surgeon. Was he really not a doctor, but still only a little boy? He glanced down at himself once more and his head was still pointed downwards when he caught a flicker of movement out of the corner of his eye. He sat frozen for a few seconds, hoping it was only a shadow cast off of one of the trees in the back yard. He couldn't hear a sound other than his own breathing, but he could feel something watching him. Cautiously he raised his head and his wide eyes drank in the horror that stood in front of him. At the end of his bed was a...creature. If James had to describe it later, the first word that came to mind was "dark." It was dark in his room, with nothing but a small sliver of silver moonlight through the closed blinds, but the shape that loomed malevolently near him was so dark that it seemed to be melting into the night around it. It was standing in one spot, but seemed to be in motion at the same time. Its own darkness left a trail of something even blacker in its wake. It had huge eyes. Sometimes they appeared like obscure sockets that disappeared into the murkiness of itself and other times, they would glow. First James thought they were red, and then white it was almost like it was purposely changing to confuse him. Its head was misshapen like a rotting potato and its arms were long and spindly with appendages that seemed to be able to reach out in every direction all at once. James could feel its evil intentions as it swung and grasped at the air, as if it had an urgent need to devour all within its path. The air in the room was heavy like the loutish thing had sucked out all of the oxygen and replaced it with its bad intentions. The thing wasn't very tall, but what it lacked in height it made up for in simple vulgarity.

SEASONS OF HEAVEN

What was this thing and what did it want from him? He didn't know for sure. What he did know was that he could feel his tiny heart pounding through his chest and the thick flannel of the pajamas his mother had put him in before tucking him into bed. His mouth was dry as he had a staring contest with the beast, waiting for it to make its move. The bloated miscreant continued to just stand there with its slithery, black tentacles reaching out, swiping at nothing in the air of the scared little boy's room. Maybe it was trying to catch his fear, James thought. Maybe that was what it fed off of. It seemed to be taunting him, wanting him to react and although the thing didn't speak it gave the distinct impression that it was annoyed at James for not screaming and crying and running away. James wanted to, there was nothing he wanted more right then but to be away from the creature, but in addition to not wanting to feed it his fear he had a feeling that this thing was like a snake...if you moved too quickly, it would strike.

He sat as still as a stone statue in his bed. He kept his eyes on the creature but he didn't move at all except to take in the occasional breath. He tried to hold it for as long as he could, partially due to his fright, but also because every time he took a breath in he could smell the foul odor of the thing at his side. The smells it was emitting smelled to James like the decaying body of a rat he'd found in the barn one day. Even to a child, it smelled like death. James didn't know how long their standoff lasted until at last and to his great relief the unholy creature disappeared.

James knew he should stay in bed, but he had a feeling the thing wasn't gone and although he was more frightened than he'd ever been, the simple curiosity of a child's imagination got the better of him. He slipped quietly out of his bed and walking softly in his bare feet, he moved towards the corridor. He peeked out the bedroom door and at first all he saw were the family photos that had hung on the papered walls for as long as he could remember and the shiny wood floor that led down the hall to the other bedrooms and the bathroom at the end. He had almost allowed himself to relax when he saw the thing reappear at the very end of the corridor. It gave him another intimidating glance and then it vanished.

He continued to tiptoe softly down the long hall, passing the bathroom. Just as he passed that door he heard a loud crack. He abruptly turned back with his heart pounding like a drum in a barrel against the inside of his chest. He was in the hospital, and the horrible thing was right behind him, close enough to reach out and touch if James had been daft enough to want to. He wasn't and he didn't, so he began to run. He ran as fast as he could to the other end of the corridor towards the stairs, The hospital looked like it had been the center of some sort of disaster. The windows were shattered, gurneys were overturned and lying in the corridors and the wooden counters were splintered and rotting. He couldn't see the thing behind him but he could feel it closing in on him. It was almost as if its evil...its bad intentions were reaching out and brushing the fine hairs on the back of his neck, causing them to rise. He could feel its darkness, and it was a cold, empty feeling.

Turning the corner, he continued to run down the second corridor. He was panting and sweating now and he couldn't block out the sound of the incessant pounding of his pulse inside his head. There were two dummies in the hallway, the kind they used for teaching in medical schools. As James ran past them they lifted their arms at the same time, pointing at something, urging him to look......James didn't stop, they didn't look trustworthy. He didn't want to see whatever they were pointing at but he was compelled to look. What he saw, for a few seconds stopped him in his tracks. It was a place suspended in air where the sky was at first a brilliant blue and the clouds looked like wisps that had been dashed across the sky by some kind of divine paintbrush. The sun was radiant...almost blindingly so. Then the blue sky morphed into night and the sun was replaced by the luminescent light of a silver moon and thousands of twinkling stars that seemed to only dangle there...like one could reach out and pluck them from the sky....

    The vision...or whatever it was faded and James got a glimpse of something beautiful. It was more of a feeling than a vision and just for a moment it consumed him and filled him with a weightlessness and light...and then it was gone and he was once again running for his life. Before he'd gotten ten more feet the floor abruptly fell out from underneath him. He fell downward, spiraling towards nothingness at such a rapid speed that his throat constricted and he could hardly breathe. It was like falling off of a cliff into a pit that had no bottom…..

There was another blinding flash of light and he was lying alone in the hall, the dreadful things had vanished once more. A suddenly adult James looked around, simultaneously hoping to see another soul that might be able to help him and glad no one else was around to find him on the floor and ask questions. He quickly pulled himself back up and began to once again walk down the empty trashed hall like a ghost. He didn't know he was in a nightmare but he was confused and his head hurt from trying to understand what was happening. He tried convincing himself it was just the stress of it all. The toll of his job and his life weighed heavily on his stooped shoulders and in the lines across his face. His hands held his aching head as he walked, hardly looking where he was going. He'd had the worst kind of day a doctor can have. It was no wonder that his head and his eyes were playing tricks on him now.

As he walked down the hall towards his unknown destination he abruptly stopped. He could smell it again, the rotting flesh. Besides that, he could feel them again. It was like the air was laden with their malevolent desires. He looked over his shoulder and saw that another one of the frightful things had begun to slink along behind him. It was soon joined by another of its kind and then another. James began to walk faster, thinking he was too tired to run again. He wasn't a kid any longer; he was a tired old man again now. His heart felt like it was ready to explode as it were, he wasn't sure that he could run if he had to.

He finally made it to the end of the corridor and allowed himself a backwards glance. The things were still there, still coming towards him. They didn't seem to be in any hurry, they just steadily followed the path he was taking. It was almost more frightening than if they just ran after him. It made them seem...confident, almost as if they knew he had no escape.

James wanted far away from them. He found out then that the human body...his body to be precise was more resilient than he'd given it credit for....He once again began to run through the empty corridors of the hospital, looking for a place to hide. He ducked into one of the patient rooms. It was empty, of course. The whole place was empty except for James and the appalling creatures that stalked him.

He ran between the two empty beds and once he was in between them and the wall, he pulled them together, making himself a barricade. James knew that creatures that could come and go from nowhere wouldn't be stopped by such a puny obstacle, but his body was so heavy from the fear and fatigue that he just couldn't go on any further. It almost felt as if the evil in the room was suffocating all of his energy. His hands were shaking and he could feel the sweat beading along his upper lip. His breaths were coming in ragged gasps as the things advanced on him, waving their slimy looking tentacles in the air.

James was sure this was the end for him. He was trying not to breathe at all now that they were so close. It felt like the air in the room was filled with their wickedness and James was afraid of breathing it in. While he contemplated what they may do to him, he found himself wishing that he'd lived a better life. What if he didn't get to go and be with Sarah and Thomas? As he pondered his mistakes in life, the creatures disappeared into the night once again as fast as they had appeared earlier. James looked around the room, his thoughts were muddled and he was second-guessing himself. It was as if the things had never been there at all. Had he imagined the whole thing? That was when there was another blinding flash of light and James woke up.

> [handwritten: So James was sleeping on the job?]

CHAPTER THREE
"BANISHED"
NEW YORK CITY, HOSPITAL

It took James a few seconds to get his bearings back and remember where he was. He'd somehow made it back to his office and he must have fallen asleep at his desk. He'd had the nightmare.... again. James stood up quickly, too quickly. The blood rushed from his head to his feet and he nearly fell over. He had to reach out for the desk and steady himself as he walked around it. He wanted to go home.

He began moving things around on the top of his desk, looking for his keys. He all at once felt like he needed to get out of this place, it was driving him crazy and he felt like he couldn't breathe. His hands shook as he moved things around on his neatly organized desk only to find that it didn't hold any keys or any other surprises. He was getting more frustrated with each passing minute. He felt an urgency to escape from this place...to be outside in the cool, wet night air where he could finally breathe.

Behind him, the rain was pelting like bullets against the panes of the large window that looked out over the hospital grounds. A bolt of lightning cut across the dark sky and caused it to light up as if someone had thrown on a switch. James didn't notice any of this. All he was focused on was finding his keys. They had to be here somewhere. He needed to get out of this place.

He went around behind the big desk and sat down in the over-sized leather office chair and began to go through the desk drawers. He'd long ago lost the intense pride that he'd had in the diplomas, certificates and commendations that hung on the wall behind him now. He'd been a doctor for so many years and the certificates hung behind him on the wall for so long, he barely noticed them any longer. They didn't mean the same thing to him that they used to. He no longer took the same pride in them, or in himself.

James had lived a charmed life for a while. He had studied first in France at the Medicine school of Paris before immigrating to the U.S. to study Cardio-vascular disorders. He had been so young then, and so full of hope. He'd been valedictorian of his class and constantly looking for new ways to nurture his desire to help his fellow man. He wanted to give back some of what he felt like he'd been blessed with right up until the time when he began to lose everything that mattered to him in his own life.

After going through each desk drawer twice and still not finding the keys, he slumped back down into the chair in defeat. His eyes landed on the pictures of his wife Sarah and his son Thomas displayed in wooden frames atop his desk. Sarah smiled out at him with her green eyes twinkling and her light auburn hair shining in the sun of the beach she had been standing on when the picture was taken. She had such an incredible aura, a charm about her that almost everyone who met her found irresistible.

The picture next to it was one of James with their boy Thomas in his arms. Thomas was such a little cherub. He had the biggest smile that James had ever seen, and the light spattering of freckles across his nose coupled with the always disheveled mop of brown hair made him look like a little rascal. He had his moments as all little boys do, but for the most part he was a great kid and there wasn't a single day that went by when James didn't miss him.

James suddenly went from defeated to angry. In one swift motion he swept all of the documents off his desk. As they flew across the room, some of them hitting the wall and others crashing to the floor, James once again switched from angry to beaten down. His emotions were all over the place, he was used to it but at a loss for how to control it. He leaned forward on the desk and put his head in his hands. Pulling at his hair with his fingers, his exhausted and tormented mind traveled back to the earlier operation.

It was such a disaster…. How could it have gone so wrong? Nevermind

He felt the hot burn of tears filling his eyes. He blinked them back and willed himself not to think about it now. There would be inquiries over it and meetings and question after question that he'd probably not be able to answer. He just didn't know how it had all gone so badly…thinking about it now was pointless. He pulled his head up out of his hands and looked at the phone lying on his desk. His hand trembled as he reached for it. The tears had escaped and were streaming down his cheeks as he put the phone to his ear and said,

"Hello? Honey…it's me."

Sarah's sweet voice floated through the phone. James could hear it, the same as he could his own and just the sound of it sent a warm glow surging through him.

"Hello? James? Why are you crying, what's the matter? You know you have to be strong, he is listening to us and he's listening to you! Why are you only calling me now? I was worried sick!"

"I feel lost, Sarah. I don't know where to turn. Everything has changed since he..." he had to stop for a second; his body was wracked with sobs. He fought through it, drawing on the strength that Sarah gave him and then he said, "Since both of you left. I wanted to call you earlier, but I was with a patient. I lost her, Sarah. It was such a disaster. She died, Sarah. Her lifeless body was just there on the table...." he had to stop again; the sobs were causing him to gulp for breath. He was such a mess.

"Don't worry, honey, you know that what we lose is never lost forever. I'll always be here for you, even though I had to go away."

SEASONS OF HEAVEN

James reached into the bottom drawer of his desk. Pulling out a dusty glass and a bottle of Bourbon, he poured himself a drink. Downing it like a shot he said,

"I know. I'm trying to remember.... It's hard Sarah."

"You're drinking again?" she asked, obviously disappointed.

"Don't worry, I'm ok..." he lied.

"When is your flight?" she asked him, changing the subject.

"In a few hours, I believe, I'll be home around eight tonight!"

"Have a safe trip," she told him before he hung up the phone.

He sat there staring at it, his mind was reeling still. He let it go back to the first time he'd gotten really drunk....

He started a fight in a bar. In his defense, it was because someone had said something horrible to him, something that no parent should ever have to hear. It was after

SEASONS OF HEAVEN

Thomas had gone missing and the entire town believed he was responsible for it...they thought he had killed his own son. After Thomas disappeared he'd done what any good, distraught father would have done; he'd gone to the police. The police had done a cursory investigation and then turned their sights on the boy's parents. The loss of a child was a devastating thing, something that no parent is built to endure, but to be blamed for that loss was indescribable. He had turned to the alcohol to numb his pain and when that idiot had opened his mouth that night, James hadn't been able to control himself. The guy ended up with a split lip and a bump on the back of his head where he'd fallen back into the bar and James ended up spending a night in jail. He would have spent more nights there, many more if they had convicted him of murdering his own son. That may have happened had it not been for the inspector in charge of the judicial inquiry. The man saved him that fate by refusing to draw any hasty conclusions as the rest of the police force and the town had done.

    James was suddenly shaken back to reality by the high pitched wail of the rain. It sounded like a siren, using her beautiful voice to lure a sailor to his doom. He got up from the chair and reached for his jacket just as another jagged bolt of lightning tore through the sky, effectively ripping it in half. He pulled the jacket off the hook it hung on and the car keys fell out of the pocket. He put on the jacket, picked up the keys and at last headed for the exit.

    James made his way to the exit door taking note that the hospital seemed to be operating normally, unlike the shambles it had been in his dream. He shivered when he remembered his nightmares and did his best to tuck that memory away in the far recesses of his brain. He hit the door at the end of the hall and began to descend the stairs; his long legs took them four at a time. When he reached the bottom floor and began to head towards the outer doors he caught sight of a small red tricycle slowly inching towards him. He stopped, riveted by the sight. It continued its gentle forward motion until it was a few feet in front of him and then it stopped. James moved towards it as if in a trance. It was Thomas's tricycle…it had belonged to his son…His chest suddenly felt heavy again and he reached out and put his hand on the handle bars. All at once there was another blinding flash and James was back in his home. The one he had shared with Thomas and Sarah.

  He was standing in the living room. Just a short time ago this room, the whole house had been filled with Sarah's decorating charms and the happy sounds of a child playing. It was a place that James craved when he was away and hesitated to leave when he was home. Now, it was nothing but a constant reminder of all that he'd lost. Everything was empty, packed in boxes and waiting out near the fireplace to be picked up by the movers. Even before the things had been packed away, it had been empty. Without Sarah and Thomas, it was like a wooden and stucco shell.

James could hear the lonely patter of the rain on the shingle roof. He turned away from the agony of the void that used to be his family's home and went out on the front porch. The water from the rain was running swiftly down the gutter making a soft metallic sound. It was the only sound on the empty street. There wasn't even a single car in sight.

James sat down and opened his bottle of bourbon and lit a cigarette. He took a deep drag off the cigarette and a drink of the bourbon straight from the bottle. He sat the bottle down and the corner of his eye caught sight of a dark shape on the left side of the courtyard. James stood up and leaving the shelter of the porch he stepped down the two steps into the pouring rain. He didn't have to extinguish his cigarette; the rain took care of that for him. Tossing it aside, he made his way deeper into the garden. He couldn't see anything except the plants and flowers that Sarah had so lovingly cared for now hanging limply from their bushes, trees or stalks. He made his way to the fence where he had seen the shape disappear, and he jumped over it. He could see the strange shape once again. The back of the house faced a wooded area and James followed the shape into the depths of the cold, dark space enclosed by large natural umbrellas made of thick tree branches and leaves. As he reached out to steady himself against one of the big trees, he could feel carvings underneath his palm. He pulled his hand away, and looked at the carving. It was a bunch of small birds that had to have been carved with a tiny little knife. He looked closer and saw that they were ortolans. Ortolans, in the past had been a delicacy in European countries, most especially in France.

SEASONS OF HEAVEN

James flashed back from his memories. He was once again in the hospital lobby. The tricycle was gone. With another tortured sigh, he continued out the main exit of the hospital. It was dark outside and everything was drenched from the rain. He slogged through the deep puddles left from the down pour. The sirens coming and going from the hospital were like background music to his life by now...he hardly heard them anymore. He made his way to the black SUV he drove, it was sitting alone in the lot. James stopped and looked at it. Alone was the story of his life since he'd lost Thomas and Sarah. He wasn't paying attention to his surroundings and he suddenly felt himself bumped in the shoulder. He turned and saw what he could only describe as a creepy looking man, passing in the other direction. James was still on edge and he hadn't realized it until now, but he was spoiling for a fight.

"Hey!" he yelled after the man, "Can't you be careful and watch where you're going?"

SEASONS OF HEAVEN

The man just made a strange sound and then giggled. That only made James more annoyed.

"Hey jerk! Don't you have any manners?"

The man stopped then and turned around. Feigning an apologetic look and tone he said,

"I'm sorry, Doc. I really am."

James wasn't buying that he was sorry. His anger and the bourbon were fueling his desire to argue the point, "Get lost, you prick before I kick your ass," he told the other man.

The man looked at him and with the semblance of a smile he said, "I know who you are...James."

"What did you say?! How do you know my name? I'm a surgeon here, dick head and I also know your name." James gestured at him then with his middle finger.

"You think you're so important because you're a surgeon. You cut people open and some live and some die. Our jobs aren't all that different, really."

James looked the man up and down and said, "What are you a butcher?"

The man smirked and said, "Something like that." He turned and walked away then and James headed on to his own car. He glanced back and saw that his car hadn't been the only one in the lot after all. The nasty little man hit the unlock button on his key fob and when the lights flashed he saw the other car. He hadn't seen it before because it was parked in the dark. It too was a black SUV like James's.

Something about that bothered him. James knew black SUV's were common, but that guy had really ticked him off. Even if he hadn't just lost a patient and even if he hadn't lost his boy...that was when everything started going wrong. The day he lost Thomas, he had proceeded to lose everything. It was like pulling a loose thread on a sweater and watching it unravel.

SEASONS OF HEAVEN

Once he was finally inside the vehicle and out of the torrential rain, he still couldn't turn off his thoughts. He reached over to his glove compartment and opened it. Reaching inside, he took out a metal flask that he'd put there earlier. It was filled with Vodka. He took off the top and downed the entire thing in seconds. Frowning as soon as he was done and realizing he hadn't made anything better at all, he dropped his head down into his hands with his long hair covering his face on both sides, and his whole body began to convulse as he wept. He was weeping for Thomas and Sarah and himself...and for the girl on the table tonight. What a terrible life this was turning out to be. He took his fist and banged it against the steering wheel, hard. That didn't fix what ailed him though so he threw the flask against the dash and then dropped his face back down into his hands. After a few minutes he was able to pull it together enough to sit up and wipe the tears from his face with his fingers. He took a deep breath and slipped his hand into the pocket of his dark, leather jacket to retrieve his keys...they weren't there. Sighing in frustration, he slipped the other hand in the other pocket...not there either.

"What the hell?" he yelled out loud inside the empty vehicle. "They were just there when I left the hospital." He checked his pockets again...still not there. "Fuck!" he yelled as he slammed his fists into the overhead of the SUV. Sometimes even the small things were just too much to bear when it felt like the rest of your life was dangling precariously over the edge of a cliff.

James sat there, not wanting to have to get out of the car again. It had started raining again. It was pounding like tiny little metal beads against the exterior of the car and the windows had all fogged up. He sat in the small space with the smell of leather and alcohol in his nose and once again felt completely removed from the rest of the world.

SEASONS OF HEAVEN

He just sat there like that for the longest time. He was like a zombie without conscious thought or reason. Then suddenly the rain eased up and something about the change in the tune of the heavy drops to the drizzle that barely resonated brought him back to reality. He reached over next to him and felt around on the passenger seat. His hand touched something metal and he picked it up, he'd found the elusive keys.

James slid the key in the ignition at last and cranked the engine. He drove out of the parking lot, leaving only a beam of light in his rear view mirror. He was still wrapped up in his thoughts. It seemed that tonight more than others he'd been unable to shake them. He began to wonder about the senselessness of life. If he was going to continue down this path and nothing was ever going to get better, what was the point?

It had been a terrible day. He reached up as he drove and flipped down the sun visor. A little picture fell out and he caught it in his fingertips before it fell to the floor. The picture was of his son, Thomas. Looking at the boy's sweet face caused him to once again become overwhelmed with emotion.

"I love you son," he said with a deep sob. "I miss you. Send me a sign…"

After a few seconds he sighed again, swallowed the tears that had begun to well back up and slipped the picture inside his jacket pocket.

****

Frank Lewis stood and watched as James sat alone in his car. Before the windows fogged up, he saw him throw back the flask and then beat the steering wheel with his fists. James was not doing well. Frank smiled. The only thing that made him happier than watching, causing or being a small part of a rich, uptight American's misery was that final breath he got to watch them take, right before he killed them.

Frank turned and walked past the other black SUV that James had thought was his. He tossed the keys into the gutter and walked several blocks before he was picked up by one of his "colleagues." As Frank slid into the red Camaro the other man asked,

"How'd it go?"

Frank nodded, "As planned. He was drunk and miserable when I left him."

****

Still drunk, upset and lonely, James made it to the highway heading out to the John F. Kennedy airport. The road in front of him seemed to stretch out in an infinite line. It was poorly lit and there were few cars out tonight, probably because of the rain. The landscape was dotted with buildings and billboards, but because of the poor lighting, James couldn't really see anything other than a few feet of black asphalt in front of him.

His thoughts continued to return to Thomas and he couldn't help but wonder if

SEASONS OF HEAVEN

Sarah had seen him. The loss of his wife had been devastating, but it was still a drop in the bucket compared to the emotional upheaval that the loss of Thomas had caused him. It tormented him night and day. At first, the alcohol helped. It numbed the feelings and took the sharp edges off of the memories. But the more used to the anesthetic his body and mind became, the less it worked its magic.

As much as James loved his son, and as much as he still held out hope that he'd see him again someday, he almost wished that he could forget that day two years ago when Thomas had disappeared. Instead, it was the clearest memory his mind held onto. It was there when he woke up and when he went to sleep, even when he finished off a bottle of bourbon. He truly knew what people meant now when they referred to a memory as "haunting."

James, Sarah and Thomas had been living in Little Rock at the time. It was a peaceful little town with friendly people and good schools. It was the perfect place to raise a family...or so he and Sarah had thought. Not long before they'd lost Thomas, strange events had begun to take place in the town, causing panic and paranoia to run rampant amongst its normally contented residents.

James hadn't been raised in a small town. He was well-educated and he had written off the ramblings of his neighbors as simply rumors fueled and spread about by uneducated people. The jest of their complaints was that they were being visited at night by a strange man, not once but several times. Some of the accounts told of the man sneaking into their children's bedrooms. Although the inhabitants of the entire county were terrified by these stories, at that point, there was no concrete evidence to back up what they were saying. James was a facts kind of guy, so he chose not to concern himself with any of it. He had a career and a family to spend his time worrying about. He didn't have the time to waste on fantasies.

Hindsight however was turning out to be a bitch. After Thomas was abducted, James and Sarah were relentlessly interrogated by the police. They thought the child was dead and that one of his parents had killed him. Luckily, the lead investigator was good enough at his job to realize that wasn't the case and he ultimately linked Thomas' disappearance with a child molestation case he was working on.

It was the largest case the county had ever been hit with. It happened at a local Children's outdoor center where kids went for day camp and learning activities. At first, the perpetrator had begun taking only their backpacks...seemingly mesmerized by stealing and touching their things. As these things go, however that had escalated to molestations. Like the investigator, James was convinced that Thomas disappearing in the midst of all of that wasn't a coincidence and the cases were linked somehow.

James was not only an intelligent man, and an excellent surgeon; he was also the son of one of the most brilliant detectives of the Paris Criminal Squad during the '50s. He'd listened to his father speak about cases for hours on end as he grew up. He was predisposed to weighing the facts and based on those facts, making assumptions. James thought about his father then. He missed him too. At the close of his career, his father was working a murder case. It was a strange case and one that local police had failed to gain any leads on. Unfortunately, his father was killed for his efforts and the case was never solved.

James finally made it to JFK. He pulled into the parking lot and parked in long term parking. Jumping out, he slammed the door and headed inside. His feet felt heavy and his legs wobbly. James was smart enough to know he was drunk, but he was stubborn enough to not admit it.

Once inside he began looking for the flight board to see if his flight was on time. The overhead announcements seemed louder than usual and James was tempted to yell,

"Shut-up!" at the top of his lungs at all of the loudly chattering people. He didn't though. This one time today, good sense prevailed.

CHAPTER FOUR
"THE QUEST BEGINS"

Yann opened his eyes slowly. He'd heard a loud bang and his eyelids could feel the heavy light pressing against them. He sat up and looked around, everything was a little blurry and the blinding light made it almost impossible to adjust. He couldn't tell where he was, but he suddenly knew who he was with. He felt a long, wet, rough tongue brush against his cheek once and then again. Ani's black coat stood out brilliantly against the hot white of the light all around them.

Ani was running around in circles, taunting the boy, wanting him to get up. When Ani wanted something from Yann, he told him what he wanted with his eyes. They communicated that way, no words needed. It was mind to mind, or as Yann liked to think of it, soul to soul.

SEASONS OF HEAVEN

All animals communicate through telepathy. It is the most basic form of communication and an ability we are all born with. Unfortunately, most humans learn to rely on verbal communication and telepathic skills get pushed to the far recesses of the brain, becoming inefficient over time; <u>Descartes and Judo Christian changed everything.</u>

Yann was different than your average human, and Ani had recognized that right away. His mind was wide open to the possibilities of magic and mystery and all of the things one couldn't see or touch. When Yann asked Ani a question, in return he would receive pictures, feelings, words, thoughts and emotions, and the same were true in reverse. It was a much more effective way of communication than the verbal route, giving the boy and his dog a virtually unbreakable connection.

Yann laughed, the message from Ani received loud and clear.

SEASONS OF HEAVEN

"Okay Ani, I'm getting up," he said. Stretching his arms and twisting his torso he finally pushed himself up with his arms. "Where are we? I feel like we have traveled. It's a really strange sensation, don't you think?" Ani was watching Yann's eyes, listening to his friend. When Yann finished speaking, Ani spoke back to Yann through his own eyes.

"You don't know either, boy? I'm sure I've never seen this place before." It seemed like a nice place, quiet and calm. There were no other people, or dogs or cars or buildings around. It was like they'd just been dropped onto a beautiful mountainside. The sky was a brilliant cobalt blue and the sun was the source of the blinding light that had been burning Yann's eyes. The trees, the meadows and the sky were completely different from anything Yann had ever known, he was sure of it. The light here was also much more brilliant. This place possessed a beauty beyond any comparison with anything he could draw a memory of. Once his eyes finally adjusted to the dazzling light, he enjoyed basking in its comfortable rays. The perfectly fluffy white clouds floated slowly across above their heads and as Yann watched them a flock of gulls appeared off in the distance, flying in perfect formation.

Yann reached down and pet Ani softly on his head.

"Maybe we're on an expedition to discover a new land," he told Ani. Ani seemed to be happy with that theory. The two best friends began to walk forward, hoping to discover where they were. The cool soft breeze felt wonderful on Yann's face. Ani walked with his tongue out to the side and his mouth cracked open. It was his smile face.

The hill sloped gently upward and they followed it that way. They were surrounded by nature and both Yann and Ani were enjoying the sights and smells of it. They were encircled by a lush meadow and a forest of trees stretched out behind that. Yann was surveying the scene when he suddenly stopped dead in his tracks.

"Do you see it Ani?"

The dog had been watching Yann's eyes but now turned towards where the boy was looking. There, he could see a huge, gray geometric shape jutting out above the line of the horizon. It looked odd there, and both Yann and Ani wondered about it. But the oddest thing wasn't that it was stuck here amidst all of this natural beauty. The oddest thing was the blue light that radiated from its surface. Neither of them could think of any logical explanation for either the structure's presence, or the light.

They continued to follow the gentle slope of the hill. It became steeper as they went and they found themselves surrounded by an opulent field of green and yellow grass that danced softly around them in the wind. Yann watched in delight as the soft ripples transformed into waves and the field began to look like a deep, green ocean. Yann reached down and picked up his canine companion. Holding him in his arms, against the backdrop of the brilliant blue of the sky they began to dance. Both of their faces radiated with warmth and happiness and they swayed along with the motion of the grass.

When their dance was done, Yann sat Ani down and the dog rolled through the grass and barked happily. Yann smiled at him and then sitting on his bottom, he slid down the verdant hill. Yann looked up once more at the sky. The beauty of it was indescribable and he had the feeling he could almost reach up and touch a star if he tried. He felt a rush of anticipation surge through his small body. He could feel that he and Ani were standing on the threshold of a grand adventure.

After a bit they began walking again, eventually reaching a plateau. They realized that they were standing at the edge of a deep forest. There was movement inside and as the boys stood frozen to their spot a large pair of glowing eyes looked out at them. Yann and Ani stayed quiet, barely breathing, and after a few seconds the owner of the eyes revealed herself. It was just a soft brown doe and she seemed as curious about them as they were about her. Sensing they were no threat, she stopped and looked them over. Once she'd assessed them both she turned and disappeared back into the thick brush. Once she was gone they continued to look in from the outside and all they could see was darkness. Unfettered by the lack of light, Ani took the lead and rushed in. Trusting his best friend's judgment and instincts, Yann followed him. Excitement ruled the moment and fear of the unknown was non-existent. As they walked through the thick and ancient looking forest, branches crunched under their feet and the smells of woody incense filtered in through their noses.

Yann could hear the soft sounds of the wind whistling as it forced its way through the thick branches of the sprawling trees. The trees reminded him of watchful guardians, a silent sentinel making the way safe for his and Ani's trek as they ventured deeper into the forest's tangled heart.

The further they traveled, the more mystical and mesmerizing it became. Huge roots twisted up out of the ground like the gnarled backs of sea monsters. The foliage became thicker and lusher as they moved forward and it formed and arch of deep green above their heads.

Then a sliver of ethereal light poked through the dense mesh. It was followed by a loom of light that filtered down in seams of gold. It chased the shadows and banished the gloom, spilling into spaces where the mist once stalked. The flute-like piping of a songbird split the silence just as the forest became flooded with light. A symphony of tweeting and warbling exploded all around them as the forest came alive with the minstrels of the trees. Yann and Ani darted between shafts of lustrous-gold light as they moved forward, and it seemed as if the forest opened up a path for them as they trudged forward. Yann was fascinated and his inquisitive mind was filled with hundreds of questions. He looked up and said,

"This light is odd, Ani. Look up on the branch; it's as if the dust is frozen. I wonder where we are."

Ani was busy, suddenly pawing desperately at the ground. He was searching for something not visible to the eye, but that a dog could "see" with his other senses.

"Hold on," Yann told him. "I'm going to help you." They dug together in the hardened ground, at last unearthing the edge of their buried treasure. "Hey...what is this?" Yann asked moving the dirt around and trying to get a better look at what they'd found, "It looks like a piece of Samurai armor. Wow, it's really nice. What is it doing here?"

Is this the post apocalyptic world?

SEASONS OF HEAVEN

He worked until he was able to catch a part of the object his hand could hold onto. Pitching in to help, Ani found a small cord attached to the armor and pulled at it with his teeth. Together they tugged it out of the earth. Yann looked at it closely and then cleaned the dirt off of it with his T-shirt. He examined it again, wondering what in the world it was doing here. It was a beautiful piece of armor. He slipped it into his backpack and told Ani,

"I'll keep it for now."

They began walking again and soon Ani's ears perked up. Yann listened to hear what it was that had caught Ani's attention. He could hear the metallic tinkling of a stream. They advanced forward until the trees parted and they could see the stream then. The water was running across dozens of little rocks and it was so clear it looked like a polished mirror of silver with skeins of white foam twirling across the surface. Huge boulders colonized the edges of the pond, covered with carpets of green moss.

SEASONS OF HEAVEN

As water met stone it caused the sounds they'd heard, a rocky gurgle, a swish a clink a swell and a clop. Yann's senses were almost overwhelmed. It seemed that sight and smell were vying for attention in this new and fascinating world he and Ani had stumbled upon.

Yann took stock of the stream and the rocks that lay across it. He was sure that he'd be able to navigate it, but Ani's legs were short and his body would no doubt be covered by the water if he attempted the crossing. Yann leaned down and picked up the dog placing his arms under his front paws and encircling him with his right hand. Trying to find his balance with his other arm held out to his side, he found that Ani was heavier when each step was risky for them both.

Each cautious step brought them closer to the other side. When they reached it a look passed between them that needed no words. From Ani, it was pure love and gratitude...from

SEASONS OF HEAVEN

Yann it was relief that his best friend was safe and the assurance he would do whatever it took to keep him that way.

"What's that, Ani?" Yann asked, looking at the tracks on the ground in the mud on the other side of the bank. It looked like the mark of horses hooves. "A horse? I wonder if he lives here or if he only came here to quench his thirst?" Yann said to his friend.

They moved forward once again, this time tracing the steps of the hooves that were embedded into the ground underneath their feet. The diamond bright light continued to push its way through the leaves and cast a tender glow across the crusty exteriors of the trees. The light pressed against the green foliage giving it a gold complexion. They idled past bushes covered in velvety soft flowers. Yann absently fingered them, caressing them softly as they passed. Eventually, they arrived at a wide glade where the trees fell away and revealed the dazzling blue sky and another lush green meadow. That was where they found the horse.

His muscular white frame stood out in front of the blue and green backdrop of the meadow and the sky as he grazed. Ani inched his way towards the horse and as the horse made eye-contact with him, Ani received pictures of a man with a long black hair and armor like the one they discovered earlier. The smells of smoke and blood were both there in his mind as well, along with pictures of a mountain and a blade. The horse broke the connection then by turning his head and noticing Yann. He locked his giant brown eyes into the boys' and there was a blinding flash of white light and Yann could suddenly see the horse lying on his side. He sensed that the horse was hurt and he wanted to help him, but he couldn't. They were in a dream...or a memory. Yann watched as the poor animal struggled to his feet. His long legs were shaking almost convulsively and his nostrils were flaring with exertion. After some time, the horse finally made it up to all fours. Yann saw then that the side the horse had been lying on was covered with blood. The dark red color of the thick liquid matted into the hair of the regal white beast and left a sharp contrast in its wake. Yann was able to see now that beside where the horse had lain, there was a bag and a bow.

Once the horse was able to find and maintain his footing, he began galloping through a seemingly endless field covered with the soft down of the green grass. He passed nothing but more field and grass for a long while. Then suddenly, the horse paused in front of a strange looking stone. It was orange and green and the water that was raining down upon it was coming from the ground and the stream was a web of vivid pastel colors. The steam rolled off of the water and the rocks, mingling with the cooler air and formed a light, rainbow-colored fog. The ground caught what was left of the hot rain when it made it back to the dirt and formed prismatic pools around the tinted boulders. Yann had no idea what he was watching but he was yet again unable to take his eyes from the amazing sight of the surreal colors. It was unlike anything he could have ever imagined coming out of the earth.

The horse continued its steady gallop until suddenly stopping again to lift its head towards the sight of a mysterious object crossing the sky. It was there and then gone, without a trace of itself left behind. Once it had disappeared the horse took off into a trot once more until it came to a small lake. The crystalline water looked cool and refreshing. The horse stopped to take a drink.... Another blinding flash passed beyond and behind Yann's eyes and he and Ani were together, alone once again.

They started back down their path, hoping to find more of the stones like the ones Yann had seen in the vision with the horse.

SEASONS OF HEAVEN

They passed more of the gently rolling hills and delighted in the way the grass rippled across them as the breeze passed through. Ani stopped suddenly, dead in his tracks and then Yann. They were standing in front of a magnificent but eerie statue.

It was a stone carving of an over-large head with heavy brows and an elongated nose with a distinctive fish-hook-shape curl of his nostrils. His lips protruded into a thin pout and his ears, like his nose was elongated and in an oblong shape. The jaw lines stood out against the abridged neck and the torso was heavy with clavicles subtly outlined in stone. The arms rested against the body and long, slender fingers relaxed along the crest of the hips, meeting at the loincloth where the thumbs pointed at the navel. The two friends ebbed closer to the statue. It was covered on one side with moss. Yann thought that it looked familiar and abruptly it came to him where he knew the statue from. It was a Moai.

An ancient statue?

"How can that be possible?" Yann mused aloud, "This is a statue from Easter Island. It's huge. Look Ani, there is an inscription on it...oh, I can't really understand these signs!"

Ani approached the statue and as he did, a brilliant light gushed out of the stone.

"Wow, that's gorgeous!" Yann said, looking towards Ani, "Did you do that?" All at once a strong wind began to blow through the statue and across the companions. It came out of nowhere, starting to the left of them and blowing across to the right. The friends had to drop low and cling to the ground to keep from being blown away. It only lasted a few seconds and then it stopped as suddenly as it had begun. It was the strangest wind that Yann or Ani had ever witnessed.

"What happened?" Yann said, confused, "That was a close one, so suddenly and now the air is so calm again...weird." Yann stood in contemplation for a few seconds and then suddenly looked down at his friend and said,

"Let's go, Ani. I think we should hurry, the sun is setting!"

Not long after, they decided to make a camp for the night. The sky was amazing and the beautiful boreal aurora were dancing in the across the limitless space. The glowing embers of the camp fire leaped and twirled in a fiery dance. Ani lay near Yann's legs as he lay there with questions swirling through his mind almost chaotically. *What was that place? Why aren't his parents with them?* He thought it must be a dream but there was also something so real about it. He ate some of the fruits they'd found during the day in this strange land to quell his hunger. Yann was a kid and so close to what life should be. His heart was pure and there was no form of life that he didn't respect. Another part of him was made magic by the autism he lived with. It made him even more unique. He thought back now to when he used to ask his parents, "Why are you eating animals? Aren't they our friends? Aren't we supposed to love our friends, and not eat them?" Yann's above average intelligence had seemed a constant source of surprise to his parents. As he lay there under the stars thinking, his eyes began to grow heavy. As sleep weighed too heavily on him for him to fight it any longer, he was serenaded by the unique and harmonious sounds of the nature that surrounded him.

He'd just slipped away into dreamland when a sound from the forest awakened Ani. He lifted his little black head and looked at Yann. Seeing he was asleep, Ani decided to investigate the sound himself. Ani had a feeling since they'd been here that he somehow knew this place, like a feeling of déjà vu. He approached the forest slowly, entering into the thick brush. He looked around with his round dark eyes in awe of what he saw there. Luminous bugs walked slowly through the trees and created a beautiful symphony of color. The forest at night seemed to take on a magical life of its own, kept secret from the rest of the world. One of the bugs stopped his busy work around the roots of the trees that were playing hide and seek with the soil, and looked at Ani. Ani received a clear picture in his head of what the bug was trying to communicate, "I work for a better place, don't bother me." Ani was aware that nature had many secrets and respecting them was an important part of life and cohabitation. As he stepped further into the forest Ani's eyes landed on another beautiful site. It was a majestic elephant, sitting calmly on the trunk of a tree. It was such an unusual picture, but at the same time to Ani, it looked so natural. The beast looked over at Ani as he approached him slowly. Ani could see or had a sense of the multitude of animals surrounding them. There were hundreds if not thousands of different species sitting or standing in the trees or down on the roots of the trees on the ground. As Ani ventured deeper they stopped what they were doing and all eyes fell on the little dog. As he met their eyes he received thousands of messages. He could see a great storm, a huge ocean...and a human with a giant boat. The boat was loaded with as many animals as it could carry. When Ani reached the big gray elephant, he sat down next to him. Ani knew he was the patriarch of this place and he looked on him with respect and awe. The great beast acknowledged the little dog with the blink of his eyes and a message of gratitude. Ani could feel that the connection between nature and all of these creatures was strong here, the strongest he'd ever felt. The energies here were all inter-connected and the Ki is strong with them. The sudden appearance of a pure white lion didn't seem to startle any of the others. Ani looked on him with curious eyes as he sat down next to the elephant. .The white lion's eyes connected with Ani's and the message he was sending was clear, "You are your friend's guard and protector. You need to keep him close on this journey to ensure that he stays safe and help him find his way. You must not leave him, no matter what."

Ani nodded at the lion and the other animals slowly began to come forth and show him gratitude. Some of the squirrels brought him nuts and others a plant. Even to Ani it was a surreal sight to see this clan of different species so emotionally and spiritually connected, that their bond could never be broken.

The grand elephant began to stand up slowly. The whole area rumbled as he got to his feet.

He gave Ani one last long look before turning and disappearing into the forest without as much as a sound. The white lion stayed behind and asked Ani to follow him; he seemed as if he had something to show him.

Ani and the lion walked until they were in the center of the forest where there was an area filled with trees that were as white as the lion. Ani had never seen anything like it. The ground was pink like a summer night and the leaves that fell from the trees looked as if they were floating to earth in slow motion. Ani heard the soft sounds of water tinkling over rock and looked towards it. There, amongst the plants and trees ran a beautiful, turquoise river. Near the river Ani could see a tombstone. The sign on it was strange with three triangles aligned on top. There was writing on them...Japanese kanji's. To a human it may have spelled out a name, but to Ani and the lion the words were only symbols. Ani was surprised to see the lady on her knees next to it, bowing her head and crying. The animals gave Ani the message that they called her 'the sadness'. She came every night here near the tomb and the lion thought it was important for Ani to see it.

    Who was she? Ani wondered. <u>She looked like a ghost with her pale, white skin</u>. She was translucent yet real at the same time. He stood there with the lion for a long time and just watched her until the first ray of the sun began to break through the thick canopy of trees.

She turned her head and looked slowly at Ani just as she began to fade. Her eyes were strange, yet familiar to him. He couldn't remember if he knew her or not. Once she was gone, the lion escorted Ani back to the edge of the forest. The lion turned and went back into the trees and left Ani alone with his friend. Yann was still sleeping by the fire and Ani went over and lay down next to his leg. He closed his own weary eyes and faded into sleep.

So you travel between worlds during sleep?

CHAPTER FIVE
"THE JOURNEY"

The boy and his best friend the dog took off on the same path they'd been following, but after a short while, they ran into a small cliff. It was just over Yann's head. He reached up and jumped slightly off the ground. He was able to grab the edge and he knew he would be able to pull himself up onto it but the problem was Ani. He couldn't climb it with Ani in his arms.

He looked at the dog and they both knew what had to be done. To Ani's credit, he didn't look nervous at all. Yann took hold of Ani around his belly with both hands. One hand rested across the front and the other along the back of his friend. He had to turn Ani one hundred and eighty degrees while leaning against his chest as he pushed him up in a single gesture onto the edge of the cliff. Yann was out of breath when he finished, but happy to look up and see Ani looking down at him, safe.

SEASONS OF HEAVEN

Yann negotiated the cliff next by grabbing on with both hands and using his feet to scale the steep side. He finally did one grand move like a pull-up and landed on his belly on top of the cliff. Ani came up to him and licked his face. Yann giggled before pushing himself up off the ground and taking a look around.

The forest was darker here, with no visible beams of light. It seemed much denser and the vegetation wasn't parting easily to allow them passage, as it had been so gracious to do in the light.

What Yann and Ani didn't see was the dark shape that slunk quietly behind them and followed them into the forest.

What they did see was that there was a light dusting of shadowy gray fog in the distance and the intense gloom of it all almost completely occluded Yann's vision. Ani led the way and as they advanced Yann couldn't help but think about how almost disturbingly inviting and cozy the forest had been in the daylight as

[handwritten note: Is this the monster from the beginning.]

compared to now in twilight when it was shrouded by an almost repellant bleakness. The poplars and oaks and ferns were covered in moss that during the day had caused the glorious green/gold reflection to bounce off of their trunks, but now it only served as further camouflage in the almost suffocating darkness.

  They passed huge trees just strewn about on the ground. In many places, they had to climb over the trunk because the tree was too large to go around. Ani seemed to be interested in one of them and Yann had to get right next to him to see what it was he was looking at. This tree trunk was hollow, and it looked like it had been hollowed from the inside out. <u>There was an opening that looked like an entrance and without discussing it with Yann; Ani wormed his way into it.</u> Yann decided to bypass it and as he went around it he could see that the trees around them looked as if they had been ripped from the ground. Their roots like tentacle sea creatures reached desperately this way and that starving for the soil they'd been planted in since long before Yann had taken his first breath. There was an entire patch not far behind them that was completely void of trees.

"I don't know what snatched those trees, Ani, but whatever it was, it was huge..."

Suddenly stillness dropped over them and Yann realized that the wind had completely stopped. The leaves on the trees no longer moved and the atmosphere around them suddenly felt colder, bleaker...

"Ani," Yann said in a whisper, "Do you feel like we're being watched?" It was a strange sensation, like a dark presence had suddenly descended over them. It was the first time since they'd begun this journey that Yann felt a true sense of fear and something even akin to loathing.

Ani sniffed the air and looked around. Then he stood completely still and appeared to be in a trance like state with his ears extended up. Yann knew he smelled the air for the scent of someone following them and listening for even the faintest of sounds. Yann stepped close to Ani. The dog let Yann know through their telepathy that he did indeed think they were being watched. He too could feel the presence of an entity with malicious intentions. They looked around together then with a mounting sense of alarm. Their eyes both fell on what had been watching them at once. It was an enormous dark creature standing frozen between the trees and the forest. The sight of him served to fuel the fear and anxiety that already dwelled in their hearts. It was as black as night and it stood motionless, staring at them with a pair of glowing red eyes. Yann felt terror grip him. It was like a heavy weight had suddenly been placed on his chest and he yelled at Ani to run.

They both began to run, through the brush that reached out and scratched Yann's arms and face and tangled itself up in his clothing. They vaulted over the massive trunks of the trees that had been ripped out of the ground and left to rot. They ducked underneath low-hanging branches and dodged the grasp of a sudden barrage of long, black arms that seemed to be reaching out for them in every direction. Yann could hear Ani's ragged breathing...or was that his own? The blood was pounding in his ears, so he wasn't sure. His heart knocked insistently against the wall of his chest as if begging to be let out.

    They ran even when they were suddenly and almost completely covered in a thick black swirl of smoke that had begun to envelope them from above. It seemed to be trying to swallow and digest them but they were moving too fast. It followed along, seemingly waiting for an opportunity. Yann was afraid that one may have presented itself as they approached a precipice. Still running he looked at Ani who confirmed what they needed to do....Jump.

SEASONS OF HEAVEN

The first clue that they had missed their mark came as both Yann and Ani's small bodies were flung against the side wall of the cliff. The second clue came as they felt themselves falling, once again striking the wall, limp as ragdolls before finally coming to a blunt force stop against the floor of a cave.

Stunned and still charged with adrenaline, the two friends looked at each other to make sure there were no serious injuries. Neither of them seemed more than terrified and exhausted. Ani got to his small feet first and watched as Yann pushed back up to his own. The two of them surveyed their new environment to discover they were inside of a cave. Ivy grew up along the sides of both walls and across the top, vying for space amongst the dried up plants. The limestone walls of the cave were wet as water seeped through the roof and ran down through the ivy that clung to the stone quenching its dark green leaves. The sound of the running water echoed off both the walls and the huge columns that also surrounded them.

"Look Ani, there's a torch." Hanging from the wall was a burning torch. Yann was so happy to have a bit of light that he didn't even stop to consider who may have lit it.

Happy to be out of the dark, Yann held up the torch and they took a better look around. He could hear the whoosh, whoosh of the wings of bats as they circled overhead, seeking out the light. As Yann twirled slowly around, he and Ani could see that the colors of the stonewalls changed subtly and mysteriously every few seconds. One moment they would be a warm azure color and the next they would fade to brown. On their second time circling around, the stonewalls changed to a fiery orange like the color of a summer sunset.

The light of the torch formed strong contrasts across the walls; some of the stalagmites were very close and exposed pleasant esthetic details. It seemed peaceful

[Handwritten margin note: The beauty of caves. Wonder if there'll be bats mentioned]

and Yann and Ani had the feeling they were safe...for the moment at least. That was just before a piercing shriek reverberated throughout the cave and the entire enclosure began to shake. Small rocks were falling but what worried Yann even more was the amount of dirt falling in on top of them. Yann was old enough to know that neither human nor dog could survive being buried alive.

"Run Ani, run!" The huge creature must be lumbering around above them, trying to find its way inside the cave. Its enormous bulk was causing the cave to fall in upon itself.

They raced ahead for their lives for the second time that evening eventually coming to the front of an uphill slope. A bright light like the one Yann had awakened to that morning was shining from it. They looked up towards the light and saw the exit. The light at the end of the tunnel.... Yann and Ani looked at each other and began strategizing their ascent to the top.

SEASONS OF HEAVEN

Yann held Ani up first, helping him climb onto a small flat area that jutted out from the rock. Then Yann grabbed ahold of one of the ruts in the stone that was as high as he could reach and pulled himself up. He was a few inches above Ani. He reached up again and grabbed another rut in the stone. As he struggled to force his arms to pull him up, he felt his friend, pushing his bottom from behind. That extra push allowed him to clear the few inches he needed to in order to place his feet in another safe position. He reached down then and with a guiding hand on Ani's back he helped the dog struggle up further until they were almost eye to eye. Yann took his turn next and with strength and will that neither of them knew they possessed they continued on until they were within reach of the top. Coming from thin air and startling them both a large white hand reached out to help.

Yann stared at the hand and then looked at Ani wondering what they should do. He couldn't see up beyond the hand, the light was too bright. Perhaps it was a trick? Did the dark creature possess some kind of magic that made him capable of transforming himself? Yann had been through so much this day that he no longer knew what to believe. What was real and what wasn't?

"Take my hand Yann; I'm here to help you." It was a woman's voice, warm and engaging. It was a choice between trusting her and being buried underneath a mountain of dirt, he decided she had to be the safer choice. Yann scooped Ani up into one of his arms and took hold of the hand. They were pulled up to the top and out into the light. A ghostly white figure in the distinct shape of a woman stood before them.

"I hope you are ok!" she said, "I'm sure you have a lot of questions, you probably wonder why you are here, you wonder about that black thing you saw, and about the statue. I know that you have lost your parents. If you want to see them again, you will have to help me free that black thing. It has been pacing up and down here for a while now... It is prisoner of this place."

Confused, Yann looked again at his companion and then back at the apparition in front of him, "But how do you want us to do that?" he asked her. "It's so huge..."

"Rest assured Yann," she told him, "You are here for a reason, but I cannot explain everything to you now. That thing holds a set of two keys that you must recover in order to activate the two towers. Once the towers are activated, a passage way will open for you."

Yann didn't say anything else but he looked skeptical. The white figure sensed his angst and she said,

"You can do this, Yann. I'm sure of that. Oh! There's one more thing...take this, it's a pendant that once belonged to that thing, a long time ago." She held the pendant out and not knowing what else to do, Yann took it. As soon as he did, the ghostly white figure began to dissipate.

"Hey...wait, don't go!" Yann yelled after her... He turned back and looked at his friend. Ani was giving him a look that was almost accusing. "Ani, don't look at me like that, I had nothing to do with this," Yann told him. Then as Ani communicated with him via their telepathy Yann said, "What? You want to smell it? Here you go..." He put the pendant down where Ani could smell it. Ani took a good whiff; they would have to follow the mysterious, hideous, awful creature using this piece of jewelry.

The companions gave each other another searching look. They knew as much about the white figure as they did the dark one...practically nothing. The difference was, the white figure was offering them salvation and a reunion with Yann's parents. They would follow her advice and pray that it led them out of the darkness and back home where they belonged.

CHAPTER SIX
"FALLING"
JFK AIRPORT, NEW YORK

[handwritten margin note: Why does the stay keep going back and forth?]

James tolerated the chaos of the airport and endured the annoyances that going through security these days entailed...barely. He was at last rewarded for it all by the sound of the voice calling overhead that his flight was boarding. He picked up his carry-on bag and grudgingly got into another line as each passenger walked across the ramp that led into the open door of the plane and found their seats. James made his way to his own seat with his boarding pass in hand and stowed his carry on in the space above. He sat down, finally able to relax...if only he could turn off his thoughts....

Looking down at the boarding pass he was holding, a strange sensation began to creep throughout his body. For years now, since the day that his son had disappeared

SEASONS OF HEAVEN

James had seriously considered suicide, more than once. Not a day went by when he didn't picture sweet Thomas' face. The only thing that kept him going was the thought...the chance...the hope they would find him and he would be reunited with his son.

James often thought that kidnapping was possibly worse than the death of a child. At least when a child dies...as horrible that was...the parent's had some sort of closure. They didn't sit and wait, and watch and pray constantly that the child was going to come home. His mind couldn't stop thinking about it. How was he supposed to? He didn't know who or what had his boy. He didn't know if he were alive or dead. He didn't know what Thomas may have to endure without his father there to help him...to protect him. There was nothing on this earth more unnatural than the loss of a child. The human spirit was strong, but no one should be expected to endure that kind of heart wrenching loss and come out the other side

> *Handwritten margin note:* Why? With a kidnapping there's a chance you can see them again.

unscathed. It wasn't humanly possible. Once you had fallen into that bottomless abyss of pain and suffering...there was no way out.

The question that James couldn't escape and the one that he couldn't stop asking...was how? How does a child just disappear? The police had no clues....no evidence ever uncovered or recorded that might give them any idea as to where Thomas went and who or what may have taken him. How does that happen? Someone had to have seen him; someone had to know where he was...

"Can I get you something to drink, sir?" James was pulled from his thoughts by the sound of the flight attendant's voice.

"Yes, I'll have bourbon on the rocks," James told her. Another drink couldn't hurt. Who knows? It might be the one that will finally dull the ache in his heart.... Soothe the pain in his soul. At the very least it would help ease him into a dreamless sleep.

SEASONS OF HEAVEN

"Ladies and gentlemen," the woman's voice came across the intercom, "The Captain has turned off the Seat Belt sign, and you may now use the lavatories. However, we always recommend keeping your seat belt fastened while you're seated. You may now turn on your electronic devices. We wish you all an enjoyable flight..."

James tried to relax but the darkness of the night outside the window and the sounds of the airplane engines whirring only served to feed his mounting anxiety. After a few minutes he signaled the nearest Flight attendant and said,

"Excuse me, I ordered a drink and it hasn't come yet..."

"It's on its way, sir," she told him.

"I don't really like to fly," he told her, "So...if you could be nice enough to hurry it up...if you can? Thank you."

After another few minutes, James received his drink. The flight attendant had brought him a bottle of bourbon and a glass full of ice.

"Thank you," James told her. Still in a foul mood he said, "It was nice of you to hurry," in a sarcastic tone.

A sudden flash of white consumed the plane and when James could focus his eyes again he was standing in the center of the aisle. Confused, he looked around at the other passengers but they were no longer human….they were mannequins, anthropomorphic mannequins, life like…but not alive.

There was another blinding flash of white light and one of the female mannequins yelled out,

"Run James!"

"Your son is dead, and he is ours!" The adult male mannequin who sat next to her said. Then the little boy mannequin who sat with them, said in a creepy little boy voice,

SEASONS OF HEAVEN

"Look for him at 10h23, maybe you'll find him...Or maybe you will only find his corpse."

It was all horrible and overwhelming, too much for James to bear. He grabbed his aching head in his hands and let out a gut-wrenching scream. James began wandering about the plane; stumbling...drunk, frightened, anguished…. The statues watched him, their eyes moving as he did. It was like truly being caught in a nightmare. James felt like time was standing still, as if he were a puppet himself. He screamed again, just to break the awful silence and this time as he did some of the mannequins began to rise to their feet. It was as if he'd awakened them. James looked at them in horror, wondering what they were up to. He found out soon enough as they began to run after him. They chased him through the humongous plane. They ran along the first floor of the two-story plane, where a game of hide and seek ensued. It was the most horrifying game that James had ever played and although he wanted no part of it he had no choice. He found a small place to hide and as he waited for them to find him and do...whatever...he could feel his heart pounding so furiously that he thought it might rip a hole in his chest. The sweat dripped slowly down the sides of his face and he tried with all of his might to control the rough and ragged sounds of his breathing so as not to give away his hiding place.

When James had at last calmed himself enough to see straight, he spotted the fire extinguisher in the seat in front of him. He lifted it out of its holder quietly and then in one grand motion he stood up and pulled the handle. A thick cloud of white began to spurt out, coloring the air so that he could suddenly see petrifying black shadows twirling all around him. They had their mouths held open as if in silent screams and some of them reached out and swiped the air around James as if trying to capture him. Still holding the extinguisher, he began to run again.... Trying desperately to find a way out. He reached the door of the cockpit and pulled hard on the latch that held it closed. As it swung open James knew he had to be caught up in a horrendous nightmare. In the pilot seat sat his dear departed wife, Sarah and their boy Thomas sat next to her as her co-pilot.

Normally James would have been thrilled to see them both, but although the things in the cockpit were dead ringers for his family their robotic movements and frozen on smiles were anything but warm and inviting. James had no idea what they were, but he knew what they weren't and that was his beautiful wife and son. He was about to close the door and the thing that was Sarah sang out,

"Bye, honey!" as if James was only leaving for work. It was Sarah's voice, only it wasn't. It was a dark, sinister version of it that sent a chill running rampant down James's spine.

SEASONS OF HEAVEN

"See you soon, Dad!" Thomas said, in a voice completely void of emotion.

James was deadly frightened now. He slammed the door, unable to look at the visions of his wife and son. He knew they weren't real, they couldn't be. It was the dark things...the things of his nightmares, trying to trick him. It wasn't what they looked like; it was what they *felt* like. They felt wrong...evil, something neither Sarah nor Thomas could ever be.

His head was pounding like a drum and he felt as if he would explode from the build-up of anxiety in his chest. He began screaming again if for no other reason than that he was hoping to release some of what was tearing him up inside. As he stood there screaming, he realized that the dark entities had found him once more. He didn't see them this time...he felt them. Like the other monsters, the ones from his childhood and in the hospital, he could feel their dark ministrations.

SEASONS OF HEAVEN

He ran up the stairs looking desperately once again for an exit. He didn't think about how high they were in the air, or that he couldn't possibly survive if he jumped. He just wanted...no, he needed out.

There was suddenly a deafening sound as an explosion ripped through the plane. James was thrown against a wall as the plane surged to the right and from where he lay in the floor, he could see the glare of bright orange and yellow flames out of one of the windows. Smoke rolled out of the plane and filled the sky with an enormous black cloud. The engine was on fire; it must have been what exploded. He didn't know what to be more frightened of the shadowy creatures or the now surely doomed flight.

He was still sliding along the windowed wall as the plane continued to tip further sideways. He reached out and tried to grab onto something, anything. He was still clutching the fire extinguisher so hard that his knuckles were white and sore. When he turned loose with one hand to try and grab something to hold onto the fire extinguisher slipped from his other hand and slamming forcefully into his head, sent him into a sea of blackness as the alarm began to screech wildly in the background.

When James came to, it was obvious that the plane was plummeting wildly towards the ground. James groped around, dazed and disoriented, only knowing that he desperately needed to find something to hold onto. He had to get to his feet...he had to get out of the plane. That made no sense, either way he was dead. Something told him that he'd rather face a free fall from thirty thousand feet or so than the eternal damnation the creatures seemed to be offering.

He was finally able to get a grip onto the back of one of the seats in front of him. With a great deal of effort because of the injury to his head and because of the sharp, downward angle of the plane he at last struggled to his feet.

The sight of the abysmal black shapes still hovering around him spurred him back into action once he was finally upright again. He began to head for the clearly marked "exit" door, but before he got there he was once again assaulted by an earsplitting sound and before he could even react to that, his body was sucked out the door that had been ripped off its hinges and he found himself suspended in the dark sky. Although relieved to have escaped the clutches of the dark, dreadful things, he knew without a doubt now that he was going to die and he began crying for a wasted life. He cried for having to leave before he knew where Thomas was and what had happened to him. That was the worst part, knowing that he'd never be able to discover what had happened to his boy. He couldn't imagine that his soul could ever rest without that knowledge, no matter how sinister the answer might be.

He watched in abject horror as the plane was ripped into two huge pieces by the violence of the storm that surrounded him. James' body was being twirled around, he couldn't stop spinning and the force of the motion caused him to become nauseated, sick...he began to vomit violently as his body continued its motion. He was hurtled through the clouds which didn't feel light and puffy at all, but as if they were coated with sharp edges that tore at his body as he passed through them. The bolts of lightning passed close, so closely that he could feel their heat and jolts of electrical currents ripping through his flesh.

His body finally stopped twisting and twirling and James began to fall now with his face turned towards the earth. His fingers and his face gathered ice as they froze and his eyes began to glaze over. He could no longer see well, but as he turned his head to the left he thought he saw a vast landmass with immense waterfalls only a hundred or so meters away, emptying out into the sky. He watched the sight, enraptured by it for several seconds and then suddenly what he'd been gazing upon just vanished as if it had never been there in the first place.

    James turned his head back into the direction of the earth, the direction that he was falling. He could see colors first and then trees. The drops of water he'd seen began to turn into lakes and the tiny little houses into huge, tall buildings. The changes were too fast for his brain to process. He closed his eyes, hoping not to see what would come last.

CHAPTER SEVEN
"CONFRONTATIONS WITH A GHOST"
QUEEN'S NEW YORK
Friday, March 3, 1990

> *[handwritten: Now it is a new perspective. These people must have something in common.]*

Tim Northman had been a criminal squad inspector, with the New York Police Department, since 1962. He'd earned several promotions and the undeniable respect of his peers after eighteen years on the force and the arrest of a serial killer who had been working in the New York area.

That arrest hadn't come quickly, or easily. Tim and his peers had worked tirelessly chasing what sometimes felt like a ghost across a city so populated that it was like looking for a needle in a haystack. Tim had ultimately been the one to solve the case and arrest the perpetrator however and because of that he had become known as the "pioneer" of modern profiling. Criminal profiling could be dated all the way back to the year 1486 when the first publication mentioned profiling in a professional manual for witch hunters, but the methods that Tim had been using were much more sophisticated than your run of the mill witch hunt.

Unfortunately, Tim's efforts had not been lauded by all. The first American profilers including Tim were virulently criticized by the press and much of the New York City police department as well. They were in fact often seen as "witch hunters" mainly because of the way they conducted interviews and examinations were so different from the way the average police officer conducted his business. It often left the profiler working the case alone and leaving his colleagues out of the loop. That method didn't go along well with the code of teamwork that officers were trained to live by. For many reasons, criminal profiling was looked upon as a "flawed science" but regardless of all of that, it had produced some amazing results. Tim had been amongst one of the first in NYPD to use the methods and succeed.

Once Tim solved that first case, he began to spend long hours going through the unsolved cases in the police archives…the "cold" cases. He looked hard at the thousands of missing person's cases that had come to a dead end because of a lack of evidence. He got so into it, he began to file and sort all of the victims by a "modus operandi," or how and where they had disappeared, ethnicity, social background, age, looks, etc. The faces from the photos of the missing, lost and otherwise misplaced souls haunted him. He felt a compulsion to at least look for them…. And a driving need to find them.

While he was working on that overwhelming task, he was invited to give conferences and seminars throughout the country in order to educate his colleagues about profiling methods. Tim never missed an opportunity to educate himself either and as the years went by, his techniques continued to improve.

Today Tim was parked in the borough of Queens. He sat in the driver's seat and his partner Eddie sat on the passenger side as they both sipped on cups of steaming hot coffee and talked about anything to fight away the boredom that a stakeout could bring about.

"Ok, tell me, don't you think it's a good idea? Getting him a dog is a way of making him responsible, or at least, that's what the doctor..." Tim started.

His partner, Eddie Nomura interrupted by saying, "I don't know, but it's a good way of teaching him life's indispensable lessons."

"You're right. And I really love dogs, I used to have one when I was a kid."

"I think it can only help your son deal with the Asperger's syndrome and..."

"And what ..?" Tim asked, wondering why Eddie had stopped.

SEASONS OF HEAVEN

"You know," Eddie said, reluctantly. He was re-thinking what he had been about to say. He didn't want to offend his partner, but they had a habit of being nothing but honest with each other so he went on to say, "We're rarely at home. We don't spend a lot of time with our families. It may help him cope with the absence of his father. You know what I mean?"

Tim had thought of that himself. He said, "You're probably right...I should convert to Buddhism. You always put such a Zen spin on life..."

"Eh, that life would be easier to deal with. It's a life philosophy...and stop that nonsense, you're a good father and a great husband. Elise is lucky to have you," he said with a laugh.

Tim smiled and said, "I know that you like her."

They were interrupted by the harsh crackle of the car radio and then the dispatcher's voice saying,

"All officers in the vicinity....903 reported in Queens, 42nd and Exeter. Suspect is reported to be armed."

Eddie picked up the radio and said, "Car 1023, responding."

The dispatcher said, "Copy 1023, back-up is on the way."

"Damn, I knew it, it's him! Maybe three days of sitting in the car drinking piss-poor coffee wasn't time wasted after all," Tim said as he was already starting the car, putting it in gear and peeling away from the curb, leaving a puff of black smoke in its wake.

The unmarked brown sedan began to weave through traffic, not stopping for red lights or stop signs and taking as many back roads as he could to get there faster. Tim drove the car up onto the curb and without turning off the ignition he jumped out with his gun drawn.

"Go around back;" Tim told Eddie, "I'm taking the stairs."

SEASONS OF HEAVEN

"Be safe! Don't try to play a hero!" Eddie yelled after him. Tim was already leaping up the stairs to the building. He ran inside and then up the stairs again to the seventh floor of the building. When his feet hit the worn landing he looked around him for any sign of life. Tim knew from his years on the force that the suspect wasn't always the only one a police officer had to look out for. The neighbors in these tight-knit "hoods" were often just as dangerous.

"Beat it, asshole!" Tim looked around again, the voice came from a crazy looking homeless man who lay forlornly in one of the doorways.

A doorway creaked open and Tim turned his gun towards it. What he saw looking out at him was uglier than the homeless man. It was a woman...at least he thought it was. She was wearing a bathrobe that looked as if it hadn't been washed since the seventies, cheap looking clown make-up and her hands were covered in what looked like paint and Play-doh. Unfazed by the gun Tim had trained on her she said,

"Hey baby, you wanna have a good time? Come on in and take those pants off, make yourself at home. My lips are magic."

Tim swallowed the bile in his throat that had risen at the thought. This building was well-known by vice. It was a hot-bed of prostitution and a den for drug addicts and dealers. Ignoring the clown-thing's offer, he moved on cautiously into the dimly lit decrepit building.

Meanwhile downstairs, Eddie had found a way into the building as well. He'd gone around the back and through a broken window. He dropped down into a laundry room. It was filthy; the rats were probably not even comfortable there Eddie thought. He saw a man and woman leaning against the wall. They appeared to be waiting for their laundry. Amped with adrenaline, Eddie yelled at them,

SEASONS OF HEAVEN

"Don't move. Keep your hands where I can see them."

A voice floated through the room from behind him and he whirled away from the terrified couple coming face to face with their perpetrator…. His name was Frank Lewis, but Eddie and Tim didn't know that yet. The despicable man held a small child against his chest, using him as a shield.

"Let the kid go," Eddie told him, his voice steadier than he felt inside, "If you don't, I'll put a bullet through your head!"

The tension in the room between the men, the child and the unfortunate witnesses was thick enough to cut. Everyone wondered who would make the first move.

Eddie gestured with his head towards the door behind him, then addressing the spectators he said,

"You can leave, go behind me." Everything's going to be ok!"

As the terrified witnesses made their hasty exit, Eddie's radio crackled to life once more. Tim's voice floated through,

"What's your twenty? Are you okay?"

Eddie spoke into the mouthpiece pinned to his chest as he said, "I'm in the basement, in the laundry room. Our suspect is here and he's brought company…. a child who he seems to think is a shield. I have my gun on him. I think I might have to shoot him in the head." Eddie said it matter-of-factly, hoping the suspect would take the hint and let the boy go.

"I'll be right there," Tim said, "Back-up will be here anytime now as well."

Eddie hadn't taken his eyes off Frank and the kid. After Tim signed off the radio he said, "Ok, if you let the kid go, we can end this peacefully. No one has to get hurt. I don't think you're going to hurt that kid, are you, tough guy?"

"I don't really have a choice inspector, sorry…" Frank said. He didn't sound sorry in the least. Before anyone could act however the light in the room began to oscillate and a strange series of sounds began to resonate in the small room. Then the light went off completely and back on again.

"What the hell is going on?" Eddie said, still with his eyes glued to the suspect.

If Eddie thought he was confused by the lights and sounds, he had no words for what happened next. As Eddie watched the hooded man vanished, leaving the kidnapped child on the ground where he had stood just seconds before.

Tim raced in as Eddie was kneeling over the child, making sure he was okay. He appeared to be in shock, terrified but breathing and unscathed.

"What happened? Where is he? Where is the kid?" Tim said; with his gun still ready to fire if need be.

"The kid's ok, I'll call an ambulance for him. I think...I mean...Shit! The guy went out

[handwritten margin note: James lost son Thomas is connected?]

the window. He must have. Go after him!" Eddie's head was spinning...he felt like the man had just disappeared, but that couldn't be possible. He must have just moved fast...that had to be it.

"Ok, back up's on the way," Tim told him, climbing out the window that Eddie had come in earlier.

"Tim!" Eddie called after him, "Be careful, there is something really creepy about this guy."

The window opened up to a narrow backstreet. It started raining while they were in the building and Tim was suddenly getting pelted with a barrage of quarter size drops of water. The cars and trashcans made the alleyway like a maze for Tim to maneuver. As he wiggled and leapt his way through he came to a pet store. Suddenly from out of nowhere a wooden crate was thrown a few inches in front of him.

Stunned, he heard laughter as he felt his feet slipping out from underneath him on the drenched ground.

"Fuck!" he yelled as he tried to regain his footing. He ran inside the back door of the pet shop, through the store and out the other side.

He came out into another alley but this one was completely deserted. Tim followed the alleyway, coming to a door in the middle of the wire netting that ran alongside of it. It looked like it was damaged at the top and upon further inspection; Tim saw traces of blood and a piece of fabric caught in the metallic fence.

"I got you, you bastard!" Tim said out loud to the empty space.

As he began to advance towards the fence he spotted a photo on the ground. He bent down and looked at it. It was a black and white photograph of a group of young boys. Tim took a glove out of his pocket and slipped it on. He picked up the picture and slipped it into the pocket of his raincoat. As he stood up again, the rain was coming down so hard that it was like a wall of water and he could barely see anything in front of him. Using his sense of touch, he climbed the slippery metal fence and dropped down into a dark warehouse. He could make out the outlines of wooden crates, but that was it. Pulling out his flashlight, he switched it on just as he heard the sounds of police sirens and ambulances in the background.

He was suddenly slammed in the face with something cold and hard. The force of the hit knocked him back and as he fought for his footing, his gun slid loose from his hand and went skittering across the ground.

"Get up inspector; you're making this too easy. Where's the challenge?" the suspect's voice echoed off the walls of the warehouse.

This time he slammed the heavy pipe wrench into Tim's back, knocking him to his knees.

SEASONS OF HEAVEN

"I...I'm going to kill you," Tim told him in a strangled voice.

The next hit was directly to his face. Tim was stunned, but still conscious. He began to crawl towards his gun, trying to reach out and grab it, but in vain. He still could barely see the outline of the suspect, but he felt him kneel down next to him before he felt the killer's hot breath on his ear,

"I know who you are inspector... We know everything about you ..." he whispered as Tim's world went black and his head and body hugged the cold, cement floor.

CHAPTER EIGHT
"NEW DISCOVERIES"
QUEENS NEW YORK

Tim woke up wet, freezing, in pain and surrounded by policemen. They had taped off the scene of Tim's assault with Tim in the middle of it. The floodlights that surrounded him burned his eyes and he tried to sit up.

"Be careful, move slowly. You've been beaten pretty badly," Eddie told him. Tim hadn't noticed Eddie right there by his side, but it figured. Eddie was a good partner; he was always there.

Tim, continuing to move let out a loud moan, "Shit!" he said, grabbing the back of his head, "Did you get him? Damn, I let him get away!"

"Stay Zen, take it easy!" Eddie told him. "We have a bunch of witnesses, on several crime scenes... An hour ago, we didn't have a thing...at least we're better off, right?"

"You're not the one who just got his head bashed in," Tim grumbled. Then realizing it was his own damned fault and not Eddie's he said, "You're right, I'm sorry. We wait...Holy shit! I almost forgot! Look at this, it fell out of his pocket I think," he pulled out the photograph and showed it to his partner.

"Looks like a bunch of school kids, with a gym in the background. I'm not sure what it means, but it's a start. See, I told you, patience. White men are always too impatient."

Tim chuckled at that and said, "Ok, let's get back to the station. We need to get moving."

"You're kidding right?" Eddie said, "You are going home to get some rest for a few days. On top of that, whoever we are looking for is going to lay low. He knows the whole force is looking for him and he knows we finally have some leads. While you're resting, I'll try to make that picture talk."

"Gentlemen, I'm sorry to interrupt," a uniformed officer said, "But we've found something strange. I thought you might want to check it out."

Eddie helped Tim up to his feet and once he was steady, they followed the officer over to one of the walls of the warehouse. They all looked at the wall in astonishment. Written there, in what looked like blood where the words,

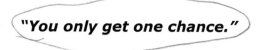

"You only get one chance."

They all had the same two questions on their minds: *What does it mean and whose blood is it written in?*

■■■

SEASONS OF HEAVEN

TIM NORTHMAN'S FAMILY HOME
NEW JERSEY—A FEW DAYS LATER

Tim had done his best to take it easy for a few days. Even if the Brass would have let him return to work right away, which they wouldn't have, he knew that it was a good idea for him to take a few days off. That was okay for two reasons: One, he hadn't had much time to spend with his son, Yann and two: he had plenty of work he could do at home.

Tim was sitting in the living room that day, watching Yann build something with his blocks. The television was on, but the sound was muted and spread out in front of Tim on the coffee table were the files of missing person's cases he'd been working on his own time. Tim looked at Yann. He was such a handsome boy with his dark hair and big, dark eyes. His heart swelled with love when he looked at him and he hoped that someday the boy would be able to understand why his father was hardly ever around. Tim's family was important to him, but they often ended up taking a backseat to his career. Tim had guilt about that, but oftentimes he would assuage that guilt by telling himself he was making the world a better, safer place for Yann's generation. For now, everything in Yann's world was organized and without chaos. That was the way the doctors had told Tim and Elise they should keep his environment. The Asperger's made him dislike any changes in his routine and have a heightened sensitivity to and become over stimulated by loud noises, lights and strong tastes or textures. Tim and Elise…. Mostly Elise because Tim was never home, did their absolute best to keep things in the home calm and quiet so as not to upset him.

Tim glanced from Yann over to the television. There was another special bulletin running about the plane crash. It had been running all night and day. The anchors were talking about it in somber voices, interviewing experts in the airline field, talking to family members and rescue crews while all the while a ticker tape ran along the bottom of the screen that said: *331 people lost or missing in the largest commercial airline tragedy in history.* Tim caught bits and pieces of it throughout the day. He didn't need the sound on to know that it was a horrible tragedy. He could see it in the eyes of the loved ones who waited at the airport for news about their family members or friends. Tim shuddered. It made him sad and once again consciously aware of the fragility of human life.

He stopped watching the screen and turned back towards his work. He was going through all of his old case files, trying to find any that had similarities with the case he was working on.... The one that they may have solved a few days ago had he not let the killer get away....Tim was his own worst critic. He expected a lot of himself, and he never took it easy on his own psyche when he wasn't able to come through.

Tim Northman had been a criminal squad inspector at the New York Police Department for a long time. He was a hard-working man, who spent at least fifteen hours away from home every day. His absence often resulted in a series of arguments with his wife Elise. He frequently thought that he hadn't embraced a career fit for a family man. He had been working on this serial killer case for the last two years, with almost no clue or evidence to work with. The killer's modus operandi was atypical and something worried Tim: No one had ever heard or seen anything about this man, leading him to believe that this man might not even exist. The press even named him "Ghost". Tim's gut told him that what happened in Queens a few nights ago definitely had something to do with it all, he just didn't know what. He was struggling with putting it all together while not feeling his best on account of the violent confrontations of that day. He needed the time off from work to recover physically and mentally, but also to try and shed some light on the recent events. Tim looked back at his son. Sometimes that's all it took to remind him that the entire world wasn't bad. He was surrounded by so much hatred and wrath that he often thought of chucking it all in.

"Nothing was able to heal such tremendous hatred," he used to say to his wife. He shook off that thought and picked up one of the files just as his phone rang. He reached over and picked up the cordless phone out of the cradle.

"Hello?"

"Hey!" it was Eddie.

"Hi, how are you?" Tim asked him.

Eddie laughed and said, "I'm fine, but I'm not the one who got my head bashed in this week, you told me so yourself, remember? How are you?"

SEASONS OF HEAVEN

"I'm doing great," Tim told him. "I need a favor," he said, looking at his copy of the photo in his hand that the killer had dropped that night. "Can you run that photo of the kids through all of our facial recognition software and see if we can match any of the faces in it and also can you have the techs start trying to find out where that gym they're in front of is at?"

"I'm on it. I don't have anything solid yet, but I will call you as soon as I do. You take it easy and enjoy your time at home."

"I'll try, Eddie."

"Zen man," Eddie said before he hung up. Tim hung up with a smile.

After Tim hung up the phone he took out the folder in his cold case files on young Thomas Marshal once more. The case had gone cold some time ago, but something about one of the boys in the photo that the man he called "Ghost" had dropped, reminded Tim of the photos he had of the missing little boy,

SEASONS OF HEAVEN

Thomas. The picture from the warehouse was grainy and in black and white so he couldn't be sure...but his instincts told him it was connected. The little boy Thomas had completely disappeared. No traces of him or any evidence of anyone taking him had ever been found. The parents had of course been suspects but were ultimately cleared when further investigation by an astute detective turned up the fact that there were other strange things happening in the little town.

First, there had been a rash of reports of thefts. Someone was stealing things from children, personal things like backpacks and journals. Then there had been the rumors, people saying that someone or "something" had been stalking their children in the dead of night. They'd seen "apparitions" at night, [Ghosts?] hovering in their homes typically near their children's beds. Then there was the sordid case of child molestations at a popular children's outdoor center in the area.... Tim was certain they were all connected. He looked at the photo in his hand once more. He wondered how this photo, his case and Thomas Marchal all connected. He looked back at his Yann and wondered how a parent could live through a loss like that. He vowed to himself that he was going to do whatever he could to figure this all out and at the very least bring some much needed closure to those grieving parents.

CHAPTER NINE
"EARLY DEVELOPMENT"
A SMALL VILLAGE IN THE NORTH OF GAUL
800 A.D

[handwritten: Constant back and forth. Village is probably related to the ghosts appearing in the book.]

Deep in the heart of the mysterious Hercynian Forest, an enigmatic territory where it was said that the rivers all flowed north and so vast that it was said one could not go from one end of it to the other in sixty days' time, the gigantic oaks grew so densely that their colossal branches intertwined. It was a place where a secret rite was held, one that was observed only by a select few insiders and took place in the bowels of the dark forest where amongst a pathless, impenetrable mass of vegetation existed a mystical corridor. This corridor was said to be the access door to an ancient underground tunnel. The tunnel had been carefully dug through the mountainous rock and according to the legend the enormous stone that blocked the entrance to the corridor opened only once a year, during the night of the winter solstice. At that moment, visitors could easily penetrate the hollow earth...If they hurried. At dawn the stone once again closed the entrance, only to open again either during the rise of a full moon.

Many adventurers waited for the great roar that signified the opening of the corridor. They fused with the darkness of the deep tunnel as they entered and began their journey, trying to make their way to the mysterious crypt that waited on the other side in the castle of the Mont Mézenc. The crypt, guarded by the druids was said to encase the treasure of the Celtic Kings of Velay. Once the fortune hunter had been swallowed up by the darkness, they were never seen again.

Legend told of evil horsemen on skeleton mounts looking after the treasure and devouring anyone trying to access it. Others believed that the visitors actually made it to the crypt, but once inside they were blinded by the sight of the splendid wealth contained there and so overwhelmed by it that they forgot to get out on time. They wasted too much time trying to grab more precious objects than the narrow corridor would allow them to escape with. Either tale would explain why the druid's treasure remained undamaged in its hiding place. It was said that things will remain that way until the day a new and wise druid will come to take the treasure himself.

The Celts that lived in this realm were said to be ferocious in battle. They didn't fear death. To them, death was a chance at a new life. They believed firmly in reincarnation and death was only something that was placed in the middle of a long life. They believed that one had to go through a certain initiation. They had to pass through multiple states of existence in order to gain necessary knowledge and wisdom. It was a druid rite.

A young man sat on a massive, freshly cut tree trunk. In front of him sat a very old, bearded druid man. His name was Olham and the younger man, Reynald had come to ask something very important of him.

"Do you know how to change things, Reynald?" Olham asked him. "I believe you do, you are sharp witted enough to come here."

"I came to see you, Olham, because you are the only one that can help me."

"Why should I help you? You know that would result in serious consequences, my dear friend."

"I have been fighting for this beautiful planet for a long time. But... you know that we are not able to control the fate of the persons we care about. Nature is always stronger."

"That is why there is a natural selection, an order," Olham reminded him. "Natural selection came about for a reason. The planet cannot accommodate everyone all the time. There has to be a "weeding out" of the weaker organisms, not the ones best adapted to their environment. It's been in play for a long time, and now you come here to ask me to disturb it. Why would I do that?"

"We do not dispose of the same forces as Evil does. He is present everywhere except for the hearts of certain persons, I am sure of that. There exists a solution to attain our goal: to choose the right people. Natural selection does not discern between right and wrong or good and evil."

"So who is going to choose them, you? You know I trust your capacity of judgment however; you cannot be the only one to decide. It is too risky."

Reynald took time to process the old man's words. He knew Olham was right about the danger of the situation, but Reynald wouldn't have come here and asked what he did of the old man if he didn't believe it to be the only way. This wasn't a decision that had come about lightly. It had come with the agony that all great decisions are wrought with. He wasn't sure how to explain it to Olham so that he would understand, but without the old druid Reynald's plan would never come to fruition.

Reynald remained silently wrapped up in these thoughts for some time. Eventually, with a heavy sigh as if the pressure of the world sat upon his shoulders, Olham went on to say,

"All right, I understand, I should have known that you wouldn't have come to me unless your plan was ready." He feared that what Reynald wanted to do wasn't as right as the younger man believed it to be, but he was torn between that and the trust and respect he had for his old friend.

Reluctantly Reynald told him, "I do have a plan and I suppose if I am to ask you to help me you have a right to know of it." He was hesitant to tell Olham, knowing the old druid would object. He knew at the same time that it wasn't fair to ask for his help without giving him all of information. "I have decided to create a place on this planet where these people could go. The good and kind people, the ones who deserve salvation. It would be a place of transition, a second chance for the chosen ones. Those who have lost their beloveds, the ones who sacrificed their lives to protect the others remain apart from their loved ones...while there are those who kill...assassinate...."

"What do you mean? How do you plan to do that? What will be your rules?" Olham asked him, obviously shocked at what he was hearing.

"I need you to trust me." Reynald told him, in a pleading tone. "Take me there. Please, Olham."

Becoming somewhat agitated Olham said, "Reynald, you have to be more explicit. I need more facts about what you plan to do. I cannot take you there just because you ask, especially armed with the information that you've already given me. I have serious concerns about it, and what you're asking me to do....It's dangerous."

"We are the only ones to know about their existence. Take me there. This is my chance to achieve my goal. This isn't for me; it's for the ones who deserve peace and a happy ending."

Olham stood up and silently stared at Reynald for a long time. Finally, and ominously he said,

"You know that from now on everything will be different." It was a warning and Reynald took it as such.

"I know." It was something Reynald had dedicated many more hours of his thoughts to, "But we have to try."

The fire crackled and the gentle light from it danced around the two silhouettes. One with a mission and the other with a heart and mind heavy with the burden of decision got up and began to penetrate the deep forest.

Reynald and Olham entered the forest through a luminous door, completely invisible from the outside. It was deeply hidden under the shrub. They began a journey through the magical forest, one that should have lasted several years. Finally, after an agonizing inner struggle Olham decided to completely trust his old friend. He told him the story of two old stones....

"They have been around since the creation of ages. They can create a passage through to another dimension." Olham told him.

Legend held that there were irradiated stones somewhere deep in this forest and the quest for those is what propelled the men forward rapidly on their journey.

Reynald knew they were on the cusp of something profound. As they journeyed, Reynald walked slowly through the tangled masses in his way, accompanied by his dog, a young female named Leia. Olham used a walking stick to move about more easily. The darkness had encompassed them but they were led by the illumination of blue and greenish lights that shone across the forest. The place they traveled was a treacherous place, said to be haunted by ghosts and the souls of evil horsemen. The two men shared their ideas as they walked and for the first time the name of the new place they were on the verge of creating was said aloud. It was to be called, Heaven.

Deep in this forest there appeared to be no sky. Above, below, in front and behind there appeared only to be thick and voluminous vegetation. Time seemed to stand still and the cold made the atmosphere heavy. The intake of breath was hard due to the weight of the air and their exhalations were marked by a white, vaporous condensation that danced around their faces before disappearing into the night.

The silence of the dark night was suddenly broken by the sound of a heavy "crack" not far in front of them. Whatever it was seemed to be moving towards them...and quickly.

SEASONS OF HEAVEN

"Lie down and do not make the slightest noise!" Olham ordered the other man and the dog.

The dog found a hiding place under a large root just as a black, phosphorescent horseman stopped in the center of the pathway. The ghostly horseman was adorned with a suit of old armor with worn out lashes hanging from it. The skinny horse that he rode tapped the ground with his hooves. There was suddenly no sound in the forest. Nothing moved and the mist that had become trapped in Reynald's hair was magically transformed into frost.

As they lay in wait, the horseman disappeared as suddenly as it had appeared. The men knew that the forest was haunted by the evil spirits of these horsemen. They had been condemned to protecting the irradiated relics. If a human were to let himself be captured, he or she would be taken into the limbo of the hollow earth.

SEASONS OF HEAVEN

The forest they wandered through had been planted where they stood hundreds of years before by numerous slaves. The slaves were all dead and the planting of the forest was done to conceal the truth about another world, the world of the Ancients. The Ancients were Reynald's people. Before disappearing into the deluge they had hidden a great number of relics of the ancient past in the heart of the earth.

Picking up the dog, Reynald placed her on a piece of cloth he'd fixed over his shoulder and carried her. They had to move slowly. The deeper they moved into the forest the more convoluted and the darker and more frighteningly dangerous it became. As they trudged forward, the path began to become steep. Each side of it contained scattered pieces of strange monuments. They resembled ones from Greek or Egyptian cultures.

The men and the dog suddenly found themselves facing a well. They look down inside of it and saw a steep, spiral staircase. Olham, appearing to not be surprised by it entered the well telling Reynald,

"Be careful! This is the way!"

"OK, but...I have an impression we are being observed...Don't you?"

Olham didn't answer the question. Instead he said, "Hurry up, follow me!"

They entered the well and began descending the stairs. Once at the bottom, they found themselves in a cave. It was illuminated by a strange light coming from its rock walls. The ground began to shake and suddenly they were facing two horrifying horsemen. The horsemen had seen them and were looking down on them through their armor with two pairs of obsidian eyes. Olham stood across the cave from them and brandished his walking stick. A sudden flash of bright light burst from the stick and seemed to terrify the horsemen.

"Go back! My light repulses you!" Olham yelled at them.

One of the horsemen disappeared but unfettered, the second one continued to charge. The old druid was able to avoid the clash and the horse and the horseman disappeared into the rock without a trace.

"They have never been very hospitable," Reynald told him with a joking tone.

"You should not take it too lightly, Reynald," Olham warned him. "Follow me, carefully." Reynald followed him and as they progressed deeper into the cave he realized that there were hundreds of apparitions watching them. He and Olham were as silent as the ghosts, trying not to draw their attention.

Suddenly Reynald spotted what the men have been looking for, "Look Olham! Here they are! What do we do now?" he asked.

Olham looked to see the two shining stones lying on a pedestal made from a matte grey rock.

"I will draw their attention to our left side, near the underground ocean. You know what you have to do next," he told his companion.

"Wait!? You are not going back upstairs?" Reynald asked him.

"You know that I have to do this. Our light could not protect us indefinitely, there is just too many of them," Olham told him.

"Olham, you know it is not possible, I won't leave you here!"

"Yes, it is possible! Do not regret the choice you have to make. I believe in you, do not worry about me brother, we will find each other. Now, take the stones and give them a second chance."

The two men hugged and looked at each other gravely.

CHAPTER TEN

"UNBREAKABLE BONDS"

JAPAN, YAMASHIRO PROVINCE 1876

A loud gong sounded across the lavish landscape that surrounded the holy temple. The crimson red temple sat encircled by verdant trees and the sound of Japanese religious chants began to float through the fragrant air.

"Tonobu Sanada Roshi."

"Kokuchi."

A man came up to a woman and took her hand signaling the end of the ceremony. They exchanged a look so vibrant and intense that it could be felt around them in the air.

The joyous occasion took place during a moment of conflict, in secret. The existence of samurais had been called into question in a country that tried to evolve while still clinging tightly to traditional culture. It had taken root one day during the attack of the village of the

Kokuchi by the rival clan the Tonobu. A young man saved a young woman who was grievously injured during the assault. As he treated her wounds in secret he also began talking to her, sharing his doubts for the future. He began to fall deeply in love with the young peasant girl. The secret marriage took place in the Yamashiro province. The reserved young man knew that if his clan learned about his relationship, he would be facing a difficult position. His family would take this marriage as an affront to their honor and the newlyweds lives could be at risk.

In the middle of the day in an ancient sanctuary, the loving couple began the purification ceremony. They married before the ancestral deities of the archipelago. They were subsequently greeted by the priests. Tonobu and Kokuchi prepared their offerings: sake and local victuals. The ceremony was imbued with calm and reverence. The couple consciously knew that the risk was daunting and that their lives were now at stake. The groom and bride began reading their vows to each other, only surrounded by priests, without any member of their families, therefore not fully respecting the purest tradition. Once bonded in matrimony, the couple gracefully exited the sanctuary.

After leaving the temple, the newly married couple hungered for some private time. Roshi took his brides hand and led her towards the natural thermal source in the heart of the little village in the south of Yamashiro. As they walked there in silence together, Roshi's thoughts went to the risk he was taking by following his emotions...his feelings towards Kokuchi, rather than the code the families had followed for centuries. He went into the union knowing full well that the consequences could be banishment...or worse. He glanced at Kokuchi walking next to him. His heart swelled with pride and the feelings he had for her that had broken through the protective sheathe he'd built around it.

SEASONS OF HEAVEN

They walked through the forest on their way to the village and Roshi breathed in every detail. Communing with nature and the feelings of peace it brought to his soul was one of the first things his father had ever taught him. "Being harmonious with this beauty that surrounded the human race is to be appreciated," his father had told him, "Not exploited."

Roshi didn't just let his eyes take in the scene around him, he opened up his soul to it all and instead of just hearing the peaceful sounds of the gentle breeze as it wafted through the bamboo and caused them to swish and click together, he felt it. Instead of looking into it and seeing green stalks, he saw a giant curtain in shades of green from the lightest to the darkest and everything in between. He could smell the earth and he could actually taste what it felt like to be a part of it all.

As they got closer to the village they could hear the soft, harmonious sounds of ringing bells. Once again he looked at his beautiful bride. She smiled at him through the long strands of silky black hair that hung down to her waist. Her skin looked like cream and Roshi suddenly longed to touch her face. She had the face of a Geisha...perfect, smooth and bright. She wasn't a Geisha however...she'd grown up in a small village with her family and she'd lived a simple life with her parents and her sisters. Kokuchi loved to write and as a girl she had taken up practicing the art of calligraphy. Her teacher was so impressed with her talent and dedication to it that he had loaned her the tools she needed to make beautiful art.

After hours of walking a temple came into sight in front of them. It was a small one, but what it lacked in size, it made up for in beauty. It had been built to blend in with the nature around it and looked as if it had grown there in the center of the forest. There were small lanterns burning around the entrance that gave the small porch an inviting glow.

SEASONS OF HEAVEN

The couple removed their shoes and entered the sacred place. Roshi had been here many times, it belonged to an old couple that were relatives of his. The old lady was there now. She looked at the two of them and greeted them with her watery brown eyes. Roshi and Kokuchi did the same in return. No words were spoken and every movement inside was slow and graceful. Preserving the quiet harmony of the temple was important and no one was willing to disturb it.

The young couple changed out of their wedding clothes and took a walk out into the garden. It was another awe inspiring place filled with giant rocks and glorious trees. In the center of it was a breathtaking waterfall that emptied into a small pond. As the rushing water hit the still ones, a beautiful mist rose up and floated around, giving the place an air of mystery. The sound of the water in the center of all of this silence is like music and it relaxes the couple even further.

SEASONS OF HEAVEN

Kokuchi looked at Roshi and breaking the silence she said, "What would you like to do now, husband?" She was speaking softly and using a certain vocabulary that in their culture extended respect and admiration.

Roshi looked into the reflection of his beautiful wife on top of the clear water and said, "My thoughts are like this water. Sometimes I have clear perceptions and they're calm like the water is now. Other times, they move too fast like the waterfall rushing into the pond and I have trouble. Right now I think of Ikigai." Ikigai meant that everything one does is in perfect harmony with one's self in every different social level. It was a word that described him perfectly at that moment.

As they spoke the trees behind Kokuchi began to move. Small monkeys covered in thick, beige fur came out from behind them. Their eyes watched the young couple but they didn't seem frightened. Some of them sat near the water and swished their hands or tails in it. A few more were having their fur groomed and checked for food by their companions. This region was their home and Kokuchi and Roshi knew that they were the visitors here. As they watched the monkeys, and enjoyed the way they attended to their lives in such a carefree manner, Roshi smiled. He thought about how human nature made people want to avoid their problems and this is one of the reasons humans loved animals so much. They sunned themselves and climbed into the trees and sat near the top of the waterfall. They were doing what some humans had forgotten how to do, paying their respects to nature by simply reveling in her beauty.

Kokuchi stepped closer to her husband and slowly put her head against his shoulder. Roshi encircled her in his arms and they stood there like that with the sounds of nature playing a symphony around them. They closed their eyes and their minds floated on the cusp of their mutual dreams. It was a dream about their future and the afterlife...where they would be reunited for all eternity.

******

University Campus
Rutgers, 1990

Matt Hawnsworth walked across the campus to his next class. He was early so he looked about at the other students as they all seemed to be hurrying along their way. That was when he spotted his friend, Shirley.

"Hey! How is it going? I didn't see you yesterday in class? What's going on with you?"

Shirley looked embarrassed as she said,

"It's complicated. Mostly I just had lots of homework to finish and frankly, I'm wrung out. I'm not even mentioning the end of the term paper. I'm not sure I'll be able to turn it in on time."

SEASONS OF HEAVEN

Matt stepped in close and kissed her on the mouth. Not stepping back, he said,

"I missed you."

"Sorry, but I... I really have to work, and I also have to go pick up Yann in a little while. You want to do something this weekend? I'll have more time then," Shirley told him.

Disappointed but understanding, Matt said,

"Ok, no problem let me know if I can help you with anything. I have to go now. My applied history class is about to start. I'll call you tonight!"

"Matt? I'm really sorry," she said.

"Don't worry about it. I understand," he told her. His voice was sincere and his look affectionate.

Shirley turned to rush off to fulfill her obligations. She was feeling truly overwhelmed which was not how she normally operated. Shirley was used to adversity in her life. She was born in 1963, in Hô-Chi-Minh-Ville, the capital of Vietnam. Her father was an enlisted soldier during wartime and worked as a communication agent before tragically dying after a bomb destroyed his compound. Given the political instability of the country at the time Shirley's mom, a British born citizen, decided to leave the country with her parents. They crossed the Pacific Ocean and migrated to Canada and then a few years later they moved to the U.S. Things were looking up until Shirley's mother then died of a ruptured aneurysm. She was raised after that by her grandparents, growing up strong and brave due to the circumstances of her life and also being shaped by the rough edges of the neighborhood in which she had lived.

At a very young age, Shirley began practicing self-defense. She never wanted to be anyone's victim. She loved dance as well and while excelling in that, she was able to maintain a high GPA and obtain a scholarship to the university. Shirley was working on her dreams of becoming a lawyer and while doing that she also stayed active in animal rights organizations and an organization that helped educate children with Autism and their parents to ensure they lived as productive and happy a life as possible. At one of the conferences she taught she met Tim and Elise Northman and their son Yann who had been diagnosed with Asperger's syndrome at a young age.

As she rushed through the parking lot towards her car, Shirley had to walk past the security guard, Mr. Norman. Something about him made her horribly uncomfortable. For one thing, he always seemed to have a glazed expression.

"Hello, Shirley," the creepy security officer said as she walked by.

Shirley smiled politely and said, "How are you today?"

"A lot better, now that I've seen you!" he said.

Feeling a little creeped out by his attentions, Shirley amplified her steps while looking for her keys in her purse. She made it to her car at last and drove away.

****

NORTHMAN RESIDENCE, 1990

The day was so bright that the light coming through the windows was almost intrusive. The birds, seemingly enjoying it were singing glorious and harmonious songs to celebrate the coming of spring. The neighborhood was peaceful and the warm rays of sunlight shone so brightly that they were even visible through the blinds of the house. Dust particles lay suspended in the air, reminding the humans that an infinite number of things exist that might not always be visible to the naked eye.

Warmly encased in his comforter, Yann opened his eyes. He could hear the birds singing through the closed window of his bedroom. He had to blink back the rays of the sun that had forced themselves into the room. Undaunted, he reached his feet down to the floor and searched out his slippers. Once he found them he sat up and put on his shirt. After buttoning it up, he dashed to the stairs. It was his birthday!

Yann had been born in 1980, in the town of Hampton. He was the son of Elise and Tim Northman, loving parents and up and coming professionals in their respective careers. At Yann's birth everything seemed to be normal. He was pronounced healthy and his parents proudly took their bouncing baby boy home to raise.

As the years passed, they began to notice things about Yann that concerned them. He was very stand-offish with people, even children his own age. He preferred to be alone and communication was difficult for him. The doctors ultimately diagnosed him with Asperger's syndrome. It's a form of autism that is characterized by poor social skills, difficult communication and extreme dependence on routine. Because of all of those traits, Yann had become a reclusive young boy despite the efforts his parents had set forth to help him.

SEASONS OF HEAVEN

Yann was enrolled in a special needs school that offered the kind of nurturing care that handicapped children needed. As he grew, he developed some very specific interests, the most important of which was baseball. His father taught him how to play and whenever they had time together it was what they did.

Yann, being left behind in a lot of areas from other boys' and girls' his age, was advancing far above them in others. He had an uncanny ability for concentration that normally eluded young children, especially boys. On his eighth birthday his parents bought him a telescope. From that moment on, he developed an unfaltering passion for the stars. Every night when favorable weather conditions presented themselves, he would scrutinize the sky.

By Yann's ninth year, his father Tim was completely absorbed in his job as a New York City Police detective. His mother worked for the United Nations and that same year her job became almost as demanding as his father's. The overwhelmed parent's, after much discussion had ultimately decided to find an experienced and well-balanced nanny to look after Yann. They met Shirley, a young Vietnamese girl during an autism seminar. She was twenty-eight years old at the time and agreed to take the job. Over time Shirley would dedicate large amounts of her time educating and caring for Yann in the absence of his parents. Yann grew to be completely at ease with Shirley and trusted her as he did his own parents. He came to love her and think of her as a second mom.

At the top of the stairs, Yann called for his mother,

"Mom? Are you there? Hey mom!"

Yann was suddenly awash with a feeling of loneliness as he stood there, arms dangling listening to the impenetrable silence that reigned throughout the house.

He was startled by the ringing of the doorbell.

"I'm coming!" he called out.

He took the stairs at top speed and vehemently clutched the front door knob when he reached it, pulling it open to reveal Shirley on the front step.

"Dear lord, this is the fastest you've ever opened the door," Shirley told him, taking him in her arms.

"I'm so happy to see you Shirley," Yann told her.

"So am I, sweetie," she said, kneeling down, "You know what day it is today, don't you?"

"It's my birthday; I'm not silly you know I never forget anything."

"Happy birthday big boy!" she told him with a kiss to his forehead. "You know I have a present waiting for you. Hold on." Shirley reached into the pocket of her coat and pulled out a medallion. "Take this, it will protect you if you feel down or go through a hard time. It can also light up your nightmares."

SEASONS OF HEAVEN

"That's not true... I know you are telling me stories, but that's ok, I love it anyhow, and I love you Shirley."

"I love you too, my sweetheart. You are really smart for a young boy. You know, when I was younger my grandma used to tell me stories before I went to sleep. She used to say that there existed a magical place... "She wandered away from him as she spoke and excitedly, he said,

"Go on, do not stop, Shirley."

Smiling at him Shirley said, "In that place it was possible to see once again the people that we love. You can find that place in your dreams. You just think very hard about the persons you love and you can travel and join them, wherever you want." She was very quiet for a few seconds and then she said, "I will tell you more about that another day, I promise."

"I am looking forward to it, Shirley," he told her.

Shirley and Yann went into the house then and Yann finished dressing and putting on his shoes and jacket. When he was ready they left out the front door, locking it behind them.

"Let's head to the Mall!" Shirley said.

The drive to the mall took about an hour and by the time they got there, both Shirley and Yann were hungry. They ate at a fast food stand in the food court. That was a big deal for Yann whose parents and babysitter normally didn't allow him junk food.

After a satisfying meal, Shirley took Yann to the arcade. The place was full of a broad mix of juveniles who were just talking and hanging out and the real gamers who were there for the challenge and the rush of winning their favorite games. To an uninitiated crowd the arcade could be a dark and electrifying place, but to Yann who had his favorite game and could block out all of the chaos around him as he played it the place was an electrifying arena of challenge and magic.

He found his game amongst dozens of arcade games with steering wheels, skateboards or old-fashioned joysticks. It was a "beat them all" fighting game with four environmentalists who attempt to arrest a gang of dinosaur poachers. It was a synopsis that might make a seasoned gangster shake in his boots. Amongst the noise and ever-changing colors Yann began his game.

Shirley allowed him to play until he'd had his fill, not thinking until they were back on the road about the traffic that would have clogged it by now. The daily routine of the traveler in their vast city involved road construction, traffic and a lot of stress. As she maneuvered the car through more than one obstacle Shirley had to wonder if the administration would ever resolve those issues.

Fortunately, the temperatures had dropped after having reached a sizzling point in the afternoon. The end of the afternoon was delicately warm, as the sun caressed the roofs of the neighborhood. When they drove up in front of the Northman's residence Yann jumped out of the car and looked up at the sun. He was dazzled by its glare and while he stood there looking up he found himself wondering if there was anything else up there...behind the sun. He burned with an avid curiosity...always. Even with the excitement of his birthday pressing down on him from all sides.

As they started towards the house Yann had a strange and sudden feeling that everything he knew was about to change. He felt a sharp, pinching pain in his stomach. It was there one moment and then gone. He shrugged it off as a reminder that he was alive and re-focused his thoughts on his parents being home soon and his birthday celebration. He hoped that they would have a present for him. Youth was that magical moment where every gesture counts, and every action embodies a dream.

CHAPTER ELEVEN
"NEW FRIENDSHIPS"
NORTHMAN'S RESIDENCE LATER THAT NIGHT

Yann sat at his chair in the dining room, finishing his dinner when Shirley called out from the kitchen,

"Do you want some more?"

"No thanks, I'm not really hungry...What's my present?"

"Golly! You are so impatient," Shirley told him with a smile, "Finish your plate first."

"It's so hard to wait..."

Shirley brought out their dessert and sat down at the table with him while they enjoyed it. Yann had almost finished his when he heard the sound of the front door unlocking.

"Daddy, Mommy?" Yann called out.

"Hello my son, I'm coming!" Tim called back.

"Finish your plate please," Shirley told him. "He'll come to you."

Tim came in then and took Yann in his arms, giving him a warm squeeze.

"I bet you are giddy about your birthday," he said to the boy.

"You have no idea; he's been spinning around the house for hours," Shirley told him.

Tim looked at Shirley and with a wink he said,

"So, how was your day? What did you guys do?"

"Tell him Yann," Shirley said.

"Ahh, what's that on your face dad? Did you fight?"

"That's nothing son, you should've seen the other guy," Tim told him, trying to play it off. He didn't want Yann to worry.

"Did you at least go the hospital, Mr. Northman?" Shirley asked him.

"I'm ok, don't worry about it Shirley," he told her. Then, looking back at Yann he said, "Ok, so do I have to beg you to hear what you've done today?"

"Ok so... we went to the mall, and Shirley took me to the arcade. It was so much fun... By the way dad, can we play baseball together tomorrow? I want to play but I can't play alone."

"Ok, I see. That was a very instructive day!" He winked at Yann, "As for tomorrow, I'll play with you, but only if you promise not to lose," he told him with a laugh.

"Mr. Northman, I'll prepare the cake, Mrs. Northman should be home any minute now," Shirley told him.

"Great idea, thank you, Shirley."

"How about my present, does mom have it?" Yann asked him, excitedly.

"Be Zen, my son, and calm yourself down by helping Shirley clear the table. You could also help her prepare the second round."

"Did you finish? I will put the leftovers in the fridge."

"Don't worry, Shirley, I'll eat later," Tim told her. He finally took his coat off and hung it on the coat rack in the hallway as Shirley and Yann cleared the table in the blink of an eye. Tim stood in the doorway for a few minutes when he came back, just watching them. If ever there was a day that he needed a reminder that the whole world hadn't gone mad, today was the day.

Not long after Tim came home, Yann heard the front door open and close again, and then he heard the sound of his mother's high heels on the shiny wood floor. He raced from the dining room into the front room to greet her. Shirley and Tim, laughing at his excitement, followed him.

"Mummy!" he yelled as he saw his mother come through the door. Elise looked professional in her perfectly tailored blue suit and heels. She normally wore her hair in a bun to work, but she had taken it out as soon as she got to her car tonight and her hair was hanging loose down her back.

SEASONS OF HEAVEN

Her job was often stressful, most recently because of the events taking place between the U.S. and Iraq. She had to spend a lot of time at work and the stress of having to spend so much time away from her family had taken its toll as well. In spite of all of that, the sight of her home and her family seemed to wash the worry from her face and the stress was replaced with a look of benevolence and hope.

"Hello honey..." she said to Yann with a smile, "Take it easy sweetie, you're so agitated." Elise looked towards his father for answers to their son's excitement. Tim smiled and said,

"Clearly he's been this way all day. Shirley was telling me that he couldn't stop pacing the room."

"Mom, it's a dog, isn't it? It's talking to me!" Yann jumped up and down, hardly able to contain the excitement that was ripping through his small body.

"How do you know?" Elise asked the boy. Then, turning towards her husband she said, "You just couldn't hold your tongue, could you?"

Tim held up his hands, palms out and said, "Nope, I haven't said a word."

"He's talking to me, it's so cool." Yann told them, only confusing his mother more. How could the dog be talking to him wasn't the most troubling question. How could he have known about the dog otherwise was what troubled her. It was apparent from Yann's face that he believed what he was saying to be the absolute truth.

A little muddled by what her son was telling her, Elise asked him, "What are you talking about?" Then she looked at Tim and said, "Did you really get Yann a dog?"

With a smile that was reserved for a parent with an ecstatic child, Tim said, "Yes we did...but apparently, it's not a surprise anymore. What do you say, should we give it to him now?"

Elise looked again towards her enthusiastic son and smiled,

"Okay, I guess we have no choice," she said.

Tim, Shirley and Yann went back into the dining room. Shirley brought the cake out from the kitchen and just as she did, Elise came into the room with a large package. She sat it on the floor next to Yann. His eyes were as wide as saucers as he stared at it, but he stayed in his chair, waiting for permission.

Tim looked at his wife and noticing the lines of worry and fatigue etched into her lovely face he asked her. "Honey, how was your day?"

"Horrible," Elise said quietly where only Tim could hear. Then she said, "I'll tell you later..."

Elise looked at her beautiful family, sitting around the table, waiting to celebrate Yann's birthday. She realized that she didn't want to talk about her awful day. She didn't want to think about it. She wanted to completely forget that a truck full of young American soldiers was taken hostage. She wanted to escape the harsh reality of life and her job that was often difficult to cope with and immerse herself in all the positive things she had in her life. The most of which was right in front of her, her family.

While Shirley put the colorful candles on the yummy looking chocolate cake, Yann squirmed in his chair. His impatience was palpable and his parents and Shirley were all able to feed off of the positively animated vibes that the little boy was radiating.

"Happy birthday to you, happy birthday to you, happy birthday to you Yann! Happy birthday to you!" Yann's face was a wide smile as his family sang to him. He stared wide-eyed at the present on the table, dying to open it. He had to be re-directed back to the cake as his mother told him,

"Go on, make a wish and blow out the candles, Yann!"

"Smile!" Shirley told him, laughing and taking a photo as the little boy blew out his candles all at once. He blew so hard that in his enthusiasm, some of the whipped cream on the cake was gusted off the top and spun around a little while in the air above the room.

"Congratulations my son!" Tim told him.

"I think it's time you opened your present," Elise said.

Looking as if he might bust Yann said, "I'm so happy, he's so cute, isn't he?"

Tim was still stumped about how Yann knew what was in the box. He whispered to Shirley, "How does he know?" Shirley shrugged, just as clueless as Tim and Elise as they all watched Yann pull the finely wrapped box towards him. He pulled delicately on the ribbon that encircled it and slowly took the lid off the box. There was a quiet moaning coming from inside and as Yann looked in two round dark eyes looked back at him. A pair of funny-looking little ears could be seen sticking out from the box and then suddenly a pair of paws was put up on the side and a little black head poked out over it. The puppy looked around at his new environment.

SEASONS OF HEAVEN

[margin note: Ani obviously.]

Yann reached in the box and took out the sweet puppy. He looked at him almost reverently, admiring the dog's shiny black coat. He had a pure white collar that emphasized the blackness of his fur and he was as soft as down to the touch. Yann brought the puppy up to his shoulder and hugged him gently. Then he held him back and looked at him again. He was so cute with his flat face and funny little ears. Yann thought he looked like a little angel.

The family watched as the two new friends got to know each other. For Yann's loved ones watching him so happy, falling in instant love with the puppy was an intense experience. It was as if for a few moments time stood still. Shirley at last broke the spell by saying,

"Oh my god, he's so cute, look at those ears."

"Mom, what kind of dog is he?" Yann asked.

"The woman at the store, Sophie said he was a French bulldog. Do you like him? He is so cute," Elise said.

"You'll have to take good care of him son..." Tim told him.

A silence pierced the room, Yann was speechless and he and the puppy were staring into each other's eyes as if an extraordinary connection was taking place. Something unexpected, magical, was happening. Yann was thinking what a wonderful present his little French bulldog was. It was love at first sight, and he didn't even realize yet how much the puppy was going to help him change his life. Yann would come out of his shell and telepathically be able to communicate with the dog. They would have their own unique language and a one of a kind relationship.

Finally, nervous with the silence Tim said, "You are not saying anything, are you ok? You know, he's delicate and a little sick, you'll have to take very good..."

"I know, I know..." Yann said, "He told me everything, but everything is going to be alright."

"What...?" Tim didn't know how to react to the fact that Yann seemed to believe he and the dog were communicating, especially since it seemed like the dog really had told Yann things that he otherwise couldn't have known.

Elise put her hand on Tim's arm. She could see the worry in her husband's face, "Give him time, and don't worry!"

Kneeling down next to Yann and the puppy Shirley said, "So, are you going to give him a name?"

"Anak...ANI! He told me that it was his name," Yann said.

"I like it, it's very nice. What do you think about that, honey?" Tim asked Elise.

Elise and Shirley both agreed that it sounded great….Ani. Ani was a little French bulldog. He was sick, suffering since birth from a medical condition called pulmonic stenosis. This condition impeded his breathing and would reduce his lifespan by half. The decision to buy Ani for Yann hadn't come lightly. Elise had read a lot of studies about pets and autistic children. Almost all of the research had been positive, but the couple never wanted to do anything that might hinder Yann's growth and development so they asked his doctors for their opinion as well, just to be sure. His doctors had been all for the idea telling the couple that it would only help Yann with acquiring the life skills and developing a taste for responsibility that he would need later on in life. They also talked a lot about how it might help him with the loneliness that came from being an only child with parents that were so often away from home.

They had then begun their search, going to almost every pet shop in town. They had found Ani at a small shop in the city and besides the fact that he was adorable, they had chosen him because they wanted to be sure that the sick puppy went to a home where he would be well cared for and have nothing but love. They knew their home was the perfect place for him, and Yann the perfect boy. The instant bonding that seemed to take place as well as the seemingly mental communication made the parents feel like they had definitely made the right decision.

The room was energized at that moment with the presence of love. The family, all with stressors and problems of their own to cope with had put everything else aside and come together united in their bliss to welcome this new member into their fold.

That night as the peaceful neighborhood they lived in began shutting off its lights for the night the little boy lay sleeping deeply, a smile tugging at the corners of his mouth as his new best friend looked around his new home. His black coat was barely visible against the darkness of the night. The only light in the room was from the sparkle and shine of the stars against the azure sky as it shone through the window. The puppy sat like a sentry on the end of Yann's bed watching over his new companion. It had only been hours since they met, but they had already forged that deep bond that had led people throughout the decades to say that a dog was "Man's best friend."

CHAPTER TWELVE
"ALLIANCES"
NORTHMAN'S RESIDENCE
1991-One Year Later

Yann woke up to the morning sun in his eyes with a smile. He jumped out of bed, eager to get his day started. There was no school today and he and Ani could work on their shed in the backyard. Ani jumped out of the bed after him. He slept in Yann's bed nightly and every night before they fell asleep, they shared stories with one another. One of the big advantages of the telepathy they had is that they could communicate in complete silence.

Yann dashed into the bathroom and brushed his teeth and put on his sweat suit. His independence had grown by leaps and bounds since Ani came into his life.

"Today we are going to finish the construction of our shed, comrade!" Yann told Ani as they raced down the stairs. Ani stopped in the kitchen and sniffed, checking for food or the presence of anyone else. The house was empty with the exception of him and Yann. Shirley was expected to come later. Ani checked out his food dish and then Yann opened the sliding glass door to let Ani outside to attend to his business.

Ani ran through the garden, sniffing around. First he sniffed a patch of grass on the left and then one on the right. He peed a little. He usually only peed a little at a time because of his sickness. In spite of his diagnoses Ani was not a sickly looking pup. He was just a little arched in his stance because of his back problems. Otherwise he had a healthy, shiny coat and an almost perpetual smile. He stopped and listened, he could hear Yann filling up his water bowl and that enticed him back inside the house.

Ani stopped next to Yann's legs and barked. Yann smiled at him as he sat the dish down on the floor and told him,

"Here, you can drink, but take it easy, keep your energy. We have to finish our shed. I have my backpack, it's full of comics. What do you think will happen in the last chapter of "Emperor's Blades?"

Ani looked up at the boy as he talked and then watched Yann walk into the living room. Yann climbed up on the couch. He sat there looking around at the family photos that hung on the walls. He was feeling curious today so he wandered into his parent's room and looked around at his father's books. Yann knew that it was a privilege to be left alone in the big 2000 square foot house. He did a lot of exploration, but he knew what the boundaries were and he respected them.

Yann smiled as he looked at all of the photos of Ani scattered around the house and pinned on the walls. The puppy had truly made his mark on this family. Then, his dark eyes fell on the red baseball bat that rested against the wall in the corner. Tim had been so busy with the serial killer case that the baseball bat had not been used very often as of late. Yann used to be good at baseball, often impressing his neighborhood friends when they played together in the street. He hoped that he wouldn't lose those skills while he waited for his father to find the time to play.

Yann's backpack was another important accessory. He took it everywhere and filled it with what he may need for the day. Today it was full of what he and Ani would need to construct the shed.

In the backyard of the house behind the trees and near the fence, Yann had built a very impressive shed. The place was magical to him, a place where he and Ani often shared their stories. The stories were always full of adventure and sometimes a touch of danger just to make it more exciting. They both loved to imagine they would someday be able to travel towards an exciting adventure together.

He slipped on his jacket, the season was changing and the air had a little bite to it early in the mornings. Satisfied that he had what he needed, he proceeded out to the back of the garden with Ani.

"It's time to finish our shed, Ani. Look, I made a list of what we need to finish it: kindling, timber, ropes, nails and a hammer."

Yann and Ani stepped into the shed and Yann searched through his backpack. Looking down at Ani he said, "Where did I put my diary? I thought I brought it out with me, but it's not here..."

Ani went immediately into the house to look for the Yann's diary. He knew exactly where it was. While he was inside he heard the front door open and ran to greet Shirley.

"Yann!" she called out, then she bent down and caressed Ani behind his ears and said, "Hey sport! How are you?" Yann heard Shirley calling and ran into the house, "Hi there," Shirley told him. "How is your day going? What have you two done today?"

"Come and see, we've been finishing the shed, come..."

Laughing, Shirley followed the two energetic males to the back yard. Yann led her to the shed and with a proud look on his face he stepped back so that she could see what he and Ani had built.

"My gosh. Yann! It's great! Can I go in? What a beautiful job!"

"Yes, but watch your head." Yann and Ani followed her in and Yann said, "See over here is the place where we tell each other our stories. Right Ani?"

Ani barked. Shirley looked at the dog and back at Yann. For a year she had listened to the boy talk about communicating with Ani. She suspected Yann was telling the truth because he wasn't prone to lying. He did have a big imagination though, so Shirley wondered sometimes if it was that. She finally asked Yann,

"You really talk to each other? How do you do that?"

Yann lowered his head. He felt like Shirley didn't believe him as he said, "I don't know

Shirley. It's been like that since the beginning, do you remember...?"

"I think it's amazing," she said, making the boy happier. She looked at Ani and said, "What does he think now?"

Ani was making eye contact with Shirley. He cocked his head to one side and then the other. Yann laughed and told her,

"He doesn't understand you, but he knows we are talking about him because he hears me."

Shirley picked the little dog up into her arms and cuddled him as she told Yann, "He really is special, and you two were meant to be with each other." She sat Ani back down and told Yann, "Well... I have some work to finish, are you coming inside?"

"Can we stay here five more minutes?" Yann asked her.

"Ok," Shirley agreed before going back into the house and into the living room.

******

SEASONS OF HEAVEN

That evening as the sun was setting; Shirley was sitting in the living room studying and Ani paced around the house while Yann read his comic book, "The Emperor's Blades." Yann was really into it. It was inspired by the true story of a Samurai named Roshi whose real name was Tonobu Sanada. The book recounted the astonishing chronicle of a man who was at war against divinities who had abducted his wife in exchange for the eradication of Samurais. He was a man who had lost everything and was willing to sacrifice everything to see his wife at least one more time, even if only at the door of the Kingdom of the death.

Yann glanced over as Ani was sniffing around Shirley's sports bag. He watched as the dog shuffled through it a bit, moving a pair of black lacey underwear up near the top. Yann moved his eyes back to his book. He didn't want to see Shirley's undergarments. Ani finally got tired of pacing and climbed up into Shirley's lap.

SEASONS OF HEAVEN

Yann looked over at them. He loved them both so much. They were living proof that "family" didn't have to mean "blood." He'd known Shirley for five years now. He couldn't imagine what his life might be like if she hadn't come into it. He knew that his parents loved her as well. His thoughts turned to Ani then. The first day they had met, when he pulled Ani out of that box and hugged him, he'd known they were going to have a fabulous life together.

They had since formed an unbreakable tie that linked them heart to heart. Yann took great care of his dog. Not only because he loved him, but also because Ani needed extra care because of his disease. He made sure that Ani always had fresh water and he would often humidify his paws to refresh him. Yann helped make sure he took his medication every day as well. The veterinarians had warned the family that his growth could be slowed significantly because of all his problems and possibly keep him from developing correctly as he grew. What the family had found was that with good care and lots of love, Ani's unfortunate disease kept him from ventilating correctly but he had grown and thrived over the past year in spite of it. Life had decided to give him a second chance to be loved by a little boy who would devote his life to loving him and protecting him.

CHAPTER THIRTEEN
"CHAOS"
UNITED NATIONS
Tuesday September 7, 1991

Elise sat in her seat at the highly varnished table amongst the thirty or so other people attending the meeting at the United Nations. She felt so tired, both mentally and physically. Her work was so stressful. She'd done this job for a long time, working in different positions and for different private funds and organizations. She has been an assistant to a multitude of influential people. She'd gotten into the field because of her degrees and over time she'd been selected for top positions because of her experience and reputation. This particular job she had worked at for a couple of years. Her main duties were to assimilate important information and deliver it properly to the authorities at the United Nations. The job brings her close to a lot of high level and even classified documentation. She never has all of the details, but from what she does have, she often knows more than she would like to. She sits in on the meetings and takes notes and receives her assignments and orders, but she doesn't take part in the decisions made there. Sometimes the helplessness of knowing too well what is going on in the world but being unable to do anything about it, rains stress down on her.

One of many groups contract she works for now is a private corporation founded by a group of billionaires doing research in different fields, they are tied up with the U.N. Because of this she is usually responsible for being the contact between them and the press who are often anxious to get any information about what the group is involved in. They have a hand in things such as industrial food, pharmaceutical companies and a lot of science research involving NASA. Some of the men she worked for had worked together to create the ethical system that we now know through highly publicized materials like The Kingsley sexual rapport, a top secret mission on the climate changing technology HAARP. The decisions that these men make on a daily basis are often highly controversial with activists and less mainstream media. Elise worried often about the explosion of the internet changing the direction of the work they do. She shook off her worries for the moment and focused back on what was going on in front of her.

There was an endless expression of ideas being shared at the table about the end of the intervention in Iraq. Too many ideas in fact. The general public had just about enough of this "crisis" and they wanted the troops called home. The government however was not satisfied that pulling the troops was the right thing to do. They worried that the rebellious troops still needed to be controlled and that the only way to do that was to maintain a military presence in the country. The active discussion hadn't amounted to an agreement amongst the professionals and as some of them bemoaned this outcome, Elise impatiently waited for the meeting to come to an end. It was Friday night and all she could think about was getting out of this darned office and to the romantic dinner that she and her husband had planned together at their favorite restaurant. Neither of them had found a moment for themselves, much less each other in four months thanks to their busy jobs.

Elise had struggled with the decision for a while, but in the end she'd known it was not only what she had to do, but what she wanted to do in order to save their family. This job had never been about passion for her. She'd taken it for the money and the travel and the respect. Elise had gotten her fill of that and now she was ready to make a change. She wanted to be a mother to her son at last. She'd already typed her resignation letter and she was ready to mail it and start a new chapter in her life. She was missing her son grow up and although Shirley did a good job with both Yann and the house, it wasn't the same thing as Elise doing it herself. She was Yann's mother and she wanted a chance to stay at home with him and do it right. She wanted to be the one to help him with his homework and take him for a stroll in the park.... And maybe, she and Tim could start thinking about having another child, maybe a little sister for Yann. Elise had actually been thinking about it so much that she'd already been picking out names. She was ready to talk to Tim about it. It was time to move their lives forward, in a new direction.

"Okay, we'll wrap up the discussion next week," the meeting chairman announced, "Linda will record the minutes and get them back to us on Monday. Enjoy your weekend everyone!"

With a relieved sigh, Elise closed her briefcase, and on the way to the elevator she pulled at the tight bun she'd wrapped her hair in this morning. As she pulled out the wrap her long brown hair spilled out and cascaded across her shoulders.

As she walked through the hallway she glimpsed something strange. There was a crowd of people in front of her and standing in the midst of them was someone, or something that shouldn't be there. It's was an inky dark silhouette from where she stood, but she had the feeling she'd seen it…or him before. Something about him…or it frightened her and she began to walk quicker, passing the elevator in her rush. It wasn't the first time today that she'd felt like she was being followed. She turned down first one corridor and then the next with a feeling of panic rising up in her chest. When she got closer to the second bank of elevators she looked over her shoulder. Standing about ten feet away a man in a black hood was watching her. She jumped into the elevator with her heart racing and pressed the "door close" button. Once the door was closed she pressed the button for the first floor and she was able to breathe a little easier.

SEASONS OF HEAVEN

When Elise hit the exit door and the fresh air outside she gulped a deep lungful of it. She was still shaking and she wasn't even sure what it was about the man that had frightened her so badly. She wasn't even sure he'd been following her.... She saw Tim's car sitting in the lot and replacing the anxiety with a smile of anticipation for their night together she walked over and opened the door and slipped into the passenger seat.

"Hi Honey. How was your...?" Tim could see from the look on Elise's face that it hadn't been a good one. He said, "Ok I get it," he said with a sympathetic look. "Hard day?"

"Yeah," she said, "It sure was..." Tim could tell that she was worried. It seemed like more than just the usual stress from work. He was about to ask about it when she said, "I had this creepy feeling all day that I was being followed. My day is stressing enough as it is, with the everlasting discussions at work about this darned conflict."

With a worried look Tim put the car in drive and headed out of the parking lot. Once they were on the road he said, "What do you mean by "followed"?"

"I don't know. I had the impression that a man was following me. I didn't even get a good look at him, yet I'm sure I've seen him before. The security of our offices is one of the tightest in the country. I can't imagine just anyone could have slipped in. I'll check with security on Monday."

"Ok, let me know if you have a problem, you know that…"

"I can take care of myself, "Mister Inspector," She told him with a smile and a kiss on the cheek.

Tim grinned and said, "Okay, fine. I'm so glad that we're getting to spend some time together, finally. Are you looking forward to our dinner tonight?"

"Of course, Hun! And I have something important to tell you. Well, actually it might even be two important things."

Tim glanced over at Elise's animated face, wondering what it was that she had to tell him. He decided to be patient; they finally had all night to talk. He drove them down to 48th street to a French Gourmet restaurant they both loved. The restaurant was done up European style with brick walls and a little wrought iron gates around the windows. There was a potted shrub on each side of the door and an old-fashioned black chalkboard out front announcing the specials.

The neighborhood around the restaurant was a noisy one with loud music drifting out from the apartment building down the street and heavy traffic going by, but once inside they felt as if they'd been transported to a quiet bistro in Paris. Soft lighting gave the place a warm atmosphere and it smelled of fresh bread and rich pastry. The sounds of Edith Piaf singing a love song floated out of the speakers and gave the impression that a French Cabaret was taking place in the background.

Tim and Elise stepped up to the podium at the front door and were greeted warmly by the maître.

"Good evening Madam, good evening Sir. Do you have a reservation?"

"Good evening, Yes we do, a table for 2, booked under Northman," Tim told him.

"Very well, one moment please."

They didn't have to wait long before they were taken to a little table in the corner with a glowing red candle in the center and a giant 1930's style painting framed in a heavy ancient frame hanging next to them. The waiter took their orders and Tim asked for a rare bottle of Bordeaux. They listened to the soft music, "Mon bistrot préféré" of Renaud playing in the background while they waited for their meals both of them caught up in their own thoughts. When their pasta was served and they'd both begun to eat, Elise said,

"Ok, let me finish what I had started in the car, and thank you for not interrupting me until I finish because this is big news and if you interrupt me I'll just get nervous. I have handed in my resignation letter. I'm done. I want to focus on our boy now." Elise laughed nervously and Tim, looking shocked in the middle of taking a bite of his pasta said,

"Are you sure?"

Elise nodded, still smiling and Tim went on to say,

"Wow, I don't know what to say. I'm so happy about that! Yann will be so happy. It will be great for his education... And I could tell that this job was ruining you..." he paused there. He knew that hers wasn't the only job ruining them. He took a deep breath and said, "Mine as well... I swear to you that this last case... It has been a living hell; we have been after that murderer for so long..."

Elise rolled her eyes and said, "See, there you go talking about yourself again...let me finish my story, I was only halfway through it."

"Ok, ok! I'm sorry, I'll be quiet!"

"I'm three months pregnant..." she blurted it out quickly. This was the part she was really nervous about. She ran her hand through her hair as she waited for his response.

Tim didn't look happy, but he tried to sound happy as he said, "Oh, ok, great! Have you known for long?"

"No... You don't look happy," she said.

"Please don't make assumptions," he told her. "I'm happy, but the world we live in... it's not easy, and it's hard for me to put a positive spin on reality with everything I'm confronted with at work. And if I could quit, I would do it."

"Do it then, it's not going to change the face of the world... stay with us, instead of chasing ghosts."

On the radio behind the counter a man was talking about the events that were happening around the world. If anyone had been paying attention, they would have found it all to be depressing news.

"*The premier general of the United States Army has been quoted today as giving the following statistics with regards to losses of U.S. lives and military equipment throughout the course of the war in Iraq. He said that 535,000 soldiers have died, eighty ships have been put out of service, six aircraft carriers blown up, two hospital ships destroyed, two submarines lost, 1,350 aircrafts, 1500 helicopters, 1000 tanks, 2000 armored vehicles and 1800 pieces of heavy artillery lost. The financial impact of all of that to the country has been staggering, the loss of human lives devastating. In other news, a massive flood in Venezuela that caused mudslides and the loss of three hundred lives is said to have been a natural catastrophe mainly triggered by global warming now by some experts....*"

"I wish I could make you understand, Elise...Shit!" Tim said in the middle of talking to his wife.

"What?" Elise said. She was shocked at how he'd yelled out the profanity in the middle of the restaurant. It wasn't like Tim at all. She started to turn and see what he was looking at when he said,

"No! Don't turn around, honey. Damn it! I can't believe that son of a bitch is here!"

"What?" Elise said again, confused. She'd heard Tim say don't turn around, but she turned around anyways. She had to see what had gotten him so agitated. Tim was on his feet, headed towards the front window. He shouted over his shoulder to Elise,

"Don't move. I'll be right back!" He made his way between the tables, pushing a waiter out of his way and pulling his gun before he reached the door. Once he pushed through the door, the man he'd seen there at the window had vanished.

He looked up and down both sides of the street. *How does the son of a bitch move so fast?*

"Damn! Damn! Damn!" he said aloud to the alarm of many of the people walking by on the sidewalk. He tucked his gun back in its shoulder holster and went back inside the restaurant. He looked at the server standing near the door and said, "Do you have a phone I can use?"

"Yes sir," the server handed him the cordless phone from behind the counter. Tim dialed Eddie's number.

CHAPTER FOURTEEN
"CRYPTIC WARNINGS"
NORTHMAN'S RESIDENCE
Tuesday, September 7TH

Yann and Ani had been playing and talking and telling stories in their room for hours when they heard the sound of Shirley's voice calling up to them. Yann got up and opened the bedroom door and that was when they both smelled the delicious aroma of dinner wafting up the stairs.

"Dinner time!" Shirley said again, "Come on boys!"

"We're coming!" Yann called down. "Let's go, Ani! Time to eat!"

The young boy and his canine best friend bounded down the stairs and rushed into the kitchen. Shirley had the table set under the bright lights and the plates were filled with a juicy steak, savory red potatoes and fresh green beans.

"What do you think?" Shirley asked Yann.

"It looks and smells delicious," he said, "Doesn't it Ani?"

Ani barked out his answer and Shirley smiled and said,

"Yours is over there little man," pointing at his food bowl. Ani walked over to his food bowl while Yann sat down at the table with Shirley. He ate one piece of his dry food at a time as he listened to the clinks and clanks of the silverware while Shirley and Yann ate a silent meal. Shirley was exhausted. She had spent the entire afternoon working on a report.

"Do you want to watch a movie after dinner?" she asked Yann. "It's two hours long, but if we start watching it early, we should have time to finish before you have to go to bed."

"No, it's okay," Yann told her. "Ani and I are going to go back into our room and read." Shirley watched him as he shoveled in and gulped down what was left on his plate. With his mouth still full he said, "Shir....I'm done. I'm going to brush my teeth and then would it be okay if Ani and I go back and read?"

"Yann! Don't talk with your mouth full. It's such bad manners! I'm not kidding, okay? It's really sloppy looking. You can go brush your teeth and read, but only for another hour, okay?"

"Okay, thanks Shirley," he said, getting up and giving her a kiss on the cheek. "Come on Ani!"

Shirley shook her head as the boy raced up the stairs towards the bathroom, taking each step with a loud thud underneath his feet. Ani slipped out the doggy door while Yann was brushing his teeth. He did his doggy business and then stopped to sniff the air. Something was about to happen…something bad. Dogs have a sort of sixth sense about those things. He listened as he heard the sounds of a fire truck pierce the otherwise peaceful night. The garden was dark in spite of the well-lit sky, shadowed by the many trees and Yann's precious shed. Ani looked up at the stars. Suddenly he saw a luminous sphere amongst them, growing in size, becoming huge as he watched. Then it suddenly vanished without a trace. Alarmed, Ani ran back inside the house with the hair on the back of his neck and down his spine standing straight up. By the time he made it to the bedroom, Yann had already fallen asleep.

Ani jumped up on the end of the bed and sat looking out at the sky. He felt his little doggy eyelids beginning to grow heavy and his head began tilting first to one side and then the other. When he couldn't hold his head up any longer, he crawled underneath the sheets and cuddled up against Yann. Yann instinctively rolled over and put his arm around the little dog in his sleep.

Downstairs, Shirley lay on the living room sofa, reading one of her textbooks. Three other books lay strewn around her as she tried to read a week's worth of assignments in one evening. She suddenly sat up straight and looked at the time,

"Oh no, I forgot to call Matt!" She put her feet on the floor, knocking over the stack of books she'd forgotten was there. Shirley sighed, she was so tired. She picked up the phone and dialed Matt's number. She was worried, afraid that he was going to be upset with her. When he answered she said,

"Hi honey. I'm sorry, I was so busy. I had to catch up on…."

Matt chuckled and said, "I know. It's okay. How are you? I miss you so much…." he said something else after that, or at least Shirley thought he did, but the words were distorted and there was a crackling sound coming out of the receiver.

"I can't hear you!" she said, "Damn phone!" Shirley could suddenly hear a woman's voice coming through the line. It sounded like she was far away but Shirley heard her say,

"One, zero, two, three….It's over."

"Hey Matt? What is that? I can't hear you!" Shirley banged the phone on the table and then put it back to her ear. She could hear Matt's voice then saying,

"Hello? Hello...the pho..." then she heard a ring and two beeps before the line went dead.

Frustrated, she dialed him back several times but each time she was unable to get through. Shirley tossed the cordless phone down onto the sofa. Stupid technology! She thought. She sat back down on the sofa with her books, hoping that he would call back when he was able. She picked the phone back up and sat it on the small table next to her. Tim and Elise should be home soon...she was just going to close her eyes for a second....

Shirley let her mind drift to thoughts of her life. She loved what she was doing with her life, although she was so tired all the time. She loved Matt and she loved the Northman's. They were the first real family she'd ever had and she hoped that when she was finally ready, she could have a family like theirs one day.

She continued to let her thoughts drift, becoming more and more relaxed. Her whole body, including her limbs felt practically weightless as she slipped into a tranquil state of REM sleep. She could see herself beside a glorious river at sunset. The intense light of the sun as it dipped its head behind the mountains made the water glitter like a thousand diamonds adorned its surface. Shirley was gazing upon that serene scene when suddenly she could see herself back in the Northman's living room, only now she was completely drenched. She could actually see herself as if she were looking into a mirror at her own reflection and she had the strangest sensation of having just been kissed.

"Yann...Ani....Are you there?" Shirley's face was as white as a sheet suddenly and she looked dazed as if just waking up from a long sleep. "Answer me, please...I..." she tried to move but she felt almost paralyzed. She fought against the feeling and slowly and progressively she began to feel each one of her limbs again. When she was finally able to rise, she ran up the stairs and flung open the door to Yann's room. It was empty. In a panic, she ran over and yanked the sheets off the bed. Nothing...no one was there.

    She was suddenly filled with anguish. She found it hard to breathe as if her distress might be causing her to have a panic attack, and the panic caused her difficulty filling her lungs with air. All at once, she could feel something behind her. Thinking it might be Yann, she spun around. To her horror, she found herself facing something so hideous that her brain could barely process it. It had the vague shape of a man, only it was bigger, maybe six and a half feet tall. It had something folded against its back that looked like wings and the worst part was that it didn't actually have a head, but two glowing red eyes the size of automobile reflectors were inset on its chest. Shirley wanted to scream, but she couldn't, the fear had trapped the screams somewhere inside of her. Fear and loathing coursed through her body and left her limbs weak and shaky.

"Stay where you are... Don't get any closer!" she told the thing as they stood facing each other only four or five feet apart.

Its voice came out slowly and had a crackling tone to it...like the sound Shirley had heard on the phone earlier, like a broken radio signal.

"We are not here to harm you, Shirley, you know that...Don't you want to join your parents?"

Shirley could feel the tears streaming down her face. Her heart was pounding rapidly in her chest and she was fighting so hard to keep air in her lungs that her breathing was audible and echoing off the walls of the room.

"Leave me alone, don't get any closer," she told it. Her voice was coming out in a high-pitched yelp. She didn't even recognize the sound of it herself. "What did you do with them, where are they?" she screamed at the thing. It took a step towards her and she realized that its giant black silhouette was made of some type of slimy, viscous material like used motor oil. Shirley was frozen to the spot, paralyzed by her own fear, at the mercy of the creature...that suddenly disappeared.

Shirley fell to her knees and cried out, "Where are you?" Tears weren't just streaming but now pouring down the sides of her face. She was petrified, in disbelief that any of this was happening. She held her hands on her head because it felt like it was going to explode. There was a flash of inky black and glowing red in front of her once more and the creature reappeared, right in front of her. It was terrifyingly close to her face as it said,

"They are ours; don't you want to join them? They command us!"

Shirley began to scream then, as the giant creature wrapped its giant black wings around her body. "Leave me alone, let go!" she yelled at it, struggling with all of her might to get away. Slimy black matter was not so much dripping as it was oozing like thick tar from its wings onto the shiny wood floor. Once it hit the floor, it would melt down into nothingness.

Screaming, kicking, clawing and even biting, Shirley was fighting for what she thought was her very life. With considerable effort she somehow managed to escape the giant creature's slippery grip and run out into the hallway, running right into the wall and falling down to the floor.

The impact left her stunned and she was having a difficult time pushing herself back up off the floor. The creature was back upon her and in the space of a second, pushed her over the ledge of the mezzanine.

Shirley screamed as her body hurtled through the air like a rag doll and came crashing down on top of the living room table. She could hear the crackly voice saying, "Stay with me, you will be safe, you might even save them..." just as the leg of the table ripped through her flesh and muscle and bone, perforating her throat.

Stunned, she pulled herself up and staggered, bleeding profusely across the room. She could see her life flashing before her eyes and she knew she was dying. She saw Yann and Ani and Matt....Their beautiful faces appeared before her and then faded to black....Suddenly there was only emptiness....

The insistent ringing of the phone brought Shirley out of her nightmare. She was still shaking and disoriented when she woke. She instinctively put her hand to her throat, feeling for the object that had impaled her in the dream. There was nothing there...it was only a dream.

She glanced at her hand as she picked up the phone...there was something on it...something red, *was that blood?*

"Hello?"

" "Hello, is this Shirley?"

"Yes it is. Who is this?" she asked, not in the mood for a telemarketer tonight. She was thinking about her nightmare still. She wanted to go up and check on Yann and Ani.

"Good evening Shirley, this is Eddie," His voice sounded anxious. It immediately got her attention; she could tell that he was calling with very bad news

Shirley listened in abject horror to the words that Eddie was speaking. The news was worse than she would have ever imagined. She began to scream with rage, the tears flowing now in real life as abundantly as they had done in her dream as she dropped to her knees and sobbed. Her breathing was ragged and she leaned forward, clutching her stomach as it reeled with disgust. She felt Ani licking her arm. He'd heard her screams and ran down the stairs to check on her.

Shirley sat back on her bottom on the floor and looked at Ani. "Dear God, how am I going to tell Yann?"

She collapsed again into a torrent of tears, wrapping herself up in her own arms, curled into a fetal position on the floor. She lay like that; sobbing non-stop for what may have been minutes or hours, or days. It was as if time had stopped and everything was just now moving in slow motion. She didn't want to believe what Eddie said even though she liked him and she knew Tim trusted him implicitly... She'd rather believe he was playing some horrible joke on her. If he was telling the truth then that meant that Elise and Tim were dead....And she had to tell Yann.

There are utterances of death a lot in this book.

CHAPTER FIFTEEN
"ORPHAN"
September, 11, 1991

Shirley and Yann drove along the road that had become like a shallow river because of the pitiless rain that had emerged from the heavy black clouds with a roar and then poured down relentlessly across the city. The sky was malevolent as it pressed down on them. Thick black clouds raced across it, so dark that they even stood out against the starless night sky.

Yann sat in the passenger seat, his skinny little shoulders leaden with grief. He was still bewildered by it all. Only days earlier, all had been right in his world. He didn't fully grasp what had happened to change all of that. He didn't really get that his parents were never coming home. He knew that something bad had happened and that things would never be the same...but he didn't understand why. Because of that, he had done his best to explain it to Ani but the dog didn't fully comprehend it all either.

"Shirley, I don't want to leave him. It's not fair..." he said with tears rimming his dark eyes as he looked at her. Shirley's heart was breaking for him, but she was doing what she knew she had to do.

"I know sweetie," she told him in a soft voice. "I'll take care of him until you get back home. I will do everything it takes to get you back."

"I don't want to go there.... I really don't. How will the other kids treat me? Please stop the car Shirley! Please! I don't want to go!"

His please were melting her heart and she wished that she had any other choice. She was trying not to cry for his sake, but that was the only thing keeping her from it,

"Listen to me, Yann. Trust me...please. Give me some time so that I can get custody of you and Ani. I promise I will get you back, and we'll all be together. Eddie said that he would help us. He knows people who can speed up the process. Trust me, Yann. Please." Shirley wanted to turn the car around and take him home. She would have done it, if not for her fear that if she didn't do this legally, someone would take Yann from her. Tim's parents had been dead for ten years, Elise's mother was in a nursing home and her father hadn't been seen or heard from in over thirty years….There was no biological family to take Yann, but Shirley wanted him…she was his family. She just had to do it right.

She pulled the car into a poorly-lit parking lot, maneuvering around the deep puddles that the rain had left behind. The majority of the lights in the area emanated from the windows of a nearby building. It was the building they were headed to and Shirley looked at it with despair in her heart. It was so lifeless and cold looking. It looked more like a sanitarium than an orphanage to her. Children shouldn't live in such a dark and dreary place….The building was immense, stretching out in all directions with hundreds of windows dotting the outside of the edifice, some were lit up and others completely black. Once they parked the car and got closer to the building, it gave Shirley the eerie feeling of a prison, like whoever went in never came out. She shuddered at the thought and glanced at Yann. He wouldn't look at her and she didn't blame him.

A woman, shorter than Shirley stood in front of the main building. Her hair was swept back into a severe bun and her dark and close-set eyes only added to the harshness of her look.

"Good evening," she said, "You must be Shirley?" the woman's voice had an edge to it, and it instantly struck Shirley the wrong way. The woman looked down at Yann and in a sharp, swift tone she said, "I assume then that you're Yann, aren't you?" The woman looked him over and her eyes came to rest on Ani who Yann was clutching in his arms. "This institution does not accept...these...you know, that black thing you have there! Animals are not allowed at Saint Josephs."

"You are?" Shirley asked her, not fond of the way the woman was speaking to Yann.

"I'm Miss Pearce, the person in charge of the children."

"We know of course that the dog can't stay…they just wanted to say good-bye." The older woman gave Yann another disdainful look and told them,

"Follow me this way." They followed her through the big main doors and began walking down a long, poorly illuminated corridor. Shirley leaned down near Yann's ear and said,

"A few days, maximum a few weeks…I promise!"

"Please Shirley. Please let me go back home with you. I don't want to stay here," Yann pleaded. Ani whimpered in his arms. Although the dog didn't understand all that was happening, he knew his best friend was sad and afraid.

Miss Pearce stopped walking and turned towards Yann, "I know this is not easy son, but we are all here to help you. We will take good care of you until we find you a real family."

"Don't worry please, sweetie! Just give me a little time," Shirley felt a tear escape down her cheek, she couldn't hold them back any longer.

"Please! I want to stay with Ani!" The little boy's voice was desperate and his eyes wide with the terror that came from being separated from everyone he loved and sent to live in such a horrid place.

"Yann, listen to me…" Shirley begged him. "Come with me to the car and we'll get your suitcase from the trunk. I'll walk you to your room. I promised you we'll find a solution to this and I meant it. Once that happens I'll be back to get you. It'll be in no time, honey. I promise."

"Come on," Miss Pearce told them over her shoulder. "I'll show you where the room is and which one is your bed. Once you've seen it we'll sign the admission papers in the office and you can get your luggage. Then Shirley and….The dog can be on their way."

SEASONS OF HEAVEN

Yann tightened his grip on the little dog, clutching him to his chest. Ani licked the boy on his neck and the side of his face. He was shaking...sensing Yann's fear.

As they walked further into the dismal place Shirley found herself thinking that a place filled with children shouldn't be such an abysmal place. It should radiate with warmth and joy. This place was as welcoming as a penitentiary and she completely understood why Yann was afraid.

The main hallway had a sign that pointed one direction for the cafeteria and the other for the administration offices. As they passed the main staircase Miss Pearce pointed out that it separates the building into two parts. One wing of the building hosted the boys and the other the girls.

The only color in the place seemed to be represented by the many drawings and doodles and old film posters hung along the walls of the long corridors. Yann was terrified, and it was only made worse by the fact that he was going to miss

Ani so badly. He hadn't left him yet and Yann's heart already ached for him.

The austere woman showed them a dull, bland room and a cold looking metal bed where Yann would be living until Shirley came back for him. Shirley shuddered once more at the bleakness of it all. The poor boy had lost his parents and now while he was still grieving and trying to understand it all, he felt like he was losing everyone else he loved.

When Shirley finished up the paperwork and went to say good-by to Yann, he was no longer begging her to go home. Now, he was silent, having withdrawn into himself. Shirley hugged him tightly and promised him again that she would be back for him. She let Ani lick his face once more and then with the little dog tucked under her arm she left him there on his bed, all alone.

Yann lay down on the bed, engulfed by the darkness and overcome by loneliness. The dormitory that housed the bed he lay on was huge with rows of beds on each side lined up with military preciseness. There was no sound in the room other than the heavy breathing of the other boys who slept there. The large windows that lined one wall of the room let in nothing but more darkness and Yann missed the window in his room, the one where he and Ani could look out and see the moon and the stars.

The thought of Ani caused another arrow of sharp pain to tear through his heart and land like a boulder in his already upset stomach. He thought about his parents then...Shirley had tried to explain things to him without coming right out and saying the word. She had said they'd had to go away...they could never come back...they were watching over him...they were in a better place. Yann had spent many hours processing all of that. He came to the realization that what she was trying to say, without saying it was that they were dead. Yann understood dead....kind of. He didn't want his parents to be dead. He missed them and he'd give anything to see them again, but he understood that he couldn't. He'd gotten through it so far by holding Ani, pressed to his chest...against his heart. It made him feel safe and warm and like everything would be okay someday. Now that he was really and truly alone, it was hard to hold on to that belief. His mood was as bleak as the building he now lived in. His emotions were as torn up as the walls and the floors. As he at last drifted off to sleep, he couldn't help but wonder how the other children here were going to receive him. Yann knew he was different and within the circle of friends his parents had created for him, he'd done just fine....But these children were not likely to be as kind and tolerant as his friends had been....

He woke up the next day and as the morning light streamed in through the dirty windows, he was able to see just how vast the room actually was. He could also see the other boys and they all seemed to be looking at him. One of the boys, much bigger than Yann started to approach him and although Yann didn't know why, fear began to coil in his belly like a snake. The door opened before the boy reached him, however and faced with a choice at that moment, Yann would have chosen the bigger boy.

In through the door marched the "general" of the orphanage. He walked briskly up to Yann's bunk with the loose and flabby skin of his body shaking and rolling with each step. Yann didn't know yet who he was or how bad his reputation fared at St. Josephs, but he was intimidated by the man's size alone.

"Yann Northman." It seemed more like a statement than a question, but to be polite, Yann said,

"Yes, sir."

"I'm Mr. Pratt. I'm the director here at St. Joseph's orphanage." The man spoke in a cold, controlled voice. His face seemed to move involuntarily as well as he spoke just above his lip like a nervous twitch or a tic. His black hair and inky little mustache stood out against his almost glowing white skin.

SEASONS OF HEAVEN

"Hello," Yann said, casting his eyes down towards the scuffed linoleum floor. Mr. Pratt didn't return Yann's greeting. Instead, he launched into his "welcoming" speech which was a litany of rules and regulations. When he finished with that he called another boy over.

"Lyle, this is Yann. You are to proctor him and make sure that he knows where everything is and keeps to the rules until he commits them all to memory."

"Yes sir," the other boy said. He looked to be a year or two older than Yann. He had strawberry blonde hair and freckles and he wore a tattered pair of blue jeans and a white t-shirt. From what Yann could see of the other boys, it seemed to be the uniform of the place. The larger boy that had started towards him earlier was still giving him the eye. Yann was trying to ignore him, but something about him seemed so threatening.

Over the course of the following weeks, Yann found out that the bigger boy was indeed threatening. He was the leader of a group of boys who liked to fight and went out of their way to make life miserable for the smaller, younger or weaker ones. Yann was not a fighter neither in terms of strength or attitude. He was blessed with a witty astuteness however and he was often forced to use it to avoid or escape a confrontation. He learned a lot of other things about his new "home" as well.

He learned that it was a place with a lot of staff…twenty total nurses and caregivers during the day and five at night, as well as a security officer or two on each shift. In spite of all the people with ample opportunity to care for children that society had all but forgotten, there was very little caring that went on. It seemed as if everyone were out for him or herself only.

The toys were always old and broken and with missing pieces. They were all donated toys and no one ever donated "new" stuff to an orphanage. The coloring books were filled with pages colored by children who were still in possession of their parents and if one was lucky enough to find a page uncolored, he colored it with broken, chipped crayons.

Personal things were practically non-existent and the reason for that was two-fold. Most of the children had no one to bring them personal items, and the ones who were lucky enough that they did rarely remained in possession of them long before they were stolen. Some of the lucky ones held onto their things by stuffing them underneath their mattresses and sleeping on them at night. Unfortunately, that only worked for the boys that were large enough not to be moved or intimidated into moving when one of the bigger boys told him to.

The bathrooms were appalling even to an eleven-year-old boy. One bathroom was used by twenty-four boys. Some of these boys had never been taught the proper way to use the toilet or clean themselves and the bathrooms were cleaned about as often as they were at the local gas station.

SEASONS OF HEAVEN

Yann found out that the holidays and birthdays were rarely recognized much less celebrated, everyone wore everyone else's clothes and the bigger kids bullied the smaller ones. Three different groups of boys constantly fought over who "ruled" which part of the orphanage. The group called "The eagles" had already been in the orphanage for a few years and felt like they'd "earned" the right to rule the entire place. They were too old to get adopted and too young to be on their own. Most of them were big and all of them were mean and it was futile to defy their orders. Yann decided that even if they had been adopted, the poor, unfortunate souls who adopted them would likely be asking for a return.

The other two groups weren't quite as threatening. The "Hares" and the "Squirrels" were what they called themselves. Their "territory" as they saw it was the toys that they fought over eternally.

SEASONS OF HEAVEN

Overall, it was not a place that someone might choose to live, and the first chance he got, Yann made up his mind, he was getting as far away from it as he could.

CHAPTER SIXTEEN
"ESCAPE"
ORPHANAGE

As the days passed, Yann spent every waking hour either practicing self-preservation or plotting his escape. The self-preservation came in the form of avoiding the attention of the gangs, or the wrath of Mr. Pratt. For some reason, the director had taken a disliking to Yann and seemed to have the staff hovering around him at every juncture looking for things to cite him over. Once a citation had been issued, Yann would be summoned in front of Mr. Pratt and Mrs. Pierce, two of the most frightening human beings that he'd ever personally known. The punishment the hefty man doled out was harsh and sometimes cruel, but preferable to Yann than standing before them. To Yann, Pratt's dark eyes seemed to be harboring a deep-seeded evil behind them, and Mrs. Pierce just appeared to be the most miserable human being on Earth.

SEASONS OF HEAVEN

Shirley visited often but not Ani. Ani wasn't even allowed to visit and sometimes when Yann thought about him, he could actually feel his heart breaking. He craved his best friend's company and he'd reached the point where he was willing to do whatever had to be done to make his way back to him. He started by observing the surveillance cameras. There were only a few and only in common areas. He wrote down their positions and in what rooms they were in inside of his diary that he kept wrapped in his extra sheets and tucked deeply underneath his cot.

The next thing he observed and wrote down was the patrol patterns of the nurses and assistants. They made rounds every half an hour. There was also a nurse on call that sat in a small room near the front exit. When she wasn't there, a guard sat in her place.

The entrance door was always locked with a key and from what Yann had been able to discover. He knew that all of the staff had keys, but he also knew that there had to be a spare set somewhere. He was sure that Pratt had one, but that would never do. Pratt's quarters were all the way on the fourth floor and getting up there and back down would be a problem in itself.

The dorm supervisor had an office just across from the cafeteria on the first floor. That was another place he was sure there had to be an extra set of keys. The office was always open; Yann would just have to find a way to get in and out unobserved.

Once he was able to get the key, he had a route mapped out. He slept on the second floor, so he would wiggle in the air vent of the second floor, and slide down to the first floor. Then he would pass by the security office while the nurse on call...a large, older woman who was rarely awake at her post, slept. It would be more difficult if the guard was there, but he was not going to let that keep him from trying. The last step would be unlocking the door and head home on foot. All he was waiting for now was the perfect opportunity for it all to come together. In the meantime, he was just surviving as he bid his time.

THE ORPHANAGE DORMITORY – NIGHT
Several Weeks Later

That night as Yann was lying on his bed and just about to doze off he suddenly heard two loud bangs. The dormitory resonated and chaos ensued. Yann didn't get up; he didn't want to be in the line of fire when the staff arrived. As it turned out, that was a good thing because Pratt himself suddenly appeared through the door. The dormitory became instantly silent, so quiet that a pin dropping would have seemed loud.

The boy who had lit the firecracker hadn't even had time to ditch the lighter. Pratt didn't ask any questions. He pulled back his fist and landed it in the center of the freckled face of the twelve-year-old pyro technician sending a wave of shock and fear through the silent observers. The boy's body suddenly looked small as it flew back a few feet, spraying blood from his nose and landed in a heap on the dirty, cracked floor.

Pratt gave a glance around with his misshapen face and dark, evil eyes and said,

"I hope you all learned a lesson!!! Everyone in bed, NOOOOW!" He stopped only to pick up the crumpled form of the unconscious boy by the collar, drag him over to his bunk and toss him on like a rag doll. Yann watched in utter horror as the surreal scene unfolded before his eyes. Pratt then stormed out the door he'd come in through and slammed it behind him, plunging the room back into darkness.

The next day as Yann ate in the crowded, noisy cafeteria, he couldn't stop thinking about what he'd seen the night before. In Yann's world, a grown man...or woman for that matter would never lay their hands on a child in anger. Yann knew from his own experience that Pratt wasn't a compassionate man in any way. He knew that he wasn't a nice man, but he hadn't known until last night just how blatantly evil the man was.

Yann tried to push the frightening images of Mr. Pratt punching the child out of his mind by calling up memories of home. He thought about Shirley and Ani and how happy they would all be once he was back at home with them. Suddenly he told himself, "Tonight is the night."

He picked up his tray right then while all of the other kids continued to eat and the staff continued to watch them for unruly behavior. He dumped his tray and slipped out into the hallway, headed for the dorm supervisor's office. He knew that he had to be quick, they'd be finished eating soon and the halls would fill with people.

As quietly as he could, he slipped into the office and tiptoed over to the desk. He began searching the drawers from top to bottom. He located a metal box in the bottom drawer that contained three identical keys with a tag marked, "Front Entrance." He slipped one of the keys off the ring and into his pocket. As he quietly slipped back into the hallway he found himself wondering why the other kids hadn't done this already. It was so easy...

****

That night as the children were all in their beds and drifting off to sleep, Yann waited. He'd begun to worry that someone would have noticed one key was missing and would be watching and waiting to see who tried to use it. He knew if he was caught that the punishment would be the most severe of anyone he'd received so far.

He lay on his bunk with his eyes closed, breathing as slowly and softly as he could, so it would appear that he was asleep. Within the first half hour, the supervisor passed and turned off the lights. The room was ensconced it darkness suddenly, only faint shards of light passed through the window from the outside. Another half hour and things were completely silent; everyone had gone to sleep.

SEASONS OF HEAVEN

Yann sat up slowly, making sure the bunk didn't creak or let out a sound. He slipped on his shoes and then standing up just as carefully, he snuck between the beds towards the door. He slid quietly out the door and into the pitch black hallway. Using the walls to guide him he made his way down the hall towards the vent. He passed a door on his way and from behind it he heard a soft whining noise and the sounds of two people's hushed voices. He didn't stop to listen he had no time to lose. He continued to fumble in the dark, into the vent and down two floors.

He made his way to the main hallway. Once he was there, he felt even more anxious than he had upstairs. He crept down the hallway until the information office came into view. The guard was there and Yann held his breath as he crept underneath it. He was so afraid when he finally made it to the front door...too afraid to even turn around and find out if he was being observed. He put the key in his right hand and slid it delicately into the lock. He turned it gently and with more stealth than even he realized he had, he slipped out into the night, closing the door behind him. He was hoping that would slow them down if they discovered that he'd left.

Yann walked quickly, not running for fear of falling and injuring himself in the dark or making unnecessary noise. He knew if he didn't get away now that he would be met with the darkest corners of the director's soul when they took him back.

The fresh air felt so good on his face. He looked up at the night sky, covered in clouds as he walked. It was completely black and impossible to see the stars, only scattered and random shards of light broke through. Yann continued his path along the sidewalk and he lowered his head every time a car passed by. He observed the road signs trying to find his way in the dark. He didn't want to waste time by getting lost.

He felt good to be away, but the fear of getting caught still silently ate away at him, feeding the terror that welled up when he considered what the punishment might be. He continued his path along the sidewalk lowering his head every time a car passed by, still observing the road signs. He felt lost but as he passed trucks and cars he feared asking for help or directions. *What if they called the police? What would they think of discovering him alone, out in the night?* He was already a few miles from the orphanage which made him feel good, but he knew that Shirley still lived quite a ways away. Her home was in a nice area. He had memorized the address and the directions. He needed to take Park Slope on the 15th St. to Flatbush Ave and then Prospect Park West to Fourth Ave. It was probably another forty minute walk, according to his calculations. That wouldn't be the problem, he was comfortable walking. The problem was that the night was growing colder and the neighborhoods that he would have to pass through in the dark wouldn't be near as nice as the one that Shirley lived in.

SEASONS OF HEAVEN

He considered his options. He could find a place to sleep until the sun came up, or he could run and get there faster. He started to run. He ran across the park, jumping over trash bags and vaulting benches. He was bound and determined to make it. It was still pitch black outside, but his eyes had adjusted and the occasional street lamp helped him find his way. He'd begun to almost believe that he was going to make it when there was suddenly an overwhelmingly bright beam of light in his eyes.

"Young man! Stop! This is the police! Come closer so that I can see your face!" It was a policeman. He would take Yann back to the orphanage...he couldn't go back there. He had to find Ani. He didn't stop, he ran even faster.

He heard the policeman yell out after him again..."Stay there!" Then he saw the swivel of the red and blue lights and heard the loud wail of the siren as the police car began to pursue him. Yann turned into a narrow street and heard the squeal of the car tires behind him. The road was too narrow and Yann too fast for them to catch him that one. One of the policemen jumped out of the car and began to pursue him on foot.

"Stop, for God's sake! We do not want to hurt you!" the breathless policeman called after him.

Yann kept running. He felt as if his heart was about to explode in his chest. He couldn't hear anything except for the sound of his own ragged breaths and the rapid pounding of his heart. Then suddenly his heart stopped. There was a loud crash in front of him and it took him several seconds to realize that the police car had hit the wall in front of him and blocked his passage out. Yann stopped running. His whole body was quivering, not from the cold but from the sheer terror that raced across every nerve in his body.

"Come on, my boy, don't move, okay? Nobody wants to hurt you. Where are you coming from?" the policeman said, shining the light again on his face.

"I...do not want...do not want to go back there...Please!"

"What are you talking about? Where is it that you don't want to go? Can we call somebody to come and get you?"

"Shirley..."

CHAPTER SEVENTEEN
"RETRIBUTION"
ORPHANAGE
The Next Day

Yann sat like a stone while Shirley and Eddie tried to figure out what was going on and what to do. They both knew that Yann didn't want to be there, but neither of them had enough information to know how bad things were, and what kind of punishment Yann would be facing when they left.

"Yann, we just need you to be patient. We'll find a solution...I promise. We'll work as fast as we can to get you back home, okay?"

Yann didn't respond. He didn't even look at Eddie. He and Shirley had been trying to talk to him for quite some time. His response had been the same.

With tears in her eyes, Shirley told him,

"Give me a kiss, the next time I will try to bring Ani, okay?" Yann didn't respond to her either. He was hurt, confused, afraid and angry and he had no one else to punish for it. Shirley and Eddie eventually left and Yann quietly returned to his bunk. He just sat there, alone for hours. He didn't know what the punishment for leaving was going to be, or when it would be doled out...but he didn't plan to still be there when it was time for it to happen. He was already thinking of retrieving the key once more. That time was a trial run...this time would be for real. He couldn't think of anything but getting to Ani. They had been separated for too long. The distance between them made it impossible to communicate and Yann felt as if a part of his soul were missing.

"Hey stupid," Yann looked up at the tall boy that had approached him. He was one of the "Eagles," a very bad kid with nothing but trouble on his mind. "Why did you come back?" the kid asked him in a mocking tone.

"I did not come back ... I was brought back!" Yann told him. He was feeling angry enough that he didn't care what this boy might do to him. "All I want is to get out of here ..."

"But you can't leave. It's not possible," the boy said. He was still obviously taunting.

Yann had been trying so hard not to cry, but the tears finally escaped their binds and began to flow freely down his face.

"I want to see my parents," he said.

"Don't cry like a baby, when somebody is dead, they're dead!"

Defiantly, Yann wiped the tears away on the back of his arm and said,

"I am not a baby...And what you said isn't true, there is always some hope!"

"Listen, I don't care about your personal stories," he said, laughing. "We all have more or less the same one." He stopped talking then and for a few moments only stared at Yann as if deep in thought. Then, with a malicious smile he said, "If you want, you can always see Eric, he may have something that will help you!"

SEASONS OF HEAVEN

"What do you mean?" Yann was confused. How could Eric help him? Eric was one of the worst boys in the place.

"Go see him. Tell him you're sad and you want to be happy," he said, laughing.

Yann's illness didn't interfere often in his life, but in this case it painted a false picture of what was really happening in Yann's mind. He saw the boy smiling and heard him laughing. He interpreted that as happy...helpful. The truth was he was hateful and what he and the others were planning was nothing that would help Yann.

The director had held a meeting earlier in the day. The boys were all told that because of his escape...and the director had been sure to point him out...the rules would be stricter and the penalties for breaking them, harsher. Their lives were about to become even more difficult. Yann didn't know it, but while he was missing and they had the police searching for him, Mr. Pratt had even put his hands on a few of the boys, smacking them the way he had the boy with the fire cracker.

Yann thought about what the boy had said. What would it hurt to just ask Eric what he could do to help him? He went downstairs to the other dormitory to look for him. He didn't notice that the other boys were watching him to see if their plan was going to work.

"Hi! Eric? I'm Yann....

"What do you want, snot-nose?" Eric snapped at him.

"That was...The other boy told me to see you..."

"Alright, I know what you want. You want to see your old folks?" He laughed and suddenly Yann though he must be okay..."Well, you came to the right place. I was wondering when you would show up."

"I just want to see my parents...And Ani..." Yann said, innocently.

"Well, if that's all...it's simple. Take these pills. Put them in your mouth and swallow them and that's it! You will dream a beautiful, magical dream. You'll see, it works well. It's the only way that any of us gets to see our parents again..."

"That's it?" Yann said, confused again.

"Are you dumb or what?" Eric said. "You swallow these pills, you keep all that secret and you buzz off! However, I warn you, if Pratt knows that I gave you those...I will destroy you!"

"All I have to do is just to eat it?" Yann asked again.

"You are nuts, dumb, deaf or what? Ivan!" he looked over at one of the other boys and said, "Get him out of here!"

"Thank you, I really thank you...you know, my father..."

Eric laughed and a beefy Ivan shoved Yann out of the room and back into the hall.

Yann found a corridor that was small and empty. He couldn't wait to take the pills...and see his parents again. He was about to swallow them when he heard a voice coming from nowhere. Yann looked around...it seemed to be coming from behind the wall Yann was leaning against. There was a small door there and he could hear the voice saying,

"Yann? Yann? Share these pills with Ani..."

"Who are you?" Yann asked, startled.

"We will guide you to your parents ... but take these pills with Ani," they told him.

"I can't, he's not with me ..." Yann was on the verge of tears once more.

"Run...Escape...Take the pills with you..." the voice faded out as if whoever was talking to him had kept moving further away.

Yann put the pills back in his pocket. He decided the voice was right. He should organize his escape first. His backpack was still ready with the bottle of water he stole from the canteen all he needed to get now was a map of New York to help him find Shirley's house. He would find Ani and share the pills with him. They could see his parents together.....

SEASONS OF HEAVEN

THREE DAYS LATER
ORPHANAGE, NIGHT

It was ten p.m. and with the map he'd stolen from the library in his hand, Yann was again standing free outside the orphanage. He'd gone through all the same steps as before, but this time he knew better how to stay on track and keep an eye out for the police.

He nervously passed the stoop of the orphanage. This was likely his last chance to get this right. He had to find Ani. Then, they would take the pills and see his parents. That thought made his heart swell with hope as he looked at the map in his hand and turned to the left down a dark, narrow street. There were trash bins scattered about and Yann stayed close to the side walls, avoiding the middle of the street.

SEASONS OF HEAVEN

He reached the end of that one and checked for cars or policemen before quickly crossing the street. Getting caught again was not an option, the punishment would be something more than what Yann could imagine, he was sure of it.

He walked for about twenty minutes before reaching a shady neighborhood. There were women standing on the streets. Yann didn't know that they were prostitutes, but they found it very curious that a little boy would be walking down the street alone at this time of night. New York in the '90's was not a safe place to be at night for a grown man. Putting a little boy on the street was like throwing a hunk of meat to a lion and expecting him to not go after it.

Yann clung tightly to his backpack. He had a few dollars inside that he'd stolen from Mrs. Pearce's wallet. The prostitutes only looked at him, however...curiously. He stumbled upon a bus stop and could see the lights of the big bus at the end of the street. Sweat was beading on his brow as he tried to think of some reason to give the bus driver if he asked what a little boy was doing out alone at this time of night, getting on a city bus. When the bus stopped, Yann stepped on.

"Good evening," the driver said as Yann put his dollars in the slot.

"Good evening, sir..." Yann said. Then he waited for it...but nothing came. The driver seemed to not even notice the strangeness of the situation. Twenty minutes later, Yann was standing in front of Shirley's residential building, breathing a sigh of relief.

Yann started towards the building, suddenly noticing Matt standing on the sidewalk. He was talking to another man. It looked like one of Shirley's professors that Yann had met once...applied science? Something like that. He couldn't tell for sure, the light was bad. They hadn't noticed Yann, so he stood with his ear to the wall and listened to what they were saying.

"I'm not sure...There is nothing written about where that place could be..." Matt was saying.

"But I'm sure, there must be something written at the entrance...It's somewhere here; there is no doubt about that. We have to take care of it before the others!" the other man was telling him.

"He doesn't mention it, even once... He explains everything except for that ..." Matt said.

Yann doesn't understand what they are talking about. He moves and his foot touches an aluminum can. The noise makes two men stop their conversation.

"What was that?" Matt said.

"I don't know, but...you have to stay close to the girl, the boy and the dog. You have to protect them. They haven't yet begun their role in the destiny of humankind."

Yann returned to the entrance of the building. The fire staircase is a good solution for him. He takes a stone with him to break a window if the upstairs passage into the building is closed.

Shirley lived on the ninth floor. As Yann made his way up the stairs, the telepathic connection with Ani came back suddenly. They were both so happy to be connected again. Ani told Yann that the window was open. Yann hurried up to find the window where he finally sees the muzzle of the dog he loved so much waiting for him.

CHAPTER EIGHTEEN
"*WINTER PARADISE AND DESTINIES* "

Yann followed the voice, still in the glorious place where he'd gotten off the train, but newly amazed as he watched the spring colors that had gleamed beneath the exacting light of the sun before now vanishing before his eyes as the snow fell from the sky and turned everything into a soft blanket of white. He trudged through the fluffy white snow, watching the puffs of dust that bounced off of his feet as they swirled up into the air and whipped around in circles before being carried off into the frigid cold air. His feet cut a path across the untouched snow towards a clump of magnificent trees. The branches hung heavy against the thick air that Yann struggled to breathe. The icicles that hung from them added weight and pulled them towards the ground. Yann's cheeks turned rosy red as the icy air bit at them.

When he got close enough to the trees, Yann could see a passageway that cut through them.

"It's so beautiful," he said looking at the winter wonderland scene that stretched out before him. Yann could hear the train in the distance. It seemed to be stopping again. As he stood and listened he looked up and realized that the extremely cold air caused the atmosphere to be clearer than ever and the Big Dipper was as visible to Yann as the trees in front of him. He was distracted by the constellation when he saw the wiggle of the shrubs in front of him out of the corner of his eye. He looked down just in time to see a small black ball of fur appear.

Ani barked and Yann said,

"You are here! Come here my love!" Yann leaned down and scooped the little dog up into his arms. The two companions, once again reunited for their final adventure. As he hugged Ani to his chest something happened...He began to have flashes of memory, a warm inviting home in the suburbs, a room full of little boy things. A place that his brain was only beginning to remember, but that his heart had along been longing for. He also saw a beautiful young woman with kind eyes and dark hair that framed her face and stopped just beneath her chin. He knew her name was Shirley and thinking about her gave him a warm feeling in his chest. He knew that she was someone special to him….His life was coming back to him now, in flashes.

They snuck between the trees with heavy steps and Yann noticed that some of the branches of the trees were lit at the tips. There was so much snow dancing in the air in front of them that it was difficult to see now. There were tracks in the snow in front of them that Yann didn't recognize. Curious, they followed them with Ani sniffing at the ground like mad. They came upon a thick patch of forest, so thick that if Yann tried, he'd be barely able to slip through. They could hear rustling and movement in the snow covered shrubs and Yann's heart nearly lurched from his chest when a very large, woodland rabbit jumped out. Laughing at himself for being scared of a rabbit, Yann and Ani turned and stood frozen as their eyes fell upon a sight that human eyes have rarely witnessed. Standing only about ten feet away in one of the thickets of the trees was a wolf. It's thick, wintery white coat was almost indistinguishable from the snow yet his violet eyes shone out like precious stones from their sockets. He looked at the boys, with disinterest and turned towards the forest to continue on his way. That was when they noticed the others...the wolf wasn't alone. A pack of beautiful wolves followed him as he walked away. They all had thick, shiny fur and glowing eyes. Behind them stood something that fascinated the boys even more...a huge grizzly bear. The beat stood on his hind legs and allowed the wolves to just walk by. When they were gone he glanced in Yann and Ani's direction with peaceful eyes, and then he turned and went on his own way as well.

SEASONS OF HEAVEN

Yann and Ani looked at each other with amazement in their own eyes before continuing on their path. Before they reached their destination they would also be witness to the lumbering's of more bear that had foregone their winter hibernation as well as the foraging of a family of deer who were looking for anything green that might yet not be buried by the snow. They traveled along through this wondrous place, beckoned by the voice and confused about where it might be coming from. It attracted them like magnets nonetheless.

Eventually the boys arrived at a peak. It was covered in ice and fresh snow clung to the surface. The brilliant sun still shown above it yet there were already stars that could be seen in the sky. A soft wind brushed Ani's fur back and Yann's hair danced with the rhythm of the wind. Yann looked down and saw that below them a massive ocean lay, covered with ice. Some of it had melted underneath the glow of the warm sun and bobbed up and down across the surface.

SEASONS OF HEAVEN

Looking to the east Yann could see a beautiful, white beast. He's crawling along the surface of the ice delicately, trying not to fall through. It's a polar bear and although he is huge and strong Yann can almost feel his vulnerability. He's afraid of drowning and he looks frightened and alone. Yann's heart went out to him. *Where is his family? Is he alone...forever? That thought made Yann suddenly wonder, Are we all alone, forever?*

Ani barked towards the bear as loudly as he could. The echo carried it from the peak but the bear didn't seem to hear it. With as much wind as he was able to muster he barked again. This time the immense white creature turned his head towards the two friends. For a moment the three of them exchanged a magical moment. Their eyes met and the bear's dark eyes shone as he realized...he was not alone after all. He stood there perfectly still, looking like a majestic statue. While Yann looked at him he got a feeling of Déjà vu, and then it was gone as the polar bear suddenly dove forward and disappeared into the icy water.

Yann made eye contact with his little friend Ani then and said, "Have you ever felt that?" Ani sent a clear picture into the little boy's head and Yann suddenly understood it all. Nature is magic, and she'll hold all of her secrets tightly until the end. Yann's heart was suddenly full and the sadness he'd been feeling was washed away and replaced with a feeling of intense happiness. He understood the purpose of life at last. He looked back at Ani and said, "I'm sorry my friend…I didn't know. No one knows."

Ani kept his eyes on Yann's face as a small smile spread across his own. His words to his friend in his head this time were, "If no one ever told you, how would you know?" Ani looked away then and Yann couldn't help but wonder, if the dog is the human's best friend, by his perspective what are we? Does he see us as a friend or companion?

SEASONS OF HEAVEN

What is our place in his world? These thought stayed in Yann's head as they forged on.

They journeyed through the thick snow and heavy air until suddenly a group of cylindrical poles appeared in front of them. They appeared to be made out of stone. Yann climbed up on one and Ani followed. Like the young boys they were, they jumped from one to the next.

As they jumped Yann suddenly felt a strange vibration. Looking down at his backpack he saw that it was the wings that he kept attached there. They were vibrating and shining with an internal light that seemed to be trying to burst out of them. That had definitely never happened before. Yann was amazed by the magical sight and he said,

"Wow, that's cool! Did you see that, Ani? Come closer, I will carry you."

Yann can see a door...an entrance to where he doesn't know. The poles are between them and it, so with Ani in his arms; he continued to jump across them until they reached it without effort. Yann felt like Ani was as light as a feather, lighter than he'd ever been before. He wondered if it was because of the magical wings.

Yann and Ani stood in front of the door, wondering what was behind it.

■■

On a beautiful beach shore... James opened his eyes very slowly. He looked around, realizing that strangely he was lying in the sand, underneath the hot sun. He could hear the whisper of a breeze and as he looked next to him, he saw Sarah. He was confused; he didn't understand what had happened.

"James...Honey... Are you ok? Do you hear me?" Sarah prodded him gently.

"Holy shit, I have a terrible headache...What happened? Where are we?" James asked her.

"Well, I guess we're on a beach. I don't quite understand, I can't recall everything..."

SEASONS OF HEAVEN

"Come, let's go find some water." James said to her. He pushed himself up off the sand and then helped Sarah up next to him.

"Look!" James pointed to a small lake he could see a ways off in the distance. He moved closer to it and waded in. It was shallow at first just over a foot and a half deep or so. He continued to walk across it when it suddenly became deep all at once and he lost his balance.

"Watch out! What is that?" Sarah called out to him. She was right behind him, close enough to reach out and grab his arm.

"I have no foggy idea, but it seemed really profound," he told her.

They both plunged under the water and were startled by what they found. There were a series of waterfalls hidden underneath the surface. They were enormous and terrifying and they realized at once they were safer on the beach. They climbed out of the water; both of them were in a mini state of shock as they climbed out and headed back to the beach. When

[handwritten margin note: Is this place a dream or possibly a beautiful purgatory?]

they got there they discovered they were surrounded by palm trees.

"We'll try to build a shelter for the night. We will wait for the rescue here, what do you think about it?"

"I don't know why should we need a rescue? We must be dreaming," she said, looking thoughtful. "Let's stay the night on this beach and tomorrow we'll try and figure it all out." Sarah told him.

"Ok," he started collecting the palm fronds to use for a shelter. Sarah pitched in to help him and they worked as the sun softly dipped down into the ocean casting a soft orange glow across the ripples of the gently waves. They worked for several hours with James lost in deep thought throughout. He decided that he'd get up early in the morning and work on figuring out what they should do next.

The shelter was small but it was sufficient for their needs. When James woke in the morning he found that the wind had destroyed much of it during the night. The bright sun was pounding in and the reflection of the turquoise ocean in his eyes was so radiant that it was almost surreal.

"Look, Sarah …" James turned to the side and realized that his wife was no longer there. "Sarah! Sarah, where are you?"

He jumped up and looked all around him. Then he ran his fingers through his hair and caught his head with both hands. Sarah's gone!

He called out to her again with tears filling his eyes, "Sarah, Sarah! For God's sake, where are you?"

He looked like a desperate man, searching the ground next to him and all around the shelter. There was no sign of her…not a trace of anything. Sarah had simply vanished. Panicking, James began picking up every leaf, every stone and every shell that he came across, looking for a clue. The entire time, he called out her name.

He was so intent on his task that he wasn't paying attention to what was in front of him. When he did look up, he was stunned by what he saw. Several feet from the entrance to the jungle was a huge stone that seemed to have a human profile. James got closer to it and realized suddenly that it was a Moai, a statue from Rapa Nui, the Easter Island.

"What the fuck? What is this doing here?"

He inched up even closer to get a better look, putting his right hand on the statue. When he touched it, it began to glow with a bluish light across its surface.

James was shocked and intrigued at the same time. "Where does the light come from?" he wondered aloud. "How the hell did I get to this place?" None of what had happened to him since he woke up on the beach seemed at all possible. It was all so confusing.

He suddenly remembered Sarah. He had to find her! He shook off the magical feeling looking at the statue had given him and anger replaced it. He started looking for his wife again, cursing loudly as he did. He almost forgot about Sarah.

But he had to find her. He gets angry, he used some coarse language.

Huge palm trees blocked his path as he tried to move forward. The dense vegetation made his progress slow, almost impossible. James began going through his pockets trying to find something he could use to clear the way. His wallet and credit cards were there and his ID and some receipts. In his back pocket, he found a packet of cigarettes and his zippo lighter.

Frustrated, he sat down and lit a cigarette. "Fucking forest..."

He smoked for a bit and then stubbed his cigarette out in the sand and got back up. He was thinking again, trying to decide the best way to make a torch and a knife before night fall. He already had what was most difficult to obtain: the fire itself. All he needed to do was find a robust branch and some sap for the torch.

Getting a knife was going to be much more difficult. James looked ahead into the dense forest in front of him. He had no idea what it might hold. Were there any dangerous animals? He needed something to defend himself, just in case. He started back into the forest, stepping around a large pile of wood on his way. He began calling out Sarah's name again. *Where was she? Did she go into the forest? Did something take her?*

James continued to yell out her name with tears streaming down his face. His voice was almost gone as he cried out,

"I lost her, I lost her." Over and over. He had no idea where he was, or how he got there. He felt almost amnesiac, but yet he sensed that his wife was still here somewhere, close by. None of it made any sense.

Suddenly, out of thin air, a strange silhouette appeared in front of him. It stared at him and began vibrating like glass during an earthquake. It began to zigzag, slowly at first and then faster and faster. James was frozen to his spot, watching it in disbelief. What the hell was it?

Suddenly it was coming closer and James yelled out at it, "Don't move! Stop! Shit!" The air temperature dropped suddenly. It was freezing and James stood paralyzed as the thing came closer and closer. He finally found his voice and began to scream.

"What the fuck do you want? Leave me alone!"

He closed his eyes with such force that the time seemed to stop for a second. When he opened them again there was a stained glass window right there in front of him. James could distinguish a dog silhouette and a long hospital corridor behind it, the scene was bathed in a greenish light that glowed in the darkness of the forest.

"What a nightmare!" he screamed, "And you? You!"

Suddenly he could see the head of his son Thomas, fixed at the top of the silhouette.

"Stop! Leave my son alone!" he screamed at it.

He was angrier than scared now, how dare it use Thomas? He began chasing it and it moved forward in a dislocated manner, trying to escape. James followed it to the entrance of a staircase that led down. The silhouette plunged into the staircase and James followed it running ten floors down, deep into the earth until at last the ground gave way underneath his feet and he fell into the void. He crashed down violently onto the ground. The place he fell into was so dark, that all he could see was blackness. He held up his hands and couldn't even see those in front of his face. As he tried to move, he felt his back twitch and spasm. Grimacing in pain he groaned out,

"Ahh! My back! I will catch you. I... I.." Suddenly remembering that he had light he reached into his pocket and took the lighter out. Lighting it up he could see everything. He was still in the middle of a jungle but the silhouette had disappeared. James wondered if it was because of the fire. He couldn't see anything around him except for the trees and vegetation but he somehow knew that he wasn't alone in this lost paradise. Trying to think quickly, he gathered up enough palm fronds to make a small shoulder bag. Then he filled it with a stock of branches. At least he would be able to make a fire if he needed to.

He knew it wasn't enough. He needed to find a weapon and he needed to get back to higher ground. If he was up high, he could at least look down and get a better gauge on his environment while he looked for Sarah. His chances would be better...

CHAPTER NINETEEN
"THE TASK"

As they stood there looking around they were suddenly approached by a soft white silhouette. Neither of them was afraid. Somehow Yann knew that the silhouette belonged to the voice and that it was here to guide them.

"You'll be far from idle," she told them, "On your journey you're going to discover two special stones. These are irradiated stones and they'll be easy to recognize because of the light they filter. One stone will be found in the south and the other in the north of this land. In order to find them, you'll have to cross an enormous field that each is surrounded by."

"What do we do when we find them?" Yann asked.

"You'll take them and place them at the top of the two towers. Once that is done, your mission will be complete. You will find your parents and the mysterious being that haunts the beauty of our place here will be liberated at last."

The silhouette vanished as quickly as she had appeared. At least the two friends knew what they had to do now. Their first decision would be which way to go first. After careful consideration, they decided the path to the south seemed easier to access, so they went that way.

■■

The forest was thick in front of them and as they entered it, they went in knowing that the horrible thing they called the Monster was roaming within. It wasn't long before they could hear it moaning and they knew they had to be as quiet and discreet as possible.

Yann told Ani telepathically that it would be like playing hide and seek. He and Ani were both good at that game. He found a tree that he could climb, trying to see where the monster was so that they didn't walk right into it. Ani did his part by sniffing the ground and using his excellent sense of hearing.

They walked like that, stopping to check again occasionally until they came to a river. Yann picked Ani up and carried him across. On the other side there was a small hill and Ani wiggled into a hole in the ground. Yann was impressed when he saw that his friend had gone to the end of the hill to push up a branch that would make it easier for Yann to climb. They were working together as a team while still maintaining their cover from the monster.

After crossing the hill, Yann stepped on something and looking down he realized it was a piece of white paper. He bent to pick it up and saw that something was written on it. It was haiku, a short, traditional form of Japanese poetry. It consisted of three phrases of five, seven and five syllables respectively.

Yann recognized that the language was Japanese, the same as in the stories he read in his comics. He couldn't understand the words, but he was hoping that he might be able to use the comic books he carried in his backpack to translate them later on.

"Someone else has been here, Ani." Yann told his friend, excitedly, "I found a writing that someone left behind."

They continued their journey through the deep forest, going back and forth between terror when the monster was nearby and they had to hide, to amazement at the awe inspiring sights they saw along the way. After hours of travel they at last came to the end of the forest. As the vegetation opened up they could see a cliff to their left. There was an entrance in the middle of it with torchlight dancing and sending up crackling sparks along each side. The sight was made much more fantastic by the fact that the fire seemed to be fed by some kind of resin that continuously ran over the side of the cliff.

Yann cautiously approached the dark entrance. He was getting the impression that someone lived there. Taking down one of the burning torches, he and Ani went inside. Yann was afraid, mostly because even with the torch it was so dark. He trusted in Ani's flair and sense of vision. The dog went ahead to check the path before Yann crossed it. There was water everywhere around them and stalactites hanging from the ceiling.

Strangely, there were wooden signs that told them where to go. Even odder, the directions were written in a Sumerian language, but Yann and Ani understood them nonetheless. They came to a place where they had to climb and jump from one side of the path to the other. At a glance, their surroundings seemed almost impossible, but the path continued to emerge as they advanced.

The oxygen was thin and because of Ani's medical problems, Yann noticed he was having difficulty getting a good breath. Yann picked him up in his arms and carried him over to the side of the path to get some water. They started on their path once again and in the darkness, Yann began to slide. As he was sliding it was as if time was passing, but in slow motion. He slid until he fell flat to the ground. He had his eyes closed and when he stopped moving them, he opened them up and saw that the place they'd been in and this one were not the same.

****

If Yann had been asleep he would have recognized what happened next as simply a nightmare, but how could he call it a nightmare when he continued to stay awake? He and Ani had gone from sliding along a muddy path one minute to sitting in the four wheel drive of Yann's parents the next. Yann was in the driver's seat with his hands on the steering wheel. He turned his head to the right and he saw Ani, sitting in the passenger seat.

As the vehicle passed the security rail of the bridge, the glass and plastic exploded into the air and the wheels took flight. A thousand feet or more underneath the car, the water stagnated and the fall of the vehicle carried Yann and Ani away. Yann watched through the shattered window of the car, powerless to do anything but be an unwilling participant in the scene. The water was dark like an inky pool and Yann tried to scream as a huge shark jumped up out of the water with its mouth wide open. He was so paralyzed with fear that no sound came out. It was all happening in slow motion and as time dragged on Yann's terrified heart threatened to beat out of the inside of his chest….Just as the entire scene disappeared and Yann and Ani were once again back in the cave.

"I have a headache, are you all right, Ani?" Yann asked, still shaking from the trauma of what they'd just gone through.

Ani barked and Yann went on to say, "Ok… that was terrifying, and so strange. It felt like I've already saw that scene... I don't know if that was real but I heard Mummy shouting..."

Ani barked again and Yann told him, bluntly, "I am sure..."

SEASONS OF HEAVEN

Yann got up and looked around. There were more signs along the wall with the same writing as were on the small piece of paper that he had found. There were two of them, attached to the strings of the samurai armor. Scattered pieces of paper were all over the ground beneath the signs.

"Look Ani, more pieces of paper. Let's pick them up and I will put them in my backpack." He picked one up and told Ani, excitedly, "Look at this one, it is really nice...It looks like...Let me see...Like a dragon."

He observed each piece as he picked it up, wondering what a samurai could have been doing in this cave. Is it possible that somebody else could have been there before them? There must have undoubtedly been others, Yann thought.

A sudden scream rattled the cave and sent a chill running through Yann's body. The mysterious thing must have found them. The air in the cave became suddenly colder and the atmosphere darker. It was as if the monster was able to announce its presence even without sight or sound. Yann's spine tingled...

Yann realized that they needed to hurry if they were going to find the stones before the creature found them.

"Let's go, Ani!" They ventured further into the dark, moist environment of the cave until they were completely engulfed in a chilling blackness. The only light was the orange and blue flicker that danced off the torch that Yann carried, casting shadows across the ovoid shaped walls that smoothly curved to the floor. Yann used the smooth wet walls to hold onto and Ani stepped lightly as the loose stones shifted and slipped underneath their feet with every step. The noise the rocks made underfoot echoed off of the dense stone walls and beyond that they could hear the sounds of water dripping into water. When Yann held the torch up high he could vaguely see the giant stalactites and bat roosts that loomed overhead. The walls became more covered with the strange writings, as the sounds of the water loomed closer. The journey through the cave was long and unsettling but the two adventurers pushed forward until at last coming to a body of swiftly running water. The water in the stream started with a crash and a foamy white rush where a curtain of white water washed over the rocks and dropped down into the wildly churning pool at the base of the cave. Yann stopped and surveyed the environment trying to decide what to do. The water seemed to be the only viable exit from the cave. Yann could see a small wooden boat tied up near the slick, rocky embankment. After some consideration he decided that it was their only choice. "Come Ani," Yann told him. They stopped in front of the boat and looked around in awe of the way the cave shimmered with blue light that seemed to be suspended from the ceiling.

"The stone has to be here," Yann said. The walls were covered with drawings of mechanisms and Yann decided that it had to be some kind of ancient workshop. Yann saw a large rock just behind them with a large puncture that opened it up so that metal or something like it could be seen from the inside.

The atmosphere suddenly got thicker and Yann knew before he saw it that the monster was close. With fear ripping through them, he and Ani got into the little boat.

"Hurry Ani! He's right behind me." They jumped into the boat but the monster wasn't deterred by the water as half of it was immersed and the other half of it remained stuck to the walls. They were both shaking from the terror, but a beam of sunlight ahead beckons them like a savior. The long, slimy looking tentacles of the terrible thing were swinging around them, grasping at the air as it tried to capture them. It was almost like the arms were so far from its brain that it had a hard time controlling them. The monster was so huge, black and shapeless that if it weren't for its terrible, glowing eyes it would have blended in with the walls of the cave. It had to be thirty feet high or more, but as large as it was, it moved quickly. Yann found himself suddenly looking into the strange orange eyes and for a second he thought he might have glimpsed something inherently human deep inside of them.

While Yann was mesmerized by the eyes, one of the long tentacles struck the boat and it was shattered to pieces. Yann was ejected and his small body was thrown against the wall of the cave and knocked into unconsciousness. As Ani plunged into the water, desperate to save his friend, Yann was scooped up by the monster and carried away. Ani swam towards the bank in a desperate hurry. He had to find his friend….

CHAPTER TWENTY
"ALIENS"?

Reynald was an exceptional man, with extraterrestrial origins. He was a member of the Ancient People, originating from Mars. Four billion years ago they used to be a very advanced people, more advanced than the human civilization. Not much evidence still exists of their inhabitation of earth.

They had to leave Mars because of the global warming and because of the excessive consumption of combustibles. As they faced environmental degradation, the leaders decided there was no other chance of their survival but to leave the planet. The entire population of the planet couldn't be evacuated however so the people who were chosen to go were children, pregnant women, doctors, intellectuals, architects and politicians. The other members of the community stayed on the planet and ultimately perished, suffering through volcanic explosions and glaciation.

The final explosion of the planet propelled billions of bacteria and germs into space. Some of these germs arrived to the Earth. At that time it was the only planet that was capable of developing organic forms of life. The local bacteria mixed with the extraterrestrial ones, resulting in an extraordinary richness of the ecosystem. Some mutations very likely caused the appearance of the Cro-Magnon man.

Those who fled the planet made their journey into the nearest solar system. They had enough supplies for a very long journey but they had to find a new planet before the provisions ran out. The leaders decided to stop on the blue planet "Earth". They explored the planet and decided that they would be able to survive there and for thousands of years they made it their home. They lived simply for all of that time, rejecting all ideas of progress and technology, communing in harmony with nature and using the resources of the planet in a way that protected themselves against the animals and the difficult climate.

Very quickly, the extraterrestrials met the humans and mixed couples began to appear. The mutations of the terrestrial endemic genes met and mingled with the genes of the Ancients. By 10,000 B.C. the humans were being helped to create the Sphinx and the Great Pyramid of Giza by the extraterrestrials. They also helped them design the empire of the Mayas and the stone spheres of Costa Rica. They were all unique monuments, meant to exist for spiritual reasons and as a gigantic calendar. The Elders served to help the humans become an autonomous civilization.

As time went on, there was some dissention amongst the terrestrial peoples. Some of them wanted to stay on Earth and continue to help humans so that they wouldn't make the same mistakes that had driven them from their own planet. Others of them wanted to quit the planet Earth and begin a new civilization somewhere else. The discourse caused a split amongst them that lasted for centuries and only worsened as the ones who advocated for leaving also tried to prohibit mixed unions, citing the disappearance of their own pure civilization.

In 5000 B.C. the birth of one man would change everything. This man was born from the last union of mixed parents. His father was an Ancient and his mother a terrestrial. They named him Reynald.

During the first years of Reynald's existence the conditions of life on the planet were harsh. A great deluge flooded a major part of the Earth, and, among other great things it destroyed the library of Alexandria. Numerous relics and documents concerning the past of the Ancient People were lost. The flood also wiped out a huge part of the civilization. Only about thirty of the terrestrials survived. A committee was created by these survivors to ensure the continuity of helping the humans. Reynald was appointed the ambassador. He lived discreetly amongst the humans, without revealing his real nature. He was present at every important human event such as the First Council of Nicaea, the construction of the pyramids, the birth of Christ and the creation of the New Testament...He was able to do this because of the particularity of children born from the mixed union that allowed them to get old very slowly and therefore their life was almost endless.

In 860 Reynald was contacted by archbishop Agobard of Lyon. He wanted to talk to Reynald about strange appearances. He had met some small grey people and Reynald thought that they could be the extraterrestrials. He used to hear these kinds of stories from his ancestors. Then, in the 12th century, Rapa Nui became a secret place of the Ancient People. They used the place to protect their memories and their own heritage. On the island they deposited their ancient vessel and this is how the story of Heaven began. Reynald wanted Heaven to be energetically self-sufficient; he needed only the energy to put it into orbit. He wanted to create for humans a possibility to live the last moments with their beloved ones, who had died somewhat too quickly. Amongst the Ancients some people were against this project and they did all in their power to delay its achievement. In 1614 Reynald assisted the marriage of Pocahontas. This event was what confirmed his desire to build Heaven. He was also impressed by the culture of the North American Indians and he recognized some similarity with himself. His last intervention in the human culture concerned the Indian Removal Act in 1830. Reynald felt profoundly shocked by its violence and hatred. He had held onto the stones that he and Olham had so painstakingly recovered ten centuries before waiting for the time to be right. Reynald had so many reasons for wanting to create a place where kind and decent people can live in harmony forever with those that they loved, but that single event solidified his plans, absolving him of any doubt he may have carried since that long ago meeting in Gaul. He was at last able to launch Heaven in 1840 and during the first forty years everything went smoothly.

Some sort of plasmatic energy covered it, so it remained invisible to the human eye. It was placed just beneath the ozone layer. It is comprised of 65% land, 30% water and 5% of the remains of its constructors. It had numerous beaches, three types of forests, mountain ranges and dark jungles, and numerous rivers that took their source at the lagoon at the Peak of Views. There was a city of a few hundred inhabitants. It was a magical place. The stars seemed to be bigger than seen from the Earth and the light was brighter. During the rain the water filtered into the Heaven. It is stored in an enormous basin, and is used for the city and for the vegetation. However, if it becomes too plentiful it has to be emptied. A special system was put into place for that. In the north-west portion of Heaven, a big white room with a small metallic cord exists. The cord can be pulled to release some of the water. The constructors used it only when Heaven was positioned above the oceans.

There was also an exit door built in. It was named "Infinite Field". Those were vast golden fields with a door frame in the center that could be activated by the system of keys/towers. The constructors made this system that was quite simple in theory. One had to put two irradiated stones on two towers. Then the towers would enter the ground and the energy created by this movement made a little hole in the infinite field, in the middle of the door frame. Only at this moment would it be possible to see the beloved persons, waiting at the other side for the great journey through the four seasons. The chosen ones would travel through winter, spring, summer and fall and as they did, the awareness... that they existed with on Earth slowly evolved into something more brilliant....an incredible level of consciousness that would allow them to exist beyond the expiration of the body they had inhabited on Earth. When not used, the towers sunk into the ground and to activate them one had to go down to the caves and move two irradiated stones first. This elaborate system was a safety measure so that the passage may be used only for the chosen ones.

    The Ancient People voted each time and that was how a human being was judged worthy of accessing Heaven to share his or her last moments of happiness with their loved ones. However, the happiness of thousands of human beings caused a great sense of envy amongst some of the Ancient People. Some of them began living cloistered in theirs homes and others who were more adamant about stopping it, became banished from the group. That was how the fantastical evil was born, the Banished. They used to live in the purple forest as normal beings, and slowly their hatred and seclusion transformed them into something dark and evil.

There exist remains of their homes in the purple forest.

****

Heaven
Reynald's office.

The office the man sat in was spacious and the grand oak desk he sat behind was centered in the room where it was bathed in the golden luminous sunlight. His longish gray hair was swept back from his face and secured at the nape of his neck. His short gray beard lay neatly trimmed against his focused face and the blue of his striped shirt matched his pale blue eyes. He was extremely focused on his work, a number of drawings of two keys...they both looked like stones.

Next to those drawings was a one of two towers. There was no sound in the big room other than that of the lead of his pencil scratching against the paper. He reached into the cabinet on his right hand side and grabbed a binder. It was very old and the pages inside were worn to the point of looking like a parchment. He sat it on his desk and quickly flipped through the pages, looking intently for something. He looked through pages of plans, a drawing of a big, white room with a ceramic tiled finish, a basin and a vessel. He closed the binder and got up from his desk then. With his hands on his hips, he went over to the window and thoughtfully looked out into the void. A door opened behind him and a man stuck his head through,

"Excuse me, sir? I am sorry to bother you, but we have found him."

"What are you talking about?" Reynald asked, turning towards the man.

"He appeared just like that, but we did not chose him, did we?" the man was agitated and Reynald said,

"What are you talking about? Please, stay calm!"

"He looks like a samurai, but he's not dead...I do not understand; it is not possible. This is the first time anything like this has happened."

It finally dawned on Reynald what the man was saying. Someone had gotten in...But that was impossible! "Do others know already?"

"Yes...We saw his horse in the fields, I am so sorry...They want to leave, they are scared, they say that anybody can come in here now... and Banished were right"

"It's not possible...I am the only one who knows the way. Please calm down, call all political parties, I am coming."

CHAPTER TWENTY-ONE
"SAMURAIS" Back to Japan?
HEAVEN NIGHT

Roshi Tonobu, still alive came into the Heaven and woke up. He looked up at the night sky, which was a dark, navy blue. The stars shone brightly across the plain. He got up gently, his muscles sore and aching still from what he'd just been through. He looked down where his wound was and realized with surprise that it had almost completely disappeared. He could still feel a strong pain in that spot. He tried to shrug off his armor so he could move freely. One of his arms and his legs were completely numb. He took a few steps forward and then stopped. He could hear a strange sound to his left. Turning his head towards it, he thought he heard something that sounded like human voices. He kept quiet, not wanting to be discovered just yet. He wanted to discover where he was and what was happening first. He didn't know if he was in a safe place...

Tucked down behind the shrubs he could hear the words of the conversation, but he didn't understand them...the language was different than his own.

He snuck under the shrubs, holding on tightly to his katana and his nagigata. He was staying vigilant, moving quietly on his knees. He was trying to move away from the voices. He's so tired; he needs to find a place to rest. He finally got up onto his feet and walked slowly and as quietly as he could. The leaves and small branches creaked underneath his weight so he progressed slowly. The light in the forest was dim and he didn't hear any sounds other than the gentle swish of the wind through the trees.

Above him in the sky he could see a strong light. It was shaped like a sphere and was flying away from him. *What is it?* He wondered. He looked away from it and realized that he was facing a field where a tree so large was standing that it actually looked as if it were touching the sky.

Tonobu made his way over to the tree and sat down underneath it. From his sleeves he took out several small pieces of paper. He suddenly had a strange feeling and he wanted to write down his last thoughts...just in case. He wanted to leave a trace of his passage through this place. Behind his belt he always carried a small inkwell and a brush; he took them out and began writing. His hand was shook as he wrote his last words for his wife, the woman whose life he saved, the woman he had married in spite of the refusal of the divinities.

As Tonobu wrote, he could feel himself becoming weaker by the second. He continued to write in spite of it, attaching all of his words to branches of the tree. His hope was that someone someday would read his story and he couldn't help but wonder if this was his payback for refusing to comply with the divinities. He had no idea where he was….certainly far away from his own home and country. This place looked like a lost paradise, and he didn't even know how he had found it.

JAPAN

Roshi was dreaming as the wind blew soft whispers through the branches of the trees. The birds sang in harmony and although the light tried hard to penetrate his closed eyelids it was hard to open them because of the heat that came from the sun. He finally opened them and got up to look out on the luxurious landscape of his beautiful country. The mountains and trees dotted the landscape as far as his eyes could see. Numerous cherry trees in full bloom were scattered along the slope of a rolling hill near Roshi and his horse grazed happily nearby.

The beauty of the land was in jeopardy...it was a country at war. Strangers had already begun arriving by boats and the constant tension between them and the Samurai's reigned. Each samurai had to pay particular attention to his honor. Once his honor was lost, he was obliged to kill himself, to commit hara-kiri. If he did not he would become "Ronin," roaming without a master and without a goal. That was to be Roshi's fate, he believed.

    He sat now in front of the mountain thinking about his deeds. He'd chosen to withdraw himself from society and to end his days. He was looking for the peace and the serenity he craved in the middle of this plentiful nature. The sky was azure blue without a cloud in sight.

    "What a beautiful day to kill oneself," he thought out loud. He mounted his faithful steed then and headed in the direction of the valley. Not far away was an old temple. Long ago abandoned. It was hardly more now than a heap of rubble but because of stories his ancestors had told over and again about it, Roshi was attracted to it like steel to a magnet.

SEASONS OF HEAVEN

The story was that hundreds of years ago, a strangely shaped meteorite crashed in the woods nearby. The shockwaves destroyed many square miles of the forest. His ancestors used to say that it was an offering made to the mother earth. A sphere of light disappeared and left behind the strange construction. No hint of an explanation as to what it really was. Roshi had to believe in this magic to be able to leave this world peacefully and to join his beloved ones beyond the grave.

Numerous conflicts ravaging his country caused death of many members of his family. That was really true for many samurais. He planned to join them all—to save his honor.

Roshi took a deep breath, feeling tight in his armor. Putting his knees to the ground one by one, he took his katana out of the sheath. With his right hand he cleaned its blade, using some water and a piece of cloth. He owed a lot to the katana's sleek blade; it had saved his life on more than one occasion. He found it almost ironic that today, the very blade that saved him so many times would be the one to take his life away. He put his gourd down next to him and with both hands touched the point of the blade to his stomach. He took another deep breath and then heard himself scream with shock as the blade cut through his armor and the soft flesh of his stomach underneath.

Roshi felt himself going into a trance. He used what little energy he had left to turn the blade to his right and continue the cut to that side of his body. Suddenly the light around him brightened and he saw a big tree in front of him. Death was taking him away.

■■

Roshi was surprised when his breath suddenly returned. He wasn't dead but the blade was still inside of his body. He was in a different place though, the forest was denser and the colors strange....He removed the katana in one swift motion. He no longer felt any pain, but he knew that he was dying.

Am I in paradise? Am I really dead? He left his weapon behind and went closer to the building in front of him. It was like a great temple made out of stone, with towers all around it. It was amazing and it made him felt better. Suddenly he knew that everything was going to be all right. He closed his eyes.

He was dreaming about his death, because he no longer felt that he had the right to live it in this life ...

Heaven

Tonobu woke up, he had been dreaming. The sun was shining brightly; he could feel the heat of it against his closed eyelids. The temperatures here were hotter than in his own country. He ran his hand over his face to wake himself up. He felt thirsty. He needed to find fresh water. Leaving behind all the haikus attached to the majestic tree he walked softly through the fields, crossing different paths and going into the forest. He sees that the vegetation in the forest is greener and he thinks that should help him find water.

He felt lost and disoriented in this strange place. He felt like he was dying and he wanted to find a better place to die. Exhaustion was weighing on every part of his body, even his mind. He removed part of his armor, hoping to be more comfortable. At last he located a clear little stream and dropped to his knees next to it. Taking the water in his hands, he gave himself small sips. His body felt numb and he knew that death was close at hand.

After drinking the water, he continued along the path through the forest. At the end of the path he found an entrance to a cave with burning torches on either side of it. He entered, walking along with the walls as support. He felt so tired, his gait was much slower now and his breathing was progressively slowing down.

SEASONS OF HEAVEN

He looked down at place where he would normally carry his scabbard and in it his precious katana. He'd left it all behind, and he felt naked...empty without it. When he carried the sword he felt powerful, connected to his ancestors and his own inner strength. His katana was no ordinary sword. His was a one that held powerful secrets. Tonobu carried it because his father gave it to him, but unbeknownst to him, the sword was what had brought about the war he'd been fighting. Roshi had mistakenly believed the men he was fighting were trying to kill him because of his relationship with his wife...a woman from the rival clan, off-limits. But the truth he didn't know was that the sword his father had given him had been stolen...from a master. Legend had it that the sword was forged by the hand of the Goddess Amaterasu. Amaterasu was the Japanese Shinto sun goddess. She was so bright and radiant that her parents had sent her up the Celestial ladder where she ruled the heavens. The main sanctuary of

SEASONS OF HEAVEN

Amaterasu is Ise-Jingue situated on Ise, on the island of Honshu. This temple is pulled down every twenty years and then rebuild in its original form. The legend told that the ancestors of the local master had found the sword Amaterasu had left there for them the first time the temple was rebuilt. He who carried the sword was said to carry great power along with it. Ironically, this was the weapon that Tonobu had used to take his own life.

  He found a spot to sit down against the wall. Taking out the paper and writing utensils once more, he began writing down his thoughts again. After he does that, he turns to the rock wall behind him and using his knife he carves the words, "The entrance to another life," in Japanese. Tonobu closed his eyes and the liquid flowed from them like tears as his heart ceased beating. He died in the cave in the center of Heaven. No one ever died there; it's a place that only those who are already dead can enter. How did he get there, and why? What would be the consequences of that?

Tonobu was about to reincarnate...

New York City
Police Department

Eddie Nomura was a brave, intelligent man. His origins were both Japanese and American. His parents left Japan after two atomic bombs were dropped on Hiroshima and Nagasaki. He was born in USA and decided at a very young age he wanted to be a policeman. He went to the academy right out of high school. Eddie was an athletic guy. He was also very religious. He's a Buddhist. He began working with Tim when the criminal office of New York opened a small profiling department. The two of them became a great team.

Eddie also became very good friends with Tim and his entire family. He loved to hang out with Tim and play baseball with him and his son.

SEASONS OF HEAVEN

When Eddie heard about Tim and his wife Elise's car accident he was devastated. If it hadn't been for the fact that he immersed himself in the investigation that he and Tim began together before his death, he wouldn't have been able to go on.

CHAPTER TWENTY-TWO
"THE VERY LAST SUMMER" *Summer is a season.*

Yann and Ani slipped easily through the door, leaving the winter season behind them. Here there was nothing but sunlight and the sights, sounds and smells of summer. It was strange, surreal even, to pass so simply from one season to the next through a door that sat in the thick of a forest. Yann and Ani were facing an extensive stretch of sand. They had entered into the season of summer. The ocean stretched out for miles on their left. The beauty of the landscape around them was once again surreal. The smell of iodine filled their noses as they looked around them. Everything was moving, the ocean rippled and crashed into the sand and the grains of sand moved with each contact of the water. The colors of the sky and the ocean and everything around them were astonishing.

A vast expanse of sand dunes lay out in front of them. Yann knew that they would have to climb and slide to cross this sea of sand, and he also knew they would slide faster if they could catch the wind blowing in the right direction. This adventure had given him an awesome feeling of freedom. Being reunited in this magical place had carved an expression of happiness into both of their faces. So far, they were enjoying their great adventure.

They began to slalom between the dunes at a great speed. Yann carried Ani in his arms, and the wings of his backpack were shining, leaving an almost imperceptible white trail in the air behind them. All at once in front of them a silhouette took shape. Yann could feel that the gentle voice that had been guiding him belonged to this silhouette.

"Follow me and do not get lost!" she told them. Her voice was firm, but at the same time it was gentle and non-threatening.

The two adventurers followed the silhouette at great speed. The beach was covered in massive rolling hills of sand and the occasional breeze stirred them up transferring the salty and rocky residue from one pile to the next. The rays of the glorious sun dazzled their eyes and t first they were having a great time, sliding on the border between the dunes and the ocean with the salty water spraying up in their faces. Yann felt free and exhilarated as he slid down with his arms held open wide, and Ani came sliding along behind him, racing along towards their next adventure.

This went on for some time as they crossed the great expanse and the silhouette became more difficult to follow. The dunes became taller and the angles sharper and the thick salty air began to consume their breathing until their chests began to hurt and the sand scoured the backs of their throats mercilessly. Their every step sank into the searing sand and their legs were heavy with exhaustion from scaling the heaped up irregularly shaped dunes. The slide down the other side became more perilous as the dunes grew steeper but as they got closer to the end, Yann knew they were on the verge of their next great adventure and in spite of the exhaustion he still that tingly feeling that spread from his head right down to his toes.

When at last they reached the end of the dunes at the bottom of the last one, they saw a beautiful lagoon that thousands of birds drank from. The sight of the birds was almost surreal. They were different colors and textures, sizes and shapes. Their long, delicate wings touched the blue surface of the water in places and the green dust that floated on the surface was illuminated by their color. Yann looked around at the line of trees in the distance, also varied in size, shape and color. It was a picture so beautiful that there were no simple words to describe it. The two friends were standing in front of a bamboo forest that was as beautiful as the rest of the landscape. Above and beyond it, Yann could see a curl of smoke. He inhaled the air and he could smell something burning. He and Ani began to walk towards where the smoke was coming from slowly. Strangely as they walked towards it, they both were filled with an incredible sense of well-being.

They were growing closer when they heard a voice coming out of the air. The voice spoke in a strange, foreign language that neither of them could understand. Yann had to push through the thick plants in order to make a path for him to move forward in places and suddenly they came upon the man...or was it a beast...that the voice was coming from. The man stood babbling until he noticed the boys. Yann was trying to process what he was seeing. The smoke wasn't helping matters; it was so thick in places that it almost made things beyond it invisible. The smoke began to form small clouds around them and for a second Yann thought he could see something familiar in one of the clouds. It was as if there was a vision being projected there and within it he saw a city. This was no ordinary city and the sight of it frightened him. It was completely devastated. The buildings were crumbling and rotted and people lay dead all over. Yann had to look away and instead he looked at his little friend. He communicated with him through his eyes,

"Can you see it, Ani? What is happening? Is it a nightmare?"

Yann could see that instead of worried, Ani seemed happy. He was confused, but at that moment he didn't insist upon understanding. He wasn't fully convinced he wanted to know.

The man suddenly began to babble again and then began moving like he was sleep walking or in a trance. He wore very thin, worn clothing and as Yann and Ani watched him he slowly began to dance. His movements were slow and easy at first but became faster and more urgent as he continued.

More horrible pictures began to appear in the smoke all around them. The pictures showed the end of humanity...destruction and chaos and the horrible slaughter of thousands of people and animals. Yann and Ani had no idea if it was real, or a vision from the future. They were frightened either way.

****

The man's movements began to slow down and he gradually stopped singing and dancing. He appeared to be "waking up" from the trance he was in and he looked at the two young friends and said,

"Don't be afraid, friends, nothing is permanent and sure."

" But what have we seen here? Could it be the end of everything?" Yann asked him.

" Nothing dies forever," the man told him. "We are all part of a huge circle. Don't forget that boy."

"Is that a premonition?" Yann asked him.

"I communicate with other dimensions and see things sometimes that haven't happened yet," he told him. "What is your name?" The man noticed the boy was hesitant so he said, "My name is Shacral, I'm a Shaman..."

" My name is Yann and my friend here he is..."

" His name is Ani. I've known him for a very long time. I can communicate with animals as well as other dimensions."

" Know him... Why are you here?" Yann asked him. "What are those visions?"

The man's clear blue eyes looked thoughtful as he said, "Don't worry, you are almost there. To be honest I'm not really here. You can see me but I'm... Somewhere else. I'm trying to find a way for humanity to survive. Dangerous times are coming."

"I want to help; we want to help!" Yann told him.

"I know you do, but you have done your part. Maybe Ani will still have some to do. The future will tell."

"So I'm useless?" Yann asked, sadly.

"No little one, don't say that. I will tell you a little secret, I think I have found a way to save humankind from their fate...They told me."

"Who told you what? What is it?"

" They told me...We need to get back to our place in the chain..."

"I don't understand...What does chain mean?"

" Every species on our planet has a specific role... Humans are the only ones who don't respect that...We have broken the system in some way."

" We don't eat things that we are supposed to eat?"

Thoughtfully again the man said, "Smart little, only from kids. Probably...I think you know enough; my role is to spread the word now before it is too late...I will have to leave now and get to my work."

" Where are you going? Where are we?" Yann was desperate for some answers.

"I can't answer your question; you have to discover it by yourself. We will meet again, don't worry. Life is magic and full of surprises. When you think it is going to end, it is just the beginning."

The man slowly faded out of sight until he was gone like a puff of smoke as the boys stood watching in disbelief.

****

James sat leaning against a tree, still recovering from the trauma of his horrific vision. *What was that thing and what did it want from him?*

The jungle surrounding him was an assault on all of his senses. The vibrant hues were in the foreground, the background and as high up as James could see. The heat and humidity pressed in on his skin, and the sounds of the birds created a symphony of nature that seemed to be calling him in deeper. The leaves brushed up against him where he sat and the air tasted both sweet and fresh as if flowers bloomed across his tongue. Everything was a glorious, luxuriant green….

"Focus James! What is this place? Where is Sarah?" With a sharp intake of breath, he said, "Oh shit! Here it comes again…."

There were more of them now, numerous two-dimensional beings. Silhouettes without mass, vaporous, distorted bodies. They moved fluidly at first and then rapidly hopping to first one side of James and then the other. Some of them danced around him in wiggly motions. Some of them appeared male and some female and some of them appeared to be running and screaming. James had a feeling they needed help...yet they were immaterial.

He tried to ignore them and stick to his goal; climb the cliff in order to see where exactly he was. He grabbed a few vines in order to make some ropes. He had to be careful. The cliff in front of him was at least sixty feet high. James didn't understand all the feelings he was having, but he suddenly believed that something...or someone important had created the cliff. The surrounding area was flat.

James was in good shape and athletic, but he'd never climbed before. The climbing holds were tiny and his hands were big, making them difficult for him to hold onto. The vine was his security guard and he managed to pass it around a small tree that grew in the center of the cliff. It was his karabiner hook. He began moving...slowly but surely advancing up the cliff.

James arrived to the top after twenty minutes of difficult climbing. He was panting and tired, but satisfied by the accomplishment of a necessary task. It was a small victory, but his first one since awakening in this place. He stood up straight and looked out upon his surroundings.

"Holy shit ... what is that place?" He was looking out on a magnificent landscape with a brilliant horizon. Every color was so intense; it was more like a painting than real life. He could see mountains, covered in lush, green grass...volcanos jutting from the rocks, leafy jungles and dense forests.... But one thing was particularly strange...There was not a trace of another human being. Where was he? James's feelings of accomplishment were being rapidly replaced by those of doubt and fear. Why was no one there? If that was the case, where had Sarah gone? He thought about his earlier vision...everything was so strange...so unsettling.

The darkness was falling and once again the magnificent colors against the sky gave the impression that the Milky Way was so close. He felt almost as if he could reach out and touch a handful of stars.

Resigned to another night in this strange place, James found some small branches to make a fire. The night air was turning cold. He would try and rest first and when the sun came up again, he would head north. He needed to find water and make some sort of compass. He thought that with all the dense, green vegetation it shouldn't be too difficult to find water.

SEASONS OF HEAVEN

The fire warmed him and he lay down, protected by a big tree behind him. His eyes became too heavy to hold open and he fell into sleep.

James woke up after a short night.... Slowly getting his bearings back. His fire was small, but still cracking. If anyone could have seen him with his tousled hair and two days growth of beard they may have mistaken him for a caveman rather than one of the best surgeons in his field. Only two days had passed since he came to this place but the stress of it already showed on the lines in his face.

He stood up to stretch and noticed something strange...A fire! James could see the thick, black smoke pouring out from the trees and he followed it. The path was long, but he was determined. He went to the other side of the cliff and further into the jungle where the trees were sparser and the precipices more frequent. He had to climb over both rocks and trees. Using vines as cords he was able to climb the more difficult rocks and after hours of roaming he was at his most exhausted. Thankfully he was able to stumble on a small body of water. He leaned forward and plunged his face into the water to cool him down. When he finished cooling off and drinking he took a good look around. It was a big lake, an amazing turquoise color, like the sea in the Fiji Islands.

"James, you have to reactivate them..." It was a woman's voice, whispering on the wind.

"Who is it? What do you want? Show yourself!" James yelled back.

"What was am I supposed to activate?" He felt like he was at the beginning of a journey that might never end. He was in a place where suddenly chaos was the new order. He stood up and walked along the ragged bank of the lake in staggering exhaustion. The line between the jungle and the water was a tangled mass of gnarled and twisted roots that started at the surface and writhed their way down. Even with the adrenaline surge he'd gotten when he noticed the fire, his feet were slowing and he could feel the vomit rising in the back of his throat. He walked until he could walk no longer and then all at once, he plunged into the water, hoping for relief from the aches and the pressure of his tired muscles...He began to swim, but his limbs were so exhausted that it wasn't so much as swimming as it was drowning. Every few strokes he had to stop and tread water and sometimes his tired, heavy body would begin to sink. His head would fall underneath the cold, clear water and he'd begin to panic and claw his way back to the sun-sprinkled surface. His head was pounding and every cell in his body screamed for some kind of relief as he continued to swim forward in a slow crawl. Getting sucked under again and again was leaving his body deprived of precious oxygen and his thoughts were beginning to become more confused and disoriented. He began to wonder if he would make it...or if this beautiful river was going to turn into a watery grave just as the far side came into view. He told himself that he was almost there. He had to keep going...just a little while longer.

When he at last was in reach of the long, gnarled roots of the trees that grew down into the water from the river bank, he reached out and grabbed hold of one and pulled himself up the slippery slope. Once he was out of the water, he collapsed down along the bank and sucked in the mud and muck, still trying to fill his lungs with air. His head was so heavy that holding it up was a chore in itself and it was several long minutes before he had the energy to at last use his arms and push himself up to a sitting position. He slowly took off his shirt. The muscles in his arms neck and back were burning. When he had it off he hung it on a bush along with his shoulder bag and liana to dry them.

"Doctor! Doctor! You have to escape, hide yourself..." It was the voice again.

"Who are you?! Show your face! Why should I hide?" James looked around and seeing no one he sighed heavily in frustration.

He sat down in a comfortable spot alongside the lake. He had to rest. He let his mind relax for a couple of hours and then tried to reassess the situation...

"I woke up here with Sarah three days ago...It seemed like an island at first...But something is wrong here!"

James thought back further and the memories began to rush in... "I was on a plane. We crashed. Where are the others? Why I am alone? And what was Sarah doing here? I don't understand!"

James was used to asking questions and getting the answers. He was a science man after all... But here in this place, his beliefs were fading away one after another. He no longer knew what was real and what wasn't.

He could feel panic seeping in and knew that he couldn't allow it to take over. Instead, he got up and continued along his path. After he'd gone a short way, right in front of him a strange object appeared. It was like a tomb, with a white stone covering the entrance.

The atmosphere suddenly became as cold as ice. James found a tree branch, used his shirt to wrap it with a piece of cloth and soaked it in sap. He entered the place and inside there was already a lighted torch. James used it to light his own.

"This fucking torch ... I am stumbling..."

After he'd gone a few feet deeper into the darkness, the ground gave way under his feet and he began to slide downward very quickly. He was still holding the torch, fearing the intense darkness. His back was hitting the rocks, his body becoming bruised and bloody along the way. After about seventy feet, he finally stopped with a jolt on the muddy ground. It looked like a place that recently held water...but now there was only mud. James stood up; he was sore and once again becoming disheartened.

He moved forward once more and came upon a strange, empty room. It was all white and the light was so bright and intense that he couldn't keep his eyes open. He had to open and shut them and when he opened them he could see that his bag was damaged from the fall.

Lost and confused, James went closer to the center of the room. There was a cord hanging from the ceiling. It looked like a power switch used on lamps back in the 1960's. James hesitated briefly and then he pulled on the cord. The light went off again and the ground gave way underneath his feet.

This time, the ground was very smooth, like a toboggan. He slid down at a great speed, feeling like every second he was barely escaping death. His limbs felt like they were on fire and they were moving along on their own. His brain was disconnected from everything other than the sound of his hammering heart and the swish-swish of blood in his ears. Adrenaline raged in his blood stream and his stomach lurched but since he hadn't eaten for so long, there was nothing there to purge.

SEASONS OF HEAVEN

The slide stopped as he was thrust into a deep pit of swirling, cold water. His muscles clenched tight against the cold water as it began to penetrate his skin and chill his blood. It felt like frost was sinking into the marrow of his bones like wet concrete and he knew that he had to get out quickly or he would drown. The thing he was in was like a giant siphon and the sides were smooth with nothing to grab onto. His already exhausted body was begging him to just give in and go under but what was left of his survival instinct, urged him to go on. He had to push against the sides with the soles of his battered feet and it took multiple attempts for him to get in a position where he could reach the top and pull himself to safety.

While his muscles were still shaking, trying to work some heat back through his body he saw three things approaching him. They were a mass of tangled limbs that projected darkness and evil. They began running towards him and he tried to duck and avoid them. They were too quick, and one entity struck out and with one touch it paralyzed him. The torch he was still holding in his hand fell down and the sparks cascaded across the grass in front of him. The entities stood back, not yet ready to flee, but watching to see what would happen. The grass began to smolder and then the flames began to lick up into tall, glowing embers. Within minutes there was a fiery dance going on around him and the things that were chasing him had begun to flee.

He tried to duck and avoid them, but they were too quick. Once the fire was established, the entities vanished, leaving horrible screams suspended in the air.

"What the hell?" James was trying to put out the fire. While he was stomping and slapping at the flames he wondered what had frightened away the entities. Was it the fire itself, or the sage that it had been burning? James didn't have the time or the energy left to ponder it at the moment. He would use both if the things came at him again. He still had his lighter and he bent down and grasped as many blades of the plant as he could hold. He tucked it into his bag so that he had it with him next time...just in case.

James went outside, thinking that this strange place could possibly serve as a shelter. He was walking again, hoping finding somebody.

"James, reactivate them! We are here for you..." It was the female voice again.

"But who the hell are you? Show yourself! I am not afraid of you!"

James's body was wrecked. He collapsed...everything was wrong. His strength was diminishing...He hadn't eaten, he was dehydrated and he was hallucinating. This place was eating him alive. He was a physician and he knew what a critical situation he was in. The water he'd been drinking did not even cool him.

He had a sudden, eerie thought...*Am I already dead?* That would at least make the events since the plane crash make some kind of sense. If that was the case however, what was he supposed to do in this place?

He got up and pushed on, continuing to wander through the dense forest, He kept wandering listening to the voices telling him to recover two stones, one in a cave, the other one in an old village.

James followed the suggestions for the next hour and ended up coming to the front of an entrance to a cave. He took one of the two torches placed on both sides of the entrance and lit it up using the sap he carried with him.

He entered the cave and suddenly he was not alone anymore. Numerous smoky shadows are following him again and once again; he began to panic.

"Go away…"

"Come, come, and do not fight. It is useless, James…" the Banished one's chirped at him.

He ran and tried to hide, but there was nothing he could do to escape them. He had the impression that these hideously evil things were eating him slowly from the inside out. He slowed down, and began hallucinating again. The walls were pushing him from all sides and then they would go away. He tried to protect himself by burning the sage.

The plant worked, chasing the shadows away. James caught his breath and once he was calmed down, he began again looking for the stone. As he moved forward, he tripped over a piece of armor lying on the ground. It was red and black...it looked like the kind that might belong to a samurai. Lying next to it James saw a naginata and a broken sword. This sword was different than any James had ever seen. It was curved at the point where it had broken. The blade was two-handed and it had a single edge. The cross-sectional area of it was around, unlike the swords James had seen in museums that had once been used by European medieval knights.

He picked them all up and took them with him, thinking that they might come in handy. He had an idea and stopped to rub the blades with the sage. He hoped that perhaps it might help him to repel or even kill the evil, dark creatures. It was a slim hope, but at least it was something. James made his way along carefully, the light of his torch lighting up only a short way in front of him. It was like walking blindly and not knowing what you would step on or into. He reached out and touched the walls as he walked. In some places they were smooth from the constant drip of water running across them and wearing them down, and in other places the water had worn jagged paths. It was cold and dank and the only sound besides James's breathing was the sound of the endlessly dripping water. His sore and tired feet slipped in places and several times he almost fell before at last stumbling into a clump of stalactites and stalagmites that hung from a low point in the ceiling. He was thrust backwards and unable to stop his fall. He struck his back and shoulders on the unforgiving rocky floor. Thank goodness he was able to spare his head the blow.

He pulled himself back upright and the only thing that propelled him forward into the unknown void was the hopes of at last finding his salvation.

He finally arrived at the end of the cave. On his left side he could see another watercourse. In front of him, inside the wall something shone out. It looked like a big screw. Curious, he used his broken sabre like a chisel and a flat rock for a wedge; he used his own weight to cleave it from the rock. He was panting and sweating by the time he finally managed to get it loose, the cave wall seemed almost reluctant to let it go. Once he had it all the way out he could see that it was a stone and it was about a foot long.

CHAPTER TWENTY-THREE
"ONE"

James put the stone in his bag. It fits easily inside. He noticed there was some kind of metal in the wall where the stone had been fixed. James wondered if it was a magnet and the stone had been fixed against it.

Just as he began moving again, a deafening noise roared throughout the cave. James continued his path towards the exit, walking along some sort of ridge line. Below him he could see numerous rocks immersed halfway in murky, dark water. One slip and fall would very likely lead to his death.

As he walked along cautiously he was pelted with pieces of rocks as they fell off the walls. Everything was vibrating and it was sheer luck that he wasn't struck down by one of the larger boulders that had been shaken loose. James looked around in a fearful state of awe as he watched things crumble. Stalactites were even coming loose and crashing down violently into the water. Something powerful had been activated.

The voices were right. The stone he just took had an effect on the surroundings and James was about to see what kind of effect.

His cautious progress finally led him outside. Once he was there in the midst of the gorgeous landscape he saw what had caused the severe vibrations. In the center of the picturesque landscape now sat at huge tower that hadn't been there when he'd entered the cave. It was surreal and James's brain wasn't sure how to process it. As he stood there looking at it a woman's voice floated on the air, reaching his ears and warning him,

"The passage is about to open, James. There is one left, one more left …"

"I know … I think I understand!" he said.

He followed a path to a set of ancient stairs that lead downward. As he descended them he saw damaged walls, covered with stems of ivy that had grown so long they were heavy like tree trunks and its tendrils cascaded out in every direction and covered everything in its path. There were weeds that grew haphazardly between the cracks in the stairs and near the bottom were clusters of defiant daffodils that chose to rear their golden heads amidst the gloom. He stepped gently, using caution because some of the stairs were damaged from weather and age. As he got closer to the bottom, the air got colder and his surroundings got darker. He lit up the torch to cut the darkness and once it was lit he could make out some writings and some signs. He continued to advance slowly as the draughts made the torch move in all directions. The wind seemed to be turning around.

    James was so cold he was shaking. He felt like time was as frozen as he and the cave around him were. He entered a space that was filled with columns. Some of them looked brand new and some of them were gravely damaged and trees had grown through the middle of them.

SEASONS OF HEAVEN

James was trying to keep warm by closing his arms on himself; he barely managed to hold onto his torch as he did. Just as he wasn't sure he could take the cold much longer the atmosphere changed once again. He could hear a continuous breath that at first he'd thought was his own. When he stood still and listened though it was like the breathing was all around him, and in the distance he could hear a disturbing moan that to a physician's ears sounded like a death rattle.

James looked to his right and then his left, terrified of what it might be. He didn't want to advance any further. He decided that he would turn around and go back.

"James..." It was Sarah's voice, calling out to him. It gave him a sense of comfort to know that he wasn't alone. He could suddenly see a new light in front of him and suddenly the cold temperature isn't bothering him any longer. There was a young boy in front of him all of a sudden. He realized with a sense of amazement that he was standing face to face with Thomas, his lost son.

"Daddy, daddy, come, follow me, we are hundreds," Thomas told him in a hoarse voice.

James suddenly felt as if his lungs were empty...devoid of all air. They burnt as he tried to suck in a ragged breath. Was this really Thomas? Had he finally found his son? His heart jumped so hard against his chest he thought sure it was about to break his ribs and rip his skin apart. His mind was reeling with so many questions, but he didn't want to go there...if he went there he would have to face the void...the emptiness that was left in his soul when Thomas was ripped away from him. If he allowed himself to believe that this was in fact his son, he at least had hope. That was more than he'd had in a very long time. He realized he'd been standing frozen to his spot. Making a decision at last he began running in the direction of his son. Every four steps he jumped, dazzled by the light in his eyes. He was no longer in the city but things had once again changed. He felt exhausted and his beard had grown down almost to his chest. His shirt was torn open and his hair was dirty...this place was sucking the life from him.

He suddenly heard a metallic sound and turning abruptly, he saw a man holding Thomas' hand. The strange man was frightening, black and gloomy. He was wearing dark pants and a black hoodie. Thomas looked terrified and James felt as if he was paralyzed, unable to react...Then suddenly the strange man began to scream. The white of his teeth cut a sharp contrast to the darkness of his face as he did. After the scream he opened his mouth again, slowly...

"He belongs to us! "

Without any thought other than for his son, James jumped on him, hitting him with his broken sabre. The stroke was violent, but nothing happened. James continued to strike and beat at it with everything he had inside of him. Even after the thing had vanished while James had been looking it straight in the eyes, he continued to shout and scream and swipe at the air with the sword and his fists until finally overcome with exhaustion he sank defeated to the floor. On his knees the tears came and he was consumed by them. He turned his face up towards the burning sun and screamed again. He thought he had his son back. How cruel was a fate that would allow him a glimpse yet once again snatch him away. James covered his face with his hands and sobbed, great hiccupping sobs until his body no longer had the moisture to form tears and his throat was sandpaper raw.

Suddenly, the light was extinguished and he felt a soft hand on his shoulder.

"Find the other stone in the purple forest..." the woman's voice told him.

"But how? Where is this village the voice spoke about?

He found himself once again in the abandoned city. His surroundings looked again like a big, cold, dark room. He stood up and ran his hands through his hair and across his face.

SEASONS OF HEAVEN

Looking down, he saw the still burning torch lying on the ground so he picked it up and took it with him.

He walked over to a big wooden door and pushed on it. It opened on a large chamber with a labyrinth in the center of it. The chamber itself had stone walls with giant old columns that probably once stood regally but were now cracked and withered from age. Dust from the stone they'd been carved out of lay at the foot of each along with chunks of stone that had rotted off and smashed to the floor, scattering in every direction. The labyrinth sat on a stone platform in the center of the room and going closer he could see that it was actually a mockup of the city he was in right now. The labyrinth is old and damaged but he could still distinguish two big towers at each end of it. Small colored pins with tiny numbers were pressed all over it.

In the center of it was a main building and a small rectangular piece of glass, like a mirror. There was a note next to it, written on paper that was yellowed and withered from age or exposure. James had to lean in close to read it. Squinting he could at last make out the words, "Through the hole." James studied the rest of the labyrinth wondering what the words meant...what it all meant. At last, knowing he needed to push on, he left the labyrinth and continued on his way, searching for an exit. He saw a small door on his left. As he slowly opened it he could see the condensation vapors coming from his mouth. The air was frigid and the humidity suggested to him that a watercourse was not far away.

He continued into that room finding an office. It was decorated with Indian masks, statues and maps of the world. It reminded him of an adventurer. There was a strange language written all over it. It looked like hieroglyphs to James. It was actually Sumerian, an ancient Mesopotamian language, but James had no way of knowing that.

The office held shelves all across the walls and the shelves held hundreds of books about religion and politics. Curiosity pushed James to open one of them. There was a lot of information in the book, but none that he found useful. He was looking for information about the place he was in. He did find a drawing of two towers and the place where two keys could be found. There was also a drawing of a small wooden door frame annotated, "Infinity Field."

There were a lot of documents about the human civilization and on the wall an impressive fresco told the story of the last twenty centuries of human history. It was full of information such as the two political factions of the Ancients. James moved over to the table and there he found sheets of paper that looked like they'd come out of a diary.

He picked them up and started to read:

My name is Reynald and this is the story of my people's origins. We originated on Mars, and were forced off the planet to save ourselves as it was dying. Twenty thousand of us too refuge, coming to the earth in a huge vessel. Our planet,

SEASONS OF HEAVEN

Mars eventually exploded and when it did, germs were released into the atmosphere. They found their way to the Earth and life here was contaminated with it. Through this contamination, numerous mutations will come about through the ages. In particular, some of the monkeys will be endowed with consciousness.

James put that paper down and began reading the next one:

The Martian civilization developed itself independently of humans, but its members went on to help the human race to build some of their most important buildings. Meant to be used for spiritual purposes, the Sphinx, the great pyramid of Giza, the buildings of the empire of the Mayas, and stone spheres of Costa Rica were all built. The Ancient People eventually divided into two clans: those who wished to continue helping the humans, and those who wanted to leave the Earth and leave the humans on their own. But, in spite of their great lifespan, the Ancients become less and less numerous. They decided not to mix anymore with humans and to forbid the mixed unions.

James wasn't sure to think about what he was reading, but he put that one down and read on:

I, Reynald was born in 5000 B.C. I was born of a forbidden, mixed family. My father was an Ancient, my mother a terrestrial.

Not long after my birth, a great deluge killed many members of the Ancient community. I grew up amongst humans and I was present at every important human event.

In 1840, I was profoundly shocked by the Indian Removal Act and that was when I decided to launch Heaven into orbit and leave the Earth. I decided that living in Heaven and being witness to the happiness of the humans that are allowed to go there, would be a more pleasant life. It was good...for a while. Unfortunately, the happiness of the humans cause jealousy amongst some of the Ancients and that was when the civilization began to decay.

SEASONS OF HEAVEN

There was a group of Ancients who refused to live in harmony with the humans. These were banished from the clan and out of those banished a fantastical evil was born. A hybrid of humans, Ancient people, magic and pain. It's imperative that they do not leave Heaven.

Suddenly, James heard a noise behind him. It was a horrible noise, one that would send a shiver down the spine of the most hardened soul. James turned towards it, already shaking before he saw the revolting sight. Shock began to push its way in as he watched the creature with its dislocated joints crawling on four paws towards him. James couldn't imagine a worse sight until it slowly stood up and revealed that even it could be unsightlier. James still didn't have it all figured out, but most likely this "thing" was one of the Banished that Reynald talked about in his writings.

"Come James, come, you belong to us!"

"Do not come any closer unless you want to be more disfigured!"

SEASONS OF HEAVEN

"Why fight? You are ours, ours …"

A fight seemed necessary. James tried to repel the thing with a sage leaf. Luckily it revealed itself to be efficient. This entity did not appreciate the plant. James used his naginata to cut more twig and he set them to burn in a circle around him.

"There's nothing you can do! Leave me alone!"

The thing wouldn't cross the circle of burning sage but it paced around the office, becoming angry and impatient, turning things over in an attempt to get at James. While the thing agonized about how to get through the burning leaves, James took action and jumped over the table. He was able to escape the room, but the thing followed closely behind. Running as fast as he could, he passed through corridors becoming quickly lost. His heart was racing, pounding against the walls of his chest. Before long James looked back and realized that more of the horrible things had joined in the chase.

"My God, they are hundreds of them," he thought. "I have to get out of here!" He ran down the stairs and into another long corridor. The chase seemed to go on forever until at last he noticed a sliver of daylight down at the far end.

He found his way out onto a veranda that seemed to be carved into the rock. Through the opening, James could see the tower he activated and he noticed water dripping from the ceiling. Going closer to it he saw a rowing boat. It was old, but it didn't look to be too out of shape to float. He jumped inside of it and found that it was moored to a small piece of wood on the shore. James tried without success to release the cord. His hands were shaking too hard and he couldn't make them work. At last, he remembered the sword and taking it out, he cut the cord. The boat began moving away from the shore.

James was rowing as quickly as he could, watching the entities come to a full stop at the edge of the water, as if they couldn't touch it. They stood watching him and the evidence of their anger at him escaping hung heavily in the air. James continued to row and he rowed until the boat reached the current of the river and the boat was suddenly taken away. James had to row furiously now, trying to avoid the numerous, jagged rocks in the water. It was like a rafting trip across the rapids and James cursed and struggled, trying only to get out of this one alive.

From a distance he could see the waterfall that fed into the stream and it had looked like a silent white stream cascading over the rocky outcrops. As he drew closer in the little boat the noise from the falls increased and became a deafening roar. Drawing closer still, he was suddenly directly in the plume of water vapor and in seconds he was soaking wet. His hair clung to the sides of his neck and around his face. James rowed mightily to get through the swirling white caps and once he made it out the other side, the river just stopped and the water became calm. James looked around and he could see that behind him the river was still flowing with the same force as it was previously. Once again confused by the strangeness of this place, he found himself facing a big city. He could see ancient houses and dense vegetation covering the major part of the buildings. The river was obviously used by the inhabitants of the city. The boat floated over and gently touched the shore and as it did, James got out of the boat and rested on the shore for a few moments. His body was wrecked with exhaustion.

When he could at last, he got up and headed to the north of the lake. The voices that he'd been hearing told him that was where the village he was looking for should be. He heard a big noise above him and looked into the sky. There was an airplane and it was passing so close that James could read "Air dream Airlines" written on the side of it against a white background. He felt thrilled and started moving his arms and yelling,

He continued on his path and as James watched them go, he began to notice something strange. The airliner was huge and noisy so James was sure it was really there and he wasn't hallucinating; but as it flew over so low that James feared it would strike a tree, nothing moved. It was like somehow it was passing by without stirring any wind or affecting the environment in any way. It was something else for James to add to the things in this place that didn't make sense. His head was full of them and the stress of that along with everything that had happened in the days past had begun to show on his face. His beard became longer now by the hour and his long, greasy hair hung limply across his shoulders. He didn't know what would happen to him and the strain of it all and his recent suffering pushed him to wander the forest like a zombie...alone and confused...

CHAPTER TWENTY-FOUR
"MOTHMAN"
NEW YORK CITY-STRIP CLUB

As Shirley dressed, she looked around the club where she worked and the people that worked here with her. They had just finished their night and she was once again thinking about Yann. Her job was a stable and honest one…but she worried about what the authorities were going to think of her being a stripper and how that would affect her bid for Yann's custody. She had to prove to them that she was capable of taking care of a young boy and whether or not that was fair, her choice of job would weigh in heavily. That was why she worked so hard at her studies. She was only doing what she had to do in order to make ends meet for now. Her end goal was to have a career…one that both she and Yann would be proud of in the years to come. Nothing was more important to her now than getting to a point where she would be able to get custody of and care for Yann. Yann was in bad shape. Shirley worried about how much longer he could take being at the orphanage. He'd already managed an escape, and being taken back only served to make him withdraw further into himself. She couldn't help but wonder what kind of long-term effects this would all have on him. She was devoting every spare moment she had to the administrative issues related to gaining custody and Matt had been helping her as much as he could. Shirley was grateful that she at least had Ani. It gave her some comfort in the face of the tragedy that had happened to the family she loved so much. It was something that she knew would change her forever...

    She slipped on her black coat and turned up the faux fur collar. The temperatures outside were so cold lately that they'd even slowed down the usual rhythm of life in New York City. Typically, because of the somewhat shady neighborhood that she worked in she had security escort her to her car for safety reasons. Tonight, she was tired and just wanted to get home, so she headed out alone.

Shirley made her way across to the parking area. The night was dark but the parking lot was illuminated by billboards and streetlights. As she looked for her car, she noticed a familiar silhouette standing at the end of the long row of cars. It was the silhouette of thing that had been in her nightmare...the night at the Northman's house...the night they had died.

"Go away! What do you want? Why are you following me?" Shirley yelled at it. She hurried to her car, stopping and searching inside of her bag for her keys.

"Shit! Where are the fucking keys?" she said, beginning to feel panic rising in her chest.

There were suddenly three men standing next to her on the right. They looked rough with torn jeans and black leather jackets. Shirley could see the gleam of a knife in one of their hands.

"Come here, whore,"

Another man, a large fat one said,

"Don't be shy.... We won't hurt you!" he let out an ugly laugh and then said, "Come on, come closer."

"Surround her!" the black man in the group told them. "She's alone." he laughed too and his sound was just as ugly.

"Leave me alone. Trust me; you don't want to come any closer."

Shirley was trying to sound tough, but she was scared to death. She knows that a fight between her and three men was already a fight lost. She had to stall for time and hope that someone else showed up to help her.

"What do you want, guys? My wallet? My car?" she tried.

"We want your ass, pretty whore. Don't pretend that you don't understand."

"Be nice to her," one of the other men said, "We don't want to scare you, precious. We want to be nice to you...real nice. We'll make you feel real good."

SEASONS OF HEAVEN

"Come on, guys, you'll regret this. I'm going to scream..."

"Go ahead, no one's going to hear you, or care if they do. This is a whore district; whores make a lot of noise! Hell, you can light the parking lot on fire and nobody would come by and piss on it."

"Hmm, that sounds like a plan. Let's set this little pussy on fire!" another man said.

Shirley was terrified. She'd been working here for two years and so far, this was the first time she'd ever had this kind of problem. It seemed to her lately like the whole world had gone mad. Things had gone so well for so long and now it was like someone had pulled on a loose string and it was all coming apart. The wheels were spinning in her head, what was she going to do? She reached her hand down into her bag and pulled out a foldable metal bar. One of the security guards had given it to her a few months back when a drunk was giving her problems. She'd not had a chance to give it back to him.

Shirley popped it open and said, "Do you still want to take your chances with me?"

The man with the knife came quickly towards her with the knife pointed towards her neck. Shirley stepped to the side and pulling back her arm, she let go with a brutal strike across his face. The man stunned and in pain, stumbled into the car and passed out on the windshield. His face was rapidly swelling where the metal bar struck it.

"Fucking whore...you killed him! Are you nuts?" the black man said.

"Bitch!" the fat man was closer than Shirley realized. She felt his fist connect with her gut before she even realized he was there. She reacted quickly, catching him in the throat with the metal bar.

Shirley had been practicing Ju-Jitsu in dojo for a long time. She hadn't had any call to use it before, but tonight, these men were getting a double dose of what she'd learned. The third man wasn't taking his chances any longer. He ran off. Shirley was left shaking; the fear and adrenaline still surged through her body. Her hands trembled and her stomach lurched. She had to bend forward and vomit onto the pavement. When she finished heaving, she felt dizzy and almost fell over as she stood back up straight. She didn't have time to worry about all that right now. She needed to get out of there. She shoved the fat, unconscious man off the hood of her car and got inside. She got onto the highway and started driving towards the comfort and safety of home. Her head was still reeling and her stomach aching as her mind went back over the events of the night.

HEAVEN DAY

Ani was all alone after the boat crashed. He made it to the surface of the water and swam to shore. He climbed up and right away began sniffing the ground urgently searching for Yann.

SEASONS OF HEAVEN

The place he was in is huge and everything was wet. The normal smells have been stirred up and washed away. He was having a hard time finding any trace of his boy.

After a long time of sniffing everything in sight, Ani finally found a trace of the smell of Yann on a wall. It was as if Yann had tried to hold onto it and save himself from the terrible monster that had taken him. Ani had a sense that he had been here before and knew where he was going. He looked around until he found the exit to the cave, stepping out onto a rocky promontory that was high off the ground. He was able to see across the expansive distance from where he stood. He could see the ruins of the trees and vegetation that the monster had left in its wake and he knew that it had passed that way.

He climbed down the rocks and ran in the direction of the forest. He stopped and looked around. He was looking for something. It was strange that he didn't know what exactly...but he knew it was here, somewhere. He finally spotted a hole in the ground and he knew that was what he'd been looking for. He sniffed around it cautiously and then stuck his head inside to take a look. It was definitely an entrance of sorts and he was sure that it would lead him to where the monster had taken Yann. Ani wiggled down in the hole. It was dark inside, but Ani felt as if he knew where he was going. He'd been here before...maybe in a dream, or a vision? He wasn't sure, but he knew this place. He walked along sure-footed, avoiding large clods of dirt and twisted, tangled roots. He knew exactly what path to take, where to turn where to stay straight, and he wasn't the least bit afraid.

Make it more like he already knew that place premonition or memories. All along the way Ani could smell traces of Yann's hands. He knew somehow that his friend was still fighting as the thing dragged him down there. Although Ani felt like he knew where he was going, he still paid close attention to the smell so as not to lose him.

SEASONS OF HEAVEN

At last he came to the end of the path. It opened into a huge room that had been fashioned in the center of a cave. It was an enormous one with a gigantic dome built around a metallic structure in the center of it. Hundreds of roots were visible from underneath from the trees and plants that grew overhead in the sunlight. The place was also filled with dark water and the light across its surface made it look almost unreal. It was the point in Heaven where all of the vegetation had its start.

Ani caught sight of the creature near the back; it looked like it was sleeping. Its large, black form was like an undefined mass of stringy, vague dimensions. It had to measure at least fifty feet long and Ani standing in front of it was a picture comparable to David facing Goliath.

Ani looked around the cave, trying to formulate a plan. Next to him on the ground he saw Yann's backpack. He took a hold of it between his teeth and dragged it over nearer to the wall. He approached the creature slowly, not wanting to wake it. Its numerous long, stringy tentacles lay strewn about and Ani snuck between them until finally he saw Yann. The boy was unconscious and after a few licks from Ani, he woke up. They carried on a telepathic conversation to maintain the silence in the cave.

"Are you all right?" Yann asked Ani. "Thank you for coming to rescue me, I thought it was over. It's weird, but in a strange way at the same time I was terrified, I had a feeling this thing doesn't really want to hurt me. It's almost like it has a split personality." He pulled himself up slowly and cautiously so as not to wake it and then went on to tell Ani, "Look what I found, the creature dropped it when we came in here."

Yann was now in possession of two irradiated stones. The two companions had made big progress in their quest. They moved slowly away from the creature. Yann took his backpack and slipped the second stone inside. They knew what they had to do now - activate the two towers.

SEASONS OF HEAVEN

They again found their way to the exit and climbed out from the cave. As the boys escaped they weren't aware that the monster was watching. He had one eye open...his plan had worked.

Once outside, they hurried to the first tower situated in the north. The sun was slowly descending. The hills were like a patchwork of green and brown whose hues would change with the shadows of the passing clouds. Yann and Ani skipped and ran through the deep carpets of grass that had embedded themselves into the rocky slopes. The entire time they climbed, getting closer to the top of the summit and seemingly the clouds, they could see the tip of the tower they were chasing and hear the crash and roll of a waterfall nearby. Once they reached the top they could see the valley below them. There was another rocky slope they would have to descend between them and valley below. The valley was thick with trees except for one spot in the center that looked like a huge meadow with nothing but rolling green waves of grass. It looked like a giant green carpet had just been rolled out in the middle of it all. Big white birds soared across the skies with their vast, beautiful wings spread open. They stood prominently out against the bright blue of the sky with only small pockets of white clouds to occasionally camouflage them.

    To their left, was a reflective white strip and upon further inspection they could see that it was water, tumbling down the hillside in a series of mini-waterfalls and roaring into the pools below. It was a magnificent sight to behold when all taken in together, possibly the most magnificent that either of them had ever seen. They stood there for a while, watching in reverence as the scene played itself out below them before Yann looked up towards the tall tower that loomed on the other side and knew they needed to start moving again. The climb down was less difficult and quicker than ascending the other side had been. But, once they reached the valley they had to pass through the trees and across the vast meadow before they could climb up the other side and reach the base of the tower.

In the midst of the trees it was dark in places with only shards of sunlight being able to penetrate through the thick canopies of branches and leaves. They spied another family of deer grazing lazily and the rabbits and squirrels played hide and seek in the trees and bushes as they passed. When they reached the thick meadow the two boys ran and sometimes tumbled through it. The grass was plush and would tamp down underneath them, only to pop back up in place as soon as they'd passed. Leaving the meadow at last, they passed through another dense forest of trees before reaching the rocky slope on the other side.

Using teamwork, as they had been all along, the travelers climbed the rocks up towards the tower. Sometimes it was a struggle for Yann's small arms to reach something to hold onto above him, but Ani was always there to lend a boost. In some places, Yann would have to lift Ani and set him up on the next rocky projection. In this manner, they finally reached the top and the base of the tower. Once they were standing next to it, a strange feeling came over them both. It was as if the tower was steel and they were magnets. They couldn't take their eyes from the majestic sight of it standing there on the hill. Although tired from the long trip they'd already made, neither of them could wait to get started climbing the perilous looking tower. It wasn't an easy climb, and it was very dangerous. A slip and fall could have been fatal. They attached themselves to each other for protection and then using only instinct they began to shimmy up the wall. They both kept their bodies and faces as close to it as they could while they moved upwards, that seemed to keep their center of balance better and kept them from falling off backwards.

SEASONS OF HEAVEN

It was a long, excruciating climb, but instead of exhausted, they both felt elated with a sense of accomplishment and the view from the top was sensational. They could see the waterfall from here from a different angle as it thundered down the mountain looking like a flash of lightning against the rocks. Shadows danced amongst the trees as the setting sun sent an army of red and orange light down on top of them. Yann could see a carpet of flowers that had sprouted up at the base of the waterfalls in an array of colors that dazzled his senses. The peaks of the summit on the other side now seemed to reach up towards the emerging moon and stars and the white birds stood out now even more spectacularly against the twilight of the sky. The stars looked huge and close enough to reach out and touch from where they stood. Yann and Ani put the stone in a bowl shaped apparatus that was situated on top of the tower. It fit the stone like a glove and as soon as it was in, the stone began to emit energy. The whole thing was like a giant magnet and Yann couldn't help but wonder what was going to happen. He didn't have to wait long to find out. Suddenly, the stone and the tower began to shake and vibrate and the building started to sink into the ground. As it sank, it turned itself into a position like a key.

Fearful of being sucked into the ground with it, Yann and Ani ran down the tower. As they ran, they had to jump and duck and dodge to avoid being smashed by the falling rocks.

CHAPTER TWENTY-FIVE
"GHOSTS"
Funeral of Tim and Elise Northman

Eddie sat at the bleak cemetery and looked around him at all the sad faces. Everyone was there, the police, Yann and Ani and Shirley. Some faces had tears streaming down them and others were simply immobilized by their pain.

Eddie tried to shake the surrealism of it all off. Tim and Elise were dead; their car plunged down over fifty feet off the bridge and into the lake. According to the experts that surveyed the scene, Tim died instantly upon impact. Elise was said to have survived the crash, but drowned in the lake. Her lungs were filled with water and Eddie couldn't shake the image of her fighting for her life.

He knew that the only way he could pay tribute to his friend and partner now was by solving the case they'd been working on...the one that was so important to Tim....

SEASONS OF HEAVEN

Eddie spent three days in Tim and Elise's home after the funerals, looking for some clue...a hint to help him clarify all that happened. He went to the French restaurant, the last place the couple had been seen alive and talked to the staff. They tell him what they remember, but no one remembered anything unusual and Eddie was thinking it might be a dead end...until he spoke with the security manager. The security manager told him there was a security camera installed on the opposite side of the street. It was set to film the jeweler's shop and the main entrance to the restaurant was also visible. Eddie was livid. Why hadn't anyone checked these before? The police who investigated the scene were obviously just writing Tim and Elise's death off as an accident. They'd looked at the scene, but not what led up to it. Eddie seemed to be the only one to think that something here was just not right. It seemed so obviously not right to him that he was furious at his colleagues for not taking the investigation more seriously. He took the tapes and went back to Tim's house with them.

He sat watching the tapes with bleary eyes and a body running only on caffeine and determination. After about five hours of recordings, at ten twenty-three p.m. Eddie saw a man wearing a hood. Something about the way he was just standing there, looking at the restaurant struck Eddie as wrong somehow. The quality of the tape was not great so he couldn't make out his face, but he still got a strange feeling about him...he seemed familiar...maybe the guy Eddie had watched vanish from the laundry room the day Tim was attacked in the warehouse?

Eddie gave up the recordings for the time being and decided to drive out to the scene where the accident took place. The investigation had concluded only that the car had swerved and passed through the guardrail...plunging off the bridge and into the lake. There was nothing in the report, or the witness accounts to say what it was that caused Tim to swerve in the first place.

Eddie didn't know why, but his gut was telling him this was no accident. He feared that it might be a murder disguised as an accident...someone wanted to get rid of Tim.

Eddie came to the place where the bridge was still cordoned off and found a spot to park his car; He walked over to the area where there were still dark skid marks and the portion of the bridge guardrail that was torn loose by the impact.

He was looking for some kind of clue...a hint that there was a link between the case that he and Tim were working on and the "accident." All the road was telling him was that Tim had swerved and braked before going through the guardrail. He walked over to where the bridge was broken, shaking the wet orange leaves from his boots. The air was frigid cold and Eddie could see his breath as it came out of his mouth.

SEASONS OF HEAVEN

He looked at where the guardrail was smashed and then he found a spot where he could walk down to the water, where the car had ended up. He took photos of everything on his way down, and again when he got near the water. He noticed tire tracks and cigarette butts...and a small piece of white paper with something stamped on it that was hardly legible any longer due to being out in the weather. He picked it up and looked at it more closely. Suddenly it dawned on him what he was looking at...

"Holy shit ... That's a parking ticket. He was there." Eddie didn't care that it would be dark soon. He went back to his car and took out the large car phone the department had just recently issued them. He called the station. He wanted the scene investigated again, right now.

By the time the crime scene techs arrived, it was almost full dark. The area was once again marked with caution tape and police emergency car lights.

SEASONS OF HEAVEN

Once again, they were examining everything. The tire tracks, the skid marks, the path the car took over the side...and he even had the pick up the cigarette butts in hopes of finding DNA on them. He was doing a good job...the best he could, but to him it didn't feel good enough. Tim was dead...and so was Elise. Yann was left as an orphan and that just didn't sit right with him. He wanted them to go faster. He wanted it solved yesterday. Zen wasn't working for him on this one.

During the second investigation a highway security camera was identified and on that tape a white Ford pickup was seen leaving the highway seven minutes after the accident. Eddie needed to find that guy and talk to him. If he hadn't been the cause of the accident, he had to have seen something.

Because of the fact he and Tim had discovered the serial killer they were looking for had been active both in Idaho and New York, the state of New York started collaboration with the

SEASONS OF HEAVEN

FBI. Eddie was worried that if he didn't find something soon, the Feds would take it over completely and it would be out of his hands.

Eddie ran the DMV for New York and New Jersey and it came back with thousands of white Ford Pick-up's registered in each city. Then, acting on a hunch based solely on the fact that the photograph of the killer had dropped the night they chased him was taken in Little Rock, he ran the plates there. He got seven possible leads. He went home and packed a bag and headed for Little Rock.

****

It was dinner time by the time he got to Little Rock. Eddie thought it might be a good idea to eat at the local diner and get a feel for the community before he started knocking on doors. He went into what seemed to be the only diner on the small street called Main in the little town. It was an old wooden building. Eddie put it at probably over a hundred years old. From the places where the paint had flaked and peeled,

Eddie could tell that it had been repainted more than once. Currently it was a dark peach color. The name on the sign out front simply said, "Dinner."

He parked his car and walked along the cobblestone sidewalk to the front of the building. All of the buildings in the town looked to be older, but they also seemed neat and well-maintained. It looked like a place out of a Hallmark movie where the neighbors got together and had pot luck dinners and church was an important part of everyone's week.

The bells on the door jangled as he opened it and walked in. The place was about half full and judging from the hearty conversations that seemed to be taking place, Eddie would guess the customers were mostly locals. He took a seat at the counter and turned over the coffee cup. Within seconds it was being filled by a waitress in a peach colored uniform. She was probably in her thirties with long red hair worn in a braid on the side of her head and dark jade green eyes.

"Hi there," she said as she was filling his cup and laying a menu down next to him. "How are you today?"

"I'm good, what about you?" Eddie asked her. She smiled and looked around,

"Another day," she said. "Let me know when you're ready."

Eddie thanked her and looked at the menu. He called her back a few minutes later and gave her his order. While she was there he said,

"Have you lived here in Little Rock long?"

"All my life," she said.

"Then you were around when the disappearances were happening...the thing with the kids?"

She gave him a suspicious look and then she said, "Yeah, I was here. That was a terrible time for this town." She put a hand on her hip and said, "Why are you asking about that?"

Eddie showed her his credentials and said, "I'm here on something entirely unrelated to that," he wasn't sure that was the truth, but no one needed to know that but him. "I'd just heard about it of course and was curious."

"So who you here looking for?" she asked.

"I'm here to talk to several people," he told her. "Maybe you could help me out with the streets so I can find these addresses more easily?"

"What streets you looking for?" she said.

Eddie pulled out his list. Folding it so that only the street addresses showed and not the names, he laid it on the counter. The waitress looked and said, "Well, Little Rock ain't that big. You'll find most of these streets over in the section of track houses by the school. It's just up the street here a way. That last one is over on the far side of town. It's not the best part of town either…"

"Great, I appreciate your help," he said. "I've got one more question. Is there a motel around here?" The waitress told him there was only one in town just off the freeway. Eddie had passed it on his way in. He finished his dinner and headed over there. He'd try and get some rest tonight and set out in the morning on his quest.

He slept fitfully, dreaming about Tim and Elise and the look on little Yann's face at the funeral also haunted him every time he closed his eyes. He had to find this guy, if for no other reason than to get some kind of justice for that little boy. After having breakfast at the same diner he set out on foot to track down the addresses of the people with white Ford's.

He walked up the street like the waitress told him to and turned left next to the little school. There was a series of track houses there and after getting turned around on a couple of "cul de sacs"; he found the first street he was looking for.

He was surprised at how nice the homes were here. It was such a small community that he wouldn't have thought the economy would be that great. The likelihood was that the residents commuted to the city for work. He made his way up a paved driveway that curved up to a quaint looking Tudor-style wooden house with leaded glass front windows. It had a steep wooden shake roof and a prominent stone chimney. His list listed a Gregory Miller as being the owner of a white Ford pick-up and living at this address. He rang the bell and within seconds an elderly woman opened the door.

"Can I help you?" she asked.

"Yes, I was looking for Gregory Miller." The smile on the woman's face melted and she said,

"Gregory was my son. He passed away last month."

"I'm so sorry for your loss," Eddie said, "Can I ask how he died?"

"Who are you?"

"I'm sorry," Eddie took out his credentials and told her, "I'm investigating an accident that happened in New Jersey a few weeks ago. I think someone may have witnessed it and that someone was in a pick-up like the one registered to your son."

SEASONS OF HEAVEN

"Oh, well it wasn't Gregory. He died five weeks ago. His pick-up is in my garage. It hasn't been driven for almost a year. He had cancer and he was in and out of the hospital the last year."

Eddie was sure this wasn't the truck he was looking for. He thanked the woman and went on his way.

The next house was three blocks away and as Eddie approached the front door he could hear the television on inside. A middle-aged woman answered the door and told him that the man he was asking about was her husband, George.

"He's at work now though. He works in the city, he's an investment banker." That explained the nice house and the expensive clothing the woman was wearing, Eddie thought. He told her who he was and why he wanted to talk to her husband.

"He doesn't ever drive the pick-up into the city," she said, "It's expensive on gas. We mostly have it to pull our fifth wheel when we go on vacations. It's in the garage if you'd like to take a look at it."

"Sure, thank you," Eddie followed her to the garage where she opened the door to reveal a white Ford pickup with a double cab. As soon as he saw it, he knew it wasn't the right one. He thanked her and headed on again.

Eddie was able to talk to four of the seven people on his list that morning. He would see the others the following day if he didn't get anything from the last one on his list. That was the one the waitress told him was on the "bad side of town."

Eddie had lunch and then drove out to find the address of the last one. The house stood alone just on the edge of town. It was not in a terrible state from the outside, yet not remarkable well kept by any means. It was probably about thirty or forty years old and it was just a square of brick walls with four windows in front that didn't add a thing to the aesthetics of the place. There was a small cement porch out front and Eddie saw a woman probably in her late fifties sitting in a folding chair looking down at him as he approached.

He introduced himself and the woman said,

"I'm Elizabeth Lewis," the woman told him.

"I'm looking for the owner of a white Ford pick-up. He may have witnessed an accident over in New Jersey a few weeks ago."

The woman had a strange way about her. She didn't seem upset or concerned or the least bit suspicious that a New York City detective was here in Little Rock asking questions about an accident that happened in New Jersey. All she said, was,

"I don't have no truck," she said.

Eddie looked at the paper in his hand and said, "It says it's registered to a Frank Lewis at this address."

"We best talk about this inside," she said. Her tone was the same, but something about her demeanor had changed.

Eddie cautiously followed the woman inside the house and after taking a quick look around, he took the seat she offered him. Once they both sat down she said, "Frank ain't been around here for a long time. I'm not sure why he would use this address."

"And Frank is?"

"My son. He's...disturbed detective. He's been in trouble most of his life." She said that with a matter-of-fact voice. She wasn't complaining, she was just stating the facts.

"Is Frank here right now?" Eddie asked.

"No, I told you, he doesn't come here anymore. I'm glad of it. The boy ain't right in the head."

"Can you tell me about him? Where does he live? How can I get ahold of him?"

"I don't know where he's at and I doubt that he's working. He don't keep a job for long."

"What kind of work does he do?" Eddie asked her.

SEASONS OF HEAVEN

"Nothing specific. He gets a job here and there...fast food, mechanics...Hell; he was even into taxidermy for a while. Like I said though, I ain't seen him in a while...."

While the woman was talking, Eddie was taking a better stock of the house around him. It was a dark...depressing little place. There were no school pictures on the walls of a young Frank...no family vacation photos.... the windows were covered with dark black curtains and the room was lit with a single naked bulb on a string in the center of the room. The furniture was old and stained and the only wall decoration in the place resembled a pentagram. The whole place gave Eddie the creeps and made him determined to find and talk to this Frank person.

"Does Frank still have a room here?"

"I ain't touched it since he left. He's got a temper...I try not to make him angry...." The old woman showed Eddie to Frank's room and she left him there. Eddie looked around at the walls, from the looks of it, Frank hadn't been here...or at least updated anything since he was a teenager. There were posters on the wall of teen movies and singers and an old dusty hi-fi system in the corner. There were stacks of clothes that had been in one place for so long they'd gathered dust. He didn't find anything special there, so he went back out to once again talk to Frank's mother.

"Mrs. Lewis, I need you to tell me everything you can about Frank, as far back as his childhood."

"Ain't much to tell. He's a "special" man. He grew up here with his Daddy and me. He was always an imaginative child. He used to tell people that we were into satanic cults and that we waited around for the darkness to come nourish itself off of our neighbors. Got some teachers and CPS workers all in an uproar over it once. He even told them I kept him in a closet when he came in from school. It were all nonsense that he made up in his head."

"Why would he tell people things like that?" Eddie asked. His inclination was to believe it. He'd found out since becoming a police officer that in cases where children reported abuse against their parents it was usually true.

"He was just always different. We was poor and I couldn't afford to take him to no fancy doctors for a diagnosis, but the truth was my family has some schizophrenia in it and I think maybe Frank got a touch of that. He tried to make himself "normal" by inventing his own world. At school he was always getting picked on and beat up for acting crazy. He used to talk to himself...all the time and he was never happy...saddest kid you ever seen. " The woman actually said that like she thought he'd deserved that kind of treatment. The poor kid probably talked to himself because he didn't have anyone else to talk to...no one who cared about him anyways. Eddie was feeling sorry for Frank...at least the child version of him. She wasn't finished yet,

SEASONS OF HEAVEN

"When he was a teenager, he stopped talking...to everyone real anyways. He talked to someone that no one else could see. He called him "Frank" too. Weird kid, I'm telling you."

"How old was he when he moved out?"

She shrugged. What kind of mother doesn't know how old their child is when they move out of the house?

"He got beat up real bad one Thanksgiving. He was out in the woods and I don't doubt he brought it on, playing with that invisible friend of his. A group of kids jumped on him and beat him senseless. He spent a couple a days in the hospital...or maybe more...anyways, he told me he was in a coma for two days."

"He told you? You weren't there?" Eddie didn't want her to stop giving him information, so he'd been trying to control his tone, but that was too much.

"I didn't know he was in the hospital until he got home. They should call us or something. He was ranting and raving about people called

"The Banished" who needed him in Heaven. I had to laugh at that, Frank in Heaven? That's a joke right there. Anyways, he packed up a bag and took off that day. He's come around a time or two since to steal from me. He got even more hateful than ever. He didn't even bother attending to his daddy's funeral."

"I need to know where you think he might be, ma'am..."

"I told you, I ain't seen him in a long time. Don't you have enough information from me?"

"No, I don't. I need you to give me some detail, something that could help me to find him. Was there a place he used to hide himself, where he felt good, maybe a kind of shelter of his? Try to remember!"

She thought about it and then finally said, "There was something like that. When he was young, after the incident with the children from the village who had sent him to the hospital he used to go the old cabin near the treatment plant. I saw him there once."

"Can you show me on the map where it was?" Eddie said, excited.

She showed him where the treatment plant was on the map and then said,

"It's up there around the back side of the plant. There ain't no real road leading to it, just dirt."

"Mrs. Lewis, what else can you tell me about Frank?"

"Like what do you mean?" she said. Eddie had to wonder if she knew her son at all even before he left.

"How about his appearance, what does he look like?"

She shrugged and said, "He's plain. He's got light hair and pale blue eyes. His skin always looks pasty when it ain't covered in acne...you know, just plain."

Eddie almost shuddered at the lack of interest this woman showed in her own offspring. "What about photographs? Do you have any pictures of him?"

SEASONS OF HEAVEN

She looked like she was thinking about it and then she got up and went over to a desk that sat in the corner. She took out an old album and handed it to Eddie. He flipped through it, disappointed to see that they were all school photos and only went up to the third or fourth grade. When he'd finished he looked at her and said,

"You don't have anything more recent than this?"

She shook her head and said, "You know, he's just plain. Who wants a picture of that on their wall?"

Eddie left with a sick feeling in the pit of his stomach. Such a lack of feeling for your own child was unimaginable to him. He'd been a cop for a long time and he'd talked to a lot of people. As far as the bad mother award goes, this woman took the cake.

Eddie at least left the Lewis house with directions to the old cabin Frank's mother said he used to stay at sometimes. The place was several miles outside of town and Eddie drove through torrents of rain and mud to get there. He finally came to a place in the road that was so muddy and slippery he could no longer get enough traction to drive. Worried about getting stuck in the mud, he got out and began to walk the rest of the way.

The air smelled terrible. The smoke coming from the treatment plant filled the air with the smell of human waste. Eddie would have liked to travel quicker and get out of the smell faster, but he was forced to walk slowly both by the weather and the conditions of the dirt path he was walking on. He had his weapon out and in his hand just in case Frank was in the cabin or somewhere in the woods along the way. After the talk with his mother Eddie was convinced that if he wasn't his guy, he was dangerous at the very least.

He walked through the woods which were marked as a "hunting preserve." There was no one else around and from the looks of the tangled brush and dead trees; Eddie guessed that it hadn't been used in a while. There was a gloomy pall that sat over the whole place and just to make it spookier a flock of black ravens flew away into the dark sky just as Eddie came to the end of the path and approached the old cabin.

The cabin was made of wood, but the roof was corrugated sheet metal and the rain made a loud tap-tap noise as it pelted down on top of it. The place was covered with brush and the wood was rotting. It looked deserted.

Eddie tried the door but it was blocked by something. Using his elbow, he broke open the dusty glass window and then using his jacket as a protective barrier he climbed inside. The room was dark and covered in dust and cobwebs Eddie shuddered to think of what kind of vermin might be resting in the corners. The smell outside had been bad, but the one in the cabin was a pungent mix of dust and mold that made Eddie sneeze repeatedly. It seemed as if no one had been there in years.

Eddie took out his little flashlight and ran it across the walls. He stopped it on one wall that was covered in newspaper clippings. Eddie stepped closer where he could see them better. They were news reports about the children who had gone missing in Little Rock all those years ago. There were also multiple Polaroid photos of various children. Most of the pictures didn't look posed, as if the children had no idea they were being photographed.

He ran the flashlight along the rest of the walls. One thing stood out, the word "Banished" had been engraved in the wood in several places and above some of them were spray painted the word, "Liberate us" in big, block letters. Eddie wondered what it all meant. Frank's mother mentioned something about him talking about the banished after he was beaten. Was it a delusion that came about after a head injury? He kept shining the light along the walls and he came to another place where the words, "You only get one chance" were written. Eddie had seen those words before. He went over and looked closer. They were written in red. In this case it was paint, or a marker he thought. The last time he'd seen them they'd been written in blood on the wall of the warehouse the night that Tim was attacked.

There was a small bookshelf in the corner with three leather-bound books on it that looked like journals. Eddie went over and took one off the shelf and opened it up. After reading the first entry he felt like he'd struck gold. He sat down on an old stump that was fashioned into a chair and with the help of his flashlight, he began to read. It seemed that Frank kept a journal detailing his conversations with what he called "the world beyond."

The first chapter said, "Who are the Banished?" Underneath that, Frank wrote: *They have been rejected by the Ancient People for a number of reasons. Some of them lied, some killed, and some of them had simply trampled on the rules of their community by collaborating with humans. These men and women lost a part of their bodies. Their behavior and their hatred turned them into dangerous creatures, shapeless and phantom like. They nourished themselves with the sadness.*

It all sounded like wild ramblings of a disturbed mind to Eddie. He kept reading however and the next sentence said: *They will do all they can to make James' journey impossible.*

Eddie wondered who James was and if the poor guy knew that there was a group of evil "banished" ones who wanted to possess him.

The most disturbing thing on the page that Eddie read said in red ink and underlined twice was:

On the Earth, Banished will guide the most vulnerable men to help them exterminate human children.

Eddie shuddered. He put that book down...for now and picked up another. The second one looked older and when Eddie opened it up, he could see why. It was Frank's journal that he'd started as a boy. He wrote about his parents and their satanic rituals and he wrote about the way his mother would lock him in a secret closet behind the wardrobe in the dark when he was only ten years old. He had printed out in excruciating detail the abuse he'd suffered at the hands of his parents and at the hands of the children he went to school with as well. He described being beaten in the woods by the kids his own age and left for dead only to wake in the hospital two days later all alone. That was the point that he decided there was no longer any point in even pretending to be a part of the human race.

    Eddie was disgusted and fascinated at the same time as he read on. Frank's journal told of his "first kill." It was a young woman that looked like his mother and he'd enjoyed it so much because it was like he'd finally gotten to kill her. Throughout the scrawling's were places where he would suddenly begin to talk about the invisible voices that told him what to do and who to kill.

After he'd killed the woman he'd left the adults alone and he'd begun killing the innocents: the children. He said the Banished asked him to get rid of the small ones. He was told to observe families and find their weaker points and use them to take the children.

Eddie had to stop reading every so often. It was almost like being in Frank's tortured mind and it was taking a lot out of him.

Frank wrote about explicit examples of how he would capture the children. He would feel bad for them sometimes and try not to kill them even though he knew that he had to do what the Banished asked of him. He would stroke their soft hair and look at them for a long time wishing that he could breathe in some of their innocence, their purity. After he killed them at last, he would keep their belongings...usually their backpacks in an effort to continue to feel close to them.

SEASONS OF HEAVEN

He had listed out the states where he'd committed these crimes: Oregon, Wisconsin, New Jersey...it even said that he'd been to an old castle in Aquitaine in France and to a farm in the south of Italy. Both places had dark history and Frank had written that these places were where the Banished "sucked" the souls from the children.

At the bottom of the page Frank had written: *The depopulation of the world has begun. Without children there is no future. The goal of the Banished was to attack humans at their weakest point...the children they loved dearly.*

Eddie felt nauseous. This was really sick stuff. He told himself one more page and then he would leave this gloomy place and have the crime scene techs come up and clean it out. The next page detailed the killing of a little boy that Eddie had heard Tim refer to in one of his cold cases. It was a boy named Thomas who had disappeared and his father had been accused of the crime.

Frank admitted in his journal that Thomas was the first child he killed. He killed him in an open air daycare center where he had worked at one time. He stabbed him and then let him die as the Banished consumed his soul

Frank had described in his journal in intimate detail how it had felt to pull the knife across the flesh of the young boy and watch as it split open and the blood began to spill out. He said that it was horrifying and exciting at the same time. He talked about looking into the little boy's eyes and the look there going from shock to terror and then nothing. The life drained out of him right in front of Frank's eyes. Afterwards, after the Banished had consumed the boy's soul, Frank thought about him a lot. He wondered about his life and if there were people who missed him. He fought the feelings of guilt that he had and eventually let it be replaced by an intense feeling of satisfaction that he had accomplished what had been asked of him and if he had to, he'd be ready to do it again.

SEASONS OF HEAVEN

Eddie suddenly had to put the book down and run outside. As soon as he hit the fresh air of the woods he began to vomit. The remains of his lunch were spewed onto the muddy ground. When he finished heaving he stood against a tree. He felt unclean just from reading Frank's thoughts. He wasn't sure who these "Banished" were or if they were even real. Frank's head seemed to be mixed up and confused between delusions and reality. What Eddie had been able to discern was that Frank was a sick son of a bitch and if these people the Banished did exist....the world was in serious trouble, on the verge of becoming as macabre as the thoughts in Frank's head.

CHAPTER TWENTY-SIX
"MONSTER"

James was moving slowly under the suddenly scorching sun. He was in bad shape; his body was marked with scars, scratches, dried blood and bruises. He was also sweating profusely and brown stains marked his neck and arms. He entered the forest, at last sheltered by the close trees from the heat of the sun. He looked around the dark place, realizing that it's much less welcoming than other places he'd seen since coming here. His mind kept going back to the things that he'd discovered in the office, and he was talking to himself like a mad man as he made his way through the gnarled forest.

"They know everything about us, humans ... My God...how is that possible? Nobody is informed about that ... Where the fuck am I?"

He questioned himself as he struggled to breathe in the dense forest. The vegetation seemed to be sucking in all of the oxygen.

SEASONS OF HEAVEN

The forest he just entered didn't let the air come in. It was difficult to breath, the vegetation was very dense. He walked and walked, eventually coming to a row of houses in the middle of the forest. James let himself through the rotting fence and examined the houses. As he'd suspected, they were deserted and in various stages of disarray. They were built in a haphazard manner, some along the sides of a stream and some were set back further into the trees. Some looked like they had been tall structures and what was left of them rivaled the trees for height. There were others that looked like a basic shelter, like the one James had built on the beach. The houses were partially furnished and looked like they'd been gone through the last time in a hurry. Now all that was left lay scattered around and covered with a fine coating of dust. Moss had found its way into the cracks of a few of them and had taken over the structures. The forest had continued its growth around them and if they'd had small yards in the past, one was indiscernible from the other now. The lazy river meandered through the center of it all and the weeds had grown up so thickly along the banks that they almost choked the water out as it tried to flow through it. It was obvious that no one had been here in a long time and he couldn't help but wonder what had made them leave in such a rush that most of their things even seemed to have been left behind. He remembered what he'd read in the journals in the office he'd passed through. This must be the place where the Banished had gone to start over when they broke away from the Ancients.

"You are already done, the second stone is just there..." a man's voice came from nowhere to tell him.

"Leave me alone!" James yelled out.

"I like that James. You're fighting back. You're becoming stronger! You're almost ready to become...."

Behind one of the houses James suddenly saw a strange violet light flashing.

SEASONS OF HEAVEN

He ignored the voice and followed the light. It led him to the entrance of a cave. Looking inside he could see that everything was illuminated. This cave was different from the others that he'd gone through since he'd been here. This one had vegetation growing in rows across the floor. James knelt down and upon closer inspection he could see that what grew there were not just abstract plants and weeds like he'd seen in the forest and jungle. Vegetables were growing, rows and rows of them.

The daylight must have been too intense for the vegetables, making it impossible to make them grow in a conventional way. James realized then that he had not seen a single flower since he came here. He'd been slowly growing accustomed to the intense rays that came from the sun but he knew that a vegetable garden would dry up and shrivel under that kind of heat. The sun here seemed closer somehow and it spilled out over everything.

SEASONS OF HEAVEN

James entered the greenhouse, and had to bat his eyes a few times against the ultraviolet light. It was actually giving him a headache the way it bounced off of everything in the cave. He lit his bunch of sage and the beam from the flame filled every corner of the cave. James had his naginata ready in case it was needed. He walked through carefully feeling the squish of the vegetation underneath his feet as he did. The cave was deep but he eventually arrived at the back of it where he discovered the second irradiated stone. It was fixed to the wall like the first one but for some reason, this one was more easily removed.

He removed it with his sabre with no difficulties and put it in his bag. He felt a sense of relief now knowing that he had both of the stones. He started back through the greenhouse, but before he made it halfway he began to become uneasy with dizziness assaulting his senses. Everything began to shake and the rocks along the walls began to shift and some of them slipped out of place and fell to the ground. Then James heard a terrible rumble that seemed to come from deep down in the belly of the earth beneath his feet. He began to run as the cave crumbled faster around him. The ground was shaking so hard now that he could barely stay on his feet. By the time he got to the entrance of the cave, the falling rocks had already begun to gather there. James had to climb over the small wall that had already formed there.

Once he was back outside he heard another rumble and then the shaking became fiercer. He ran back towards the forest with panic in his chest as the structures around him began to cave in around their own foundations, falling and striking the ground with a mighty impact that sent dust and mud flying and crushed whatever was underneath it. James ran stumbling across the shaky earth until at last he was under the cover of the trees in the forest once more.

The shadows began to come at him again and he once again used his sage and naginata to try and protect himself. This time though he could feel their violence inside his body. It was as if they were passing through him, going in and out of his body as if he didn't exist. It was painful and exhausting. He forced himself to continue forward and at last he came to the exit and ran outside, heading towards the village.

James was running...he knew he was, but it felt as if time around him had slowed down. He felt dazed and he could feel the presence of something in the air. He stopped for a second, unable to move because of the presence that stood before him. This time the presence was different than the others. He could feel the presence of two entities, but these were light...good, not dark and evil like the others. The feeling that there were two other people there with him, next to him only lasted for a few seconds and then it was gone.

James had just intersected with the future although he didn't know it. His destiny had crossed paths with Yann and Ani in the pursuit of theirs. As soon as he knew he was alone once more and could continue to move forward he did, and in the distance he could hear the hubbub of the Banished increasing in volume. He ran for a few feet before at last collapsing and for James, everything went black.

■■

HEAVEN
REYNALD'S OFFICE

Reynald was hurriedly gathering documents off his desk, shoving them into larger books so that he could carry them with him. He was trying to take as many as he could, grabbing the important ones first....

An anxious looking man stuck his head into the office and asked, "Are you coming? We are waiting for you!"

SEASONS OF HEAVEN

"I am coming!" Reynald snapped back. He was agitated as he stuffed the rest of what he had in his hands into his bag. He followed the man out into the magnificent, bright landscape. He was at the top of the city with about twenty other people.

"Pardon! Please, listen to me... This day is a particular day. A man appeared in Heaven without being asked to do so! You see, we cannot completely control nature; it has its own ways. This man is dead here, in Heaven. Normally that's not possible, only the dead can come in here. However, this is what happened, he is dead here and that means that we could have been wrong..."

"Where did he come from?" a man asked. "He brought a horse with him..."

"It doesn't matter! What's important is you! Start over, build a similar place, other civilizations need hope. They need you.

"You are leaving us?" was the question of numerous voices at once.

SEASONS OF HEAVEN

"No, this is merely a shift in power... you can do it better than me..." Reynald told them.

"What do you mean...?" was the question asked by the voices almost in unison.

"Please calm down. You have to carry on. Find another place and bring hope into it. I have to stay here..."

"Who will guide us?" One of the men asked.

"She will ... You knew that would happen one day, Titias! Come here, it is your turn...Guide them well!"

"I will do so," the beautiful woman said.

"But what do we do with ... you know ... with the Banished?" the man asked.

"I am the only one responsible," he said. Then after a long pause he said, "They are staying here. When you leave, I will lock the keys! And now, go! Hurry, to the Infinity Field!"

Everyone took their personal effects. They would be heading south to the place they're supposed to leave from...Infinity Field. It's a door that makes it possible to travel in time and space. What's left of the Ancient's were about to do that...travel beyond death.

After they were gone Reynald returned to the city. He made his way down the stairs, jumping on each fourth step. He arrived to the ground floor and pushed a door that was hidden so well that one who didn't know it was there would hardly notice it. He entered a long corridor and came to another set of steps that went down.

The second set of stairs led him down about three hundred feet into the dark. They ended outside and he was back in the forest. The exit itself underneath the vegetation. Reynald created this place; he knew all of the details.

He headed quickly west then, the south tower coming into view as he did. Its ochre color along with the rocks that floated mysteriously around it gave it a surrealistic quality.

As he exited the forest he faced a flat stone lying on the ground. On either side of it was a big statue, a Moai made on the Rapa Nui

Island and brought here by those that helped him create this place. Reynald pushed on the stone. It resisted because of the tangled vegetation but suddenly opened up.

There were more stairs and Reynald went down them. These stairs ended in a room that was over two hundred and fifty square feet. There was a mirror in the center of the room about three feet high by six feet wide. It shone as bright as a star in the clear night sky. It used to be the heart of the vessel...a sort of hydrodynamic magnetic engine...a secret source of energy. The engine was capable of recognizing feelings and thoughts, technology that was coveted by humans. This was the main thing that made the construction of Heaven possible. When Reynald got closer to it the mirror turned off. The light ceased to emanate and the ground began to shake. The towers and the keys were locking themselves.

SEASONS OF HEAVEN

"Maybe one day... You will reactivate yourself. I hope you will feel their hope, their despair, their sadness..." he said.

He took the path upstairs towards the exit and once outside he put the flat stone back on the entrance. He had to leave now. He knew that without its heart this place was dangerous. It would begin to eat up his and anyone else here's thoughts. It could easily drive a person mad. Reynald had never found the solution for that problem.

"We are only souls in this place and if the soul cannot share its feelings with the surrounding nature, it is lost," was how he explained it.

Reynald came back to the lower entrance of the city, not far from the dock. He took a bunch of keys out of his pocket and opened the small door.

He entered a room that looked like a small hut. He pushed in on another door and entered another small room. In the middle of the room lay a man. The man was maintained in an artificial coma, he was breathing using artificial breathing assistance. Through the astral journey, he was connected to someone else on the Earth. Two cables exited his spirit and outside the cabin, plunged into a splendid lake.

Reynald had created this system as an emergency way to go back to the Earth.

Now, all the books and notes he had in his bag were a real treasure of knowledge. He was nervous but happy at the same time, about to see the planet he cherished so deeply. He couldn't take anything with him. He had to memorize everything. Even if he had left his original plans on the Earth, he disposed of the documents on the walls and started reading all the information out loudly. For the next twenty minutes his highly effective brain was in maximum focus.

He took two cables and his shoulder bag and then he ran and jumped into the lake. He plunged more and more deeply and finally he lost consciousness.

This wasn't Reynald's first experience with astral travel. He knew that once his body reached an optimal level of relaxation as it had now, his consciousness would simply be lifted from his body. He would be aware of things then, but outside of his physical body. He would be free then to float weightlessly and to see things from a different vantage point. The world when he was on an astral journey held no boundaries and seemingly no time. The places between the beginning of his journey and the destination held only calmness and beauty and light.

GREENLAND

Once at his destination Reynald would again lose consciousness only to be pulled back into it by the freezing cold of the water around him. He was completely submerged and overhead he could see ice that was inches thick making an

SEASONS OF HEAVEN

essential tomb of the water. Reynald knew what to look for however and when he found it, he began to swim upwards towards it. There was a perfect round hole in the ice. The hole was just large enough for Reynald to pull his body up through. Once he was on top of the ice he reached up and opened the door of the office that was carved out of ice. It was a part of the landscape and if one didn't know it was there, it was hardly visible. Once inside, Reynald dropped to the floor. Every one of his muscles ached and as he lay there on the floor drooling he was "waking up." He finally got up slowly, holding his head in both of his hands. He felt sick and began to vomit. He tried to grab any receptacle to use it, but in vain. He coughed hard; the travel was more than exhausting. It used every muscle and nerve fiber in his body and placed a great deal of stress on them. He vomited an orange liquid, a kind of ectoplasm, energetic rejection that appeared during the astral journey. He did it before only once and it was just as violent.

SEASONS OF HEAVEN

He was in his office which resembled the one he used in Heaven. The other twin was lying on a stretcher, connected to numerous cables. Reynald got close to the wall and began stripping of the wet clothes he was in. He was freezing. Once he'd gotten them off he took a thick towel and dried himself off from head to toe, using friction to warm his aching cold muscles. He wrapped himself up in a thick, thermal blanket and sat for a while until his body temperature had returned to almost normal. Then he went over to the closet against the wall and took out dry clothes, put on thermal long underwear first and then pants and a long sleeved shirt. Then he put on snow pants that had a bib that connected over his shoulders like a pair of overalls. He slipped on a heavily padded jacket then, a thick hat with ear muffs attached, insulated boots, gloves and then a scarf. He opened the door and in front of him as far as he could see was the icy desert. The snow was all around and the temperature is under -20°C. The building he just left resembled a metallic dome.

He took the path in front of him. On his right he saw the housings of the Inuit's. He always appreciated the people living close to nature. He stopped in front of a small house and rang the bell. A man came out, they know each other. The two of them exchanged a few words in Eme-sal, a fine version of the Sumerian language.

Reynald entered the courtyard, and the man disappeared into the house. He came out again right away accompanied by five sled dogs. They were magnificent, resembling wolves.

Reynald stroked their heads and attached them to the sled. It took only a few moments to get his means of transport ready. The two men exchanged few more words before saying goodbye.

The sled got moving very fast, the five animals were particularly strong. Reynald had to go to the city of Nuuk and start his new life there as a terrestrial. He knew that he had to be careful not to lose his way in the middle of this white plain. He took all he needed to nourish himself and to make a fire. The journey was going to last at least a dozen days.

During the journey, he started writing down all the information he had memorized before leaving Heaven. His account started like this...

"This story will let you travel through time, live the life of different characters, immerse yourself into the different periods and various religious beliefs that exist. You will live through the eyes of many innocent people. The hardness of my tale takes its roots in the obscurity of the evil locked up on our planet, the evil which expresses itself in the desire of men to seize power over other people. But as long as the physical evil exists, its opposite has to exist as

well, in order to keep the balance between both of them. All the choices made by love serve as the shield against the evil. Through life and death, between the earth and Heaven, through time and seasons, men and women have to untangle the mystery of this grievous story. In this compendium I will mention, as precisely as my memory permits it, the moves and the actions of these heroes that created this unique feeling, proper to their species: love."

CHAPTER TWENTY-SEVEN
"DESTINIES COLLIDE" *Everyone meets up?*
JAPAN

Tonobu "Roshi" traveled to the ancient temple in the center of Hamanashi City.

The streets were calm, and the moonlight seemed to freeze everything that tried to move. Henchmen from the Roshi clan had come to get rid of him. What was supposed to be simple revenge was about to become a terrifying slaughter. Tonobu was a strong warrior, but armed with the legendary katana he was virtually invincible.

He entered the temple gently, assassinating a few men and disemboweling them. The fight lasted a few hours and many of the men he killed never even saw him coming.

At the center of the temple was a garden where the final confrontation took place. Each dead henchman from his own clan left a trace of himself in Tonobu's spirit.

In the garden he created a moment of panic. The temple was completely devastated and the final fight took place on a white floor, with only a few trees left.

After the confrontation, Tonobu escaped his village, leaving dozens dead in his wake. He himself was injured.

He took his horse and headed north, setting out on a long journey. Still losing blood, he arrived at the old sanctuary. He arrived at the entrance just as he loses consciousness.

The darkness turns to blinding light as Heaven appears and then fades away. Eddie Tonobu knelt inside his temple sanctuary praying to his God...

DAKOTA
Buddhist Temple

Eddie exited the Buddhist temple of the city he was in, Dakota. The police units were waiting for him; he was determined to end this enquiry today.

Numerous amounts of evidence gathered in New York and in Little Rock made it possible to find the suspect. Now at last came the moment to arrest the killer.

There were two dozen police cars and the US Marshal truck.

Eddie got into the car and he could feel the tension. It was thick enough to cut with a knife. A few miles between the center of the city and the small cabin felt like an eternity.

A helicopter could be seen in the air, following the dozen police cars as they headed up the narrow trail to the cabin. The police arrived at full speed and skid to a halt in front of the small, discreet cabin.

Eddie opened the car door and put his foot out on the ground.

*****

SEASONS OF HEAVEN

HEAVEN ~~I can't determine if people are~~ dead
As James seemingly lay in a coma, his but it
mind went somewhere else. It traveled across seems
time and space and settled in the life of his
father. He was able to see Lionel Marshal; the that
detective as he investigated his last case...James way.
lived the time through his father's eyes. The case
was related to the Banished and to Monster.

James found himself...or his father really, standing in front of the entrance to the woods. There was a road sign in front of him with the name of the village written on it. It's red and white like the village signs in France. His father was about forty years old and his age shown through slightly in streaks of gray in his hair and beard. His hair was slicked back from his face and he was wearing an old leather jacket. In his right hand he held an old colt .45 and in his left a radio controlled trigger. He leaned back against an old 1950's Renault.

Lionel was talking on the radio, informing his back-up that he is about to go to somewhere.

SEASONS OF HEAVEN

Twenty-three children were missing, accompanied by two teachers, they had just totally disappeared. It had been nine months since any of them had been seen.

Lionel entered the forest. He was hyper-alert, vigilant. On his path, it began to rain. It was a cold autumn day, and as he walked he could feel the ravens observing him. When he gets closer to them most of them fly away in a rush. The twigs and branches on the ground snap and creak under Lionel's weight. After about twenty minutes of walking, Lionel is guided by the children laughter. It seemed to be carried to his ears on the gentle autumn breeze floating through the trees. Other than the laughter, the sounds of nature, trees rustling and ravens calling played in the background.

Directly in front of Lionel was a fence made of stone and behind that, an old castle.
The castle consisted of two twisted towers that made a dark and morbid impression on the sky behind it. The stones were grey and some of

them were completely covered in ivy. On either side of the stairs that climbed up into the dark and spooky castle, two stone lions stood guard.

Lionel notices there were roundabouts and swings. He got the impression that children were not far away. He needed to enter the castle to better assess the whole situation.

Moving slowly, he approached the entrance, pushed open the glass door and snuck inside. The temperature inside the stone castle was even lower than it was outside. He could see his own breath in the air.

Once inside he faced a long corridor. Medieval armors were posted in front of each door along the corridor. Ancient paintings clung to the walls and on his right was an old wooden table that held a bird cage. Inside the cage an ortolan sat on his swing. When he saw Lionel, he cried out.

"Shut up, old parrot!" Lionel said to it. He suddenly froze…it sounded like he'd heard someone saying his name. Listening intently, he picks up the sounds of a conversation coming from somewhere on his right.

He heard a man say, "The cop is dead, I burrowed him under the tree ... these Americans ..."

A woman's voice came next saying, "Very good ... we almost got caught ... You will have to stop playing with them!"

"I know, I know," the man said, "How many kids are left? They keep asking for more, they are so active. Are they still talking to you?"

"Oh you! You do not believe me!"

Lionel did not quite understand the conversation, but one thing was certain, a cop had been killed and some children were in a grave danger. He felt someone coming from behind him before he turned and saw him. It was a man, running towards him, carrying a sickle. Lionel shot him several times and the man collapsed. The gunshots resonated throughout the castle. Lionel ran through the corridor, taking the door on his left and closing it behind him. He heard the voices coming closer.

He crossed the room and saw that there was a huge mirror in it. The decor was quite strange; it looked a little bit Chinese.

He was facing a door. He opened it slowly and was faced with complete darkness. Stepping in he realized it was a stairwell. He took the first two but his foot missed the third one and he fell down about six feet before he hit the ground. His arm hit so hard that the sound of his bones breaking screamed out across the room. Lionel screamed too, losing his gun as he hit the ground. He immediately reached his left arm out to search for it, but he groped around in the dark vain. He was startled then by a strong light cutting through the darkness. He blinked several times until his pupils adjusted just enough to allow him to see a silhouette.

It was a man with a mask, sitting on a wooden horse, a medieval instrument of torture. His mask had pointed and shapeless ears, scarce hair and a terrifying face. It was like the face of a harlequin made out of plastic, and melted in a few places.

The man was holding Lionel's weapon ...

"You can't do anything, they command us ... we execute ..." the man said.

He took aim at Lionel's head with the cop's own weapon and pulled the trigger. The bullet passed cleanly through Lionel's head. The man with the mask crossed the room on his wooden horse and leaned over Lionel as the blood rushed from his head and pooled underneath him on the floor. . Then he climbed off the horse and a violet substance oozed out of his body and penetrated Lionel's.

HEAVEN

The transformation was complete... James had become the Monster. James opened his eyes and looked at his hands.

"What was that nightmare?" He wondered.

He could feel something new inside his chest. It was an unknown sense of power. The color of his skin looked violet to him and all around him he could see the same forest as before only the colors were different. Everything looked as if he were wearing a pair of colored sunglasses.

He pulled himself up and as he did he noticed that he was strangely taller, closer to the tops of the trees. There were white and black flashes all around him, making it difficult to see. It took him several minutes to process what was happening but it finally dawned on him that he was no longer himself. The voices he used to hear outside of his head were now inside. The substance all around him and inside of him were the creatures that had been following him. He was lost...no longer in control of himself. The Banished had control of his body now and they would progressively destroy anything that was left of him.

James could hear their voices in his head, expressing their desire to conquer the Earth.

✶✶✶✶✶✶

HEAVEN TOWER

The young companions were getting ready to climb the second tower. The way up seemed as difficult if not more so than the first one. It was full of traps. Ani was panting, the day was about to end and the sun was still hot. Ani used any little shadow to protect himself. Yann was doing his best not to feel dizzy he didn't think it would be a good idea when they were up so high.

Once on the top of the high tower Yann and Ani, in a complete silence, saw above them an airplane. There was no sound and the plane was leaving behind a luminous trace. It was an unrealistic scene.

SEASONS OF HEAVEN

On the top of the tower, Yann and Ani activated the mechanism and the second tower started sinking into the ground, rotating on itself. They had to go down quickly again, avoiding all sorts of traps. On the way down Yann notices that the white silhouette is with them again.

"Follow me!" she told them.

Yann and Ani had made it, they activated two towers. The white shape accompanied them all the way down. The night was coming fast and the incredibly bright, close stars began to shine. The friends followed the voice that led them into the forest, in the direction of the Infinity Field when suddenly a shrill cry rang out all through Heaven. The monster was following them, hot on their heels, and it seemed furious. The boy and his dog began to run with everything they had inside of them as the hideous monster chased them. It was hard to breathe as he got closer to them, it was as if his evil reached out somehow and stole the oxygen from the air.

SEASONS OF HEAVEN

They ran through a wheat field and were surprised to find a sparkling door frame in the middle of it. The light from it became stronger as they approached and they could see a long corridor stretched out inside of it. Yann and Ani realized before they reached it that the Monster had caught up. They threw themselves to the ground and curled into a ball for protection. Strangely, the Monster passed above them and headed to the door frame. It threw itself to the door and as it reached it, black shadows began to dislocate themselves from it and one by one they passed through the door.

Yann, Ani and the white silhouette sat in horrifying witness of all of this. It was a disturbing sight and they were helpless to do anything about it. Something abysmal had just happened, the Banished left Heaven and made its way to Earth.

On the ground, was a man who had been left behind by the shadows. He pulled himself up and with his hands on his head he looked around, confused.

"Where am I? Ah, my head ..."

"Who are you, sir?" Yann asked him.

"Eh...I don't know. They were in my head!" he yelled out loudly, "Where are they? Oh my God, they managed to do it..."

"What are you talking about? Please, calm down, you're in shock..."

"The Banished ... I heard them in my head ... They want to destroy the Earth ... They want the children ... Oh no, what have I done?" His voice and his facial expressions were a mixture of horror and anguish. Then suddenly, he stopped talking. He was staring the space between Yann and Ani. The silhouette that for them had only been a white shape for James was much more. It was Sarah...his wife. He'd found her at last.

"My dear Sarah!"

"I see you ... Finally," she told him.

"I missed you so much, I..." James was crying.

"You know each other?" Yann asked, confused. There was nothing but silence for several minutes before he went on to ask, "You are the voice, aren't you?"

"Yes, my dear boy," Sarah told him before looking back at James.

She put both of her hands on the sides of his face and said, "I know what you've been through ... but it is time to go now!"

"I thought I lost you forever ... We have to stop them, you know what they want, don't you? They want to take back all our hope!"

"You can't do anything more in this life, you have done so much already. I love you. I love you, do you know that? Trust me; you will be able to help in another life."

"How is that? Another life? Is this the end of the journey?" Yann asked.

"No, my boy, this is only one stage of this long trip ... This life is much longer than the life itself ... But it is time to go now, we have to move."

"And our son?" James asked her, "Thomas? Did you see him?"

"He is waiting for us on the other side of the season ..."

"I let them do what they wanted ... that was them who killed our son ... all they want is children ... and me, ah, what did I do, I was so weak ..."

"You must not feel guilty ... You did everything you could ... Come, it is time to leave all of this to others ... We are going to find our son."

"Yann, can I have the pendant...the one that I gave you to track the monster?"

Yann took the pendant from around his neck and gave it to Sarah. James was looking at it with wide eyes as she held it out to him. "Thomas's pendant. I thought I'd lost it...."

"No, Yann's been keeping it safe for you," she said. Sarah had known that as long as Yann held the relic the monster...James would not be able to harm him. It was all that James had left of his son and he had cherished it.

"Do our parents wait for us as well? On the other side?" Yann asked her.

"Yes, this is a magical place; you will find your parents there. Just pass this door …" she told him.

Yann went closer to the door and Sarah crouched down in front of Ani,

"But you, my dear, your time did not come yet! You still have some things to do in here … You know that, don't you? You are the only one to know this place as anyone else and you love the Earth so much … I can see it in your eyes …"

"But why? How? No, I want you to come with me, Ani!" Yann scooped the little dog up into his arms and held him against his chest. "I love you; you know …

"Do not worry, he will be happy, trust me," Sarah told him.

SEASONS OF HEAVEN

Tears were streaming down Yann's face as he clutched on to the little dog. If one looked closer, they could see the tears gathering in Ani's eyes as well. Yann looked at Sarah with wide, pleading eyes and said,

"You don't understand, to take him away from me is the same as if you cut out a piece of my heart...Ani and I need each other...

Sarah gave Yann a sympathetic look and said, "It's hard to understand, I know. It's just not his time. His work on earth is not finished."

The tears flowed down Yann's cheeks and spilled onto Ani's shiny coat. He told her, "I don't know how to say good-bye to him."

Sarah smiled and said, "Just tell him how you feel, from your heart."

Yann held the little dog so that they were face to face. He was holding him so tightly against his chest that he could feel the little dog's heartbeat and it felt like it had merged with his own. "You're not just a part of my heart, Ani. You are imprinted on my soul. I will never, ever forget you. I'm going to love you until time no longer exists. You will always be my best friend. I love you, so much and I will wait for you...forever if I have to."

His words were hard to understand because as he said them he was sobbing so hard that he could barely take enough air into his lungs to speak. His longing for Ani was a physical ache in the center of his chest and the little dog had yet to leave his arms. He didn't know how he was going to let him go.

As if she could read his thoughts, Sarah said, "You can do this Yann. You can do this because you hold not only love in your heart for each other, but now you also have hope in your heart for the day when you'll be reunited."

Yann hugged his dog once more and Ani whimpered, sadly. Whispering in the little dog's ear Yann said, "I'm not going to say good-bye old friend. I will say so long for now. I'll be waiting for you. Take care of Shirley for me. Kiss her and

SEASONS OF HEAVEN

remind her of me and how much I love her...I love you Ani!

CHAPTER TWENTY-EIGHT
"NEW BEGINNINGS"
SHIRLEY'S APARTMENT

Ani opened his eyes slowly ... The sound of Sarah's voice telling him that his time hadn't come yet still resonated in his ears. He looked around to see that he was now lying on the wooden floor in Shirley's apartment.

Shirley was panicking, trying to resuscitate Yann. She'd already called for the ambulance and the dispatcher told her the police were on their way as well. She used mouth-to-mouth resuscitation but it wasn't working and she was becoming desperate. There were pills scattered across the floor, the same ones that Yann had taken at the orphanage. Ani got himself up and Shirley was looking at him with despair in her eyes.

"Oh, my God, please, help me!" The tears flowed like a river down her lovely face and she sat on her knees in the floor. Ani went to her and

[handwritten margin note: Yann was in coma due to possible drug O.D.]

she took him into her arms and hugged him tightly against her chest. The ache inside of her was so deep that she had to scream to let it out or her chest would have ripped wide open.

The ambulance attendants rushed in through the door she'd left open and started taking out their equipment. Ani wiggled loose from Shirley's grasp and went over to nestle himself against Yann's cheek. He lay down next to his best friend and closed his eyes.

Two flashes take place between the best friends and suddenly they're together again in the midst of a magnificent field for a short instance...a train was not far.

∎∎∎

NEW JERSEY HAMPTON CEMETARY
Five days later.

Late in the morning, Shirley, Matt, Eddie and Ani were in front of the Northman's tomb. Shirley leaned over Yann's stone and kissed it. Matt stood next to her, deeply moved by her grief. On his shoulder was a bag with a very old book sticking out the top and in his hand was a bouquet of magnificently bright colored flowers. He laid the flowers down on the tomb and stepped back to make room for Eddie.

Eddie looked rough and haggard. His hair stuck out from his head in different angles and there were deep, dark circles underneath his eyes. He leaned down and took Ani into his arms, stroking his head gently. No one was speaking and only the sounds of nature and the distant hiss of traffic penetrated the silence. They were each lost in their own sense of grief, pain or longing as the brilliant sun shone down upon them.

Eddie had initiated a probe into the orphanage after what happened to Yann. He was still on the other case, but the men who headed up the probe kept in touch with him. One of the detectives told him about what a strange man the director, Mr. Pratt was. In spite of his important status, they had found strange things he used to dress himself up in in his room. He'd made something of a shrine to Miss Pratt, his assistant which they found strange as well.

The boys had told them many stories, once they were sure Pratt wouldn't be around to punish them any longer. They told horror stories of neglect, mistreatment and abuse that seemed to often be of the military torture variety. One of the boys told them that after Yann escaped the first time he was punished for several days by Mr. Pratt. Part of the punishment the man liked to dole out was isolation. It was a terrible thing for a young boy to be deprived of any sight or sound other than four small walls and his own cries.

Pratt had tried to refuse to leave the orphanage, rambling on about his closet and how he couldn't leave it. He said the voices told him secrets about disappearing children and other dark things. That caused the police to check out any local disappearances, but none were connected to Pratt. He was forced to leave and he lost his license. The orphanage was closed and the children re-located.

Mr. Pratt now lives on the streets and is often seen shouting at the voices in his head.

DAKOTA SUPERMARKET

The stocky man was doing his shopping in a small grocery. He whistled leisurely as he put milk and cornflakes into his cart. Taking them up to the counter, he paid for his purchases and put them in a paper bag. He smiled at the cashier, at everyone around him and at no one in particular. He took his groceries out to his car and once he was inside he began to drive towards the forest.

He drove as far as the forest path and then parked the car. Taking his shopping bag he slammed the car door and took the small set of stairs that lead up to a small cabin.

Inside the cabin was really small. It was cluttered with things that were mostly used by a hunter. There was a cross-bow hanging on one wall and a couple of rifles leaning against another. The place was dusty but there were prints on the floor where the dust had been disturbed recently by someone's boots. A pile of clothes was heaped in one corner, jackets and blue jeans and men's underwear. The place smelled of dirt and old sweat and had an underlying smell of decaying meat. There was very little furniture and what there was looked as if it had been fashioned out of logs and stacked up to form a chair or a table. There were no real pictures or photographs on the walls, but the ones that were there were hand drawn and all of the banished. One wall was lined with small backpacks in various styles and colors, leaning there as if the children would be returning for them soon.

    There was a small sketch of a door frame on the wall and as Frank carried his groceries over to the counter a black shape passed through it. There was a simultaneous knock on the front door. His first instinct was to pick up his knife and hold it behind his back. The kitchen counters were full of knives, not the kind you buy for culinary use, but the ones with the serrated edges that were used for hunting…and killing. The knocking got louder and more impatient…Frank touched the handle of his knife and went over to the door, opening it abruptly.

Frank stood frozen as he finally laid his eyes upon the Banished. His face registered first shock and then turned quickly into a smile. Nobody had ever cared about him and finally, someone was paying attention.

"Finally, we meet each other …"

■■■

END OF SEASONS

Many trains came through the seasons as Yann waited for Ani. It was a beautiful, happy place and Yann had grown content here passing the time and convening with nature in the arms of his loving parents as he waited for his best friend Ani to join them.

When Ani arrived on one of the trains at last, the two friends rejoiced in their reunion. Yann picked up the little guy and hugged him into his chest tightly, never wanting to let him go again. He'd been happy here, but without Ani he hadn't felt complete.

"Come Ani, I want to show you around."

Ani followed Yann across the expanse of rich, jade grass and in between two grand trees that marked the entrance to a forest. The leaves on the trees were rich with color, oranges, yellows and reds lit them up as if they were on fire and the flames were licking up towards the sky. Thousands of colors floated slowly to the ground as the leaves shed from the trees. Every so often one would softly brush against a cheek or land on a shoulder. The sounds of the natural opera around them made them want to dance and as they danced their way further into the forest they discovered even more of nature's magic.

Here and there brown squirrels with big, fluffy tails chased their acorns across the roots and soil. When one was caught they would sit and nibble quietly at it and the look in their little eyes made it apparent they were savoring it. Yann and Ani realized that the group of squirrels was a family. The mother squirrel was just a little bigger than the other and Ani wondered if she was expecting. He went towards them slowly and then sat down where he could watch them. The squirrels took him in with their eyes and then they looked at Yann. It seemed like they were trying to communicate, but Yann was having trouble understanding their signals. He watched as one of them reached its small paw out and placed it gently on the side of Ani's face. That was when he understood. There were no words they were trying to convey...it was a feeling, the most important one of all, love. As Yann watched in awe, the little squirrel family collected around his friend in a circle. They all reached out and put one of their tiny paws on Ani's fur. At that moment, Yann had a memory of their long trip, the contact with the Shaman, and every animal along the way. After the squirrels finished offering vows to Ani, they turned and disappeared back into their trees. Ani looked at Yann and his face was illuminated by the sun. He looked happy and his eyes were shining like the surface of one of the perfect lakes they had seen on their adventure.

    Just to their left the ground began to rumble and the trees to shake. Instead of floating to the ground, the leaves began to fall by the handfuls. As the rumbling grew louder, the friends could see a massive black silhouette approaching. They were paralyzed once more simply by the virtue of how unexpected it was…and how magical. A huge black rhino was coming in their direction. Yann knew that the black rhino was one of the rarest on earth. His father once told him that legend said they have been here so long that they have seen everything about the history of the humankind. This beautiful and massive creature walked past them with a glance in their direction, but he didn't stop. The boys watched him until he was gone and then moved on. After coming out of the other side of the dense forest they arrived at the edge of a huge cliff. The trees were thick along the slope of it and each one grew in a different shape and direction. The artist's pallet was never as rich as the colors that danced around them. The vibrant hues of Autumn had arrived on the new chill that crept in to the air. It wasn't the bite of a wintery bluster, but just a nip to let them know a new season was at hand. Beyond the nature coated leaves of the trees the brilliant blue sky was blanketed with soft clouds that attempted to block out the brilliant glare of the sun as it began to descend in the sky, preparing itself for a night's rest.

Yann and Ani go closer to the cliff's path. The void was infinite as the air passed through it. From a distance they could see the plain with its usual flow of life.

Yann's wings begin to flap...gently at first and then harder. A luminous halo surrounded them and Yann leaned forward and took Ani into his arms. He kissed his muzzle and stroked his ears. They looked calmly into each other's eyes and the short moment seemed like an eternity. Then holding tightly to his little companion Yann ran and jumped into the void. His wings stiffened and caught on the wind. They were gliding through the air and the moment was so full of sensations that with words it would be indescribable.

As they soared across the sky the day was replaced by night and the clouds separated to reveal the stars. Yann gazed upon the constellations he loved; he could see Perseus and Canis Minor.

After a dozen minutes of flight, they were in the middle of the plain. There were numerous animals and humans. Yann suddenly felt a hand on his shoulder. It was Tim, his father. The family was finally together, and Elise took Ani into her arms.

"We've been waiting for you ..." Elise told him.

Smiling, Tim said, "Are you ready, my son? It is time to turn the page, huh? Ani, you took your time coming here." It was two long years between the time that Sarah sent Ani back to earth and the time that Ani was brought into Seasons on the train. Two full seasons had passed in Heaven and although Yann spent his days in a place that both stimulated and calmed every one of his senses, virtually wrapped in a blanket of peace and security, shadowed by the love and adoration of his parents, he had missed the part of his soul that Ani had taken back to earth with him, and he had longed for nothing more than the day they would be reunited.

Now that Ani was here, the family could enter the end of seasons and their new lives could at last begin.

"Where are we going, dad?" Yann asked his father.

"Don't worry ... "Elise told her son, "You'll see, my dear, everything will be all right!"

"Do you see that little chalet, over there?" Tim asked him, pointing to it. "This is where people are going ... Isn't this plain beautiful? Look, a flock of birds, they're flamingos! They're going to the same place we are ... We are all the same, my boy, shadow and dust. I wish our time could have been longer." Tim was crying.

"Come on, my heart, let's go. It is our new start," Elise told him.

Looking at Ani, Yann said, "Are you ready? You have so much to tell me ... It will stay engraved in our genes." The boy took the dog he loved so much into his arms for the last time. Yann and Ani would always love each other, but they would love each other in different places and in different forms throughout the centuries to come. From one life to the next, their souls would recognize each other instantly and their past lives together wouldn't be conscious memories any longer but simply the overwhelming feelings of love that happens between souls that are destined to travel through time together. As Yann held his little friend in his arms for the last time, they shared a vision; perhaps it was a hint or a reflection of another life yet to come.

TOKYO 2023

A small girl approached a tiny kitten, alone on the street. She leaned forward and took it in her arms.

In their native language of Japanese, the little girl said, "Look, Mammy, Daddy, a kitten! Can we take it home? It looks sick."

"Well," her father said, looking at her mother, "I guess we can." With a smile he said, "I think it is a girl cat, look."

"Oh yes, it is "so cute"!" the little girl said.

"You will have to give her a name, my darling," her father said.

"Darling! That's a nice name, isn't it, mom?"

******

NEPAL 1973

A man was sitting on an armchair covered with colored plaids. He seemed very comfortable. In his room, there were plenty of different trinkets. He was writing a book. His feet were stretched out close to the chimney and the fire crackled. He's almost unrecognizable from the strapping young man he'd been for so many centuries. It was Reynald and he was at last becoming visibly older with glasses and greying hair.

SEASONS OF HEAVEN

As the last descendent of the Ancient People on Earth, he's writing his memoirs. He closed the notes and stretched before getting up off the sofa. He had to pick up the little beige dog that was lying across his knees. She was a French bulldog and he put her into his jacket. At his feet another one just like her only male lay in the floor.

His wife approached and kissed him on his cheek.

"I am going to pick him up." Reynald told her, "It is time..." he sighed heavily.

"He is waiting for you up there," his wife told him.

"Thank you ... Thank you for all..." he said.

She stared at him for a long time and then smiled. Reynald left the house then, stepping out into the beautiful, clear day. The sky is a brilliant blue and the sun splashed light and color across the valley.

The little house was built high in the mountains, on the slope of a steep ridge, at the heart of Nepal. Reynald went up the green hill above their house, with the dog still snuggled inside his jacket.

A young boy sat waiting in the grass.

"Hello father," Matt said as his dad approached.

"What a beautiful day it is, isn't it? How are you today?" Reynald asked his son.

"I don't know. Did you finish?"

Reynald handed the finished book to his son and sat down next to him. They are both sitting in the middle of the deep grass, rippling in the breeze. The little dog Leia climbed out of Reynald's jacket and sat between the boy and the man.

Matt looked at the dog and said, "She follows you everywhere, doesn't she?"

"She never abandoned me ... There is no other companion as faithful as her. This is the time for you to know the truth about me as well as about the role you will play...Treat this book like a bible. Follow its rules and lead the Circle of

SEASONS OF HEAVEN

Light. The right one has to be found...the Hero that can unleash the power of the Ancient one and save our future." Reynald ran his hand through his son's hair and gave him a light hug. Matt looked down at the book in his hands. On the first page of the book, in the Navajo language it is written:

"Seasons of Heaven."

Reynald was passing on the book to his son because although he had lived a long and very productive life, he knew that it wouldn't be forever. Reynald's life eventually ended in 1974 in the city of Nepal. He was 6553 years old...

HOLLOW EARTH

After separating himself from Reynald, Olham penetrated a small cavity. At the end of it was a cave about three hundred feet long. It contained numerous stalactites and a number of horsemen wandered the cave like ghosts, protecting the remains of the ancient city. It was about 20 feet high and there were blocks of stones that hung from the ceilings with a number full of stalagmites. There were narrow holes that led off here and there into narrow blind chambers, and walls completely made of stalagmitic material. Olham passed through a widened passage sneaking in gently, that entered into another wide chamber with successive rows of pillars that were about twenty feet high. He had a plan.

He wanted to draw the attention of the horsemen so that Reynald could recover the irradiated stones.

The cave was dark, the only light coming from a yellow halo left on the walls by the ghosts.

Olham hit the ground with his walking stick, creating a beam of a blue light that smashed one horseman who disappeared in a flash. In the following second, all of the horsemen rushed towards Olham.

SEASONS OF HEAVEN

He created a sphere of energy that protected him and killed some of the horsemen that touched it.

Olham then jumped onto the rock shaped as a toboggan and began sliding. The other horsemen started chasing him.

Olham believed that now Reynald was certain to recover the stones. The old druid arrived at the bottom of the rocky ramp and started running towards an inland lake, a cold heart of the inner land.

According to the ancient stories, there were numerous connections between the inner earth and the outside, but nobody knew the details. Olham had to find the exit by himself, but at least he got rid of the horsemen. They could not touch the water because of their energetic shield.

Olham kept running until he reached the lake shore. He entered the lake slowly and progressively. He could see the horsemen out of the corner of his eye. There was a small army of them. They sat on sickeningly frail horses staring at him with eyes that were barely more than empty sockets. Their noses were completely sunken and their faces stretched tight across their skulls with teeth showing through their lips and jaw. The water was freezing cold in the swiftly running lake. It was being fed constantly by the many waterfalls that surrounded it. The sandy, rocky bank was littered with the vibrant greens and yellows of the vegetation that grew alongside and on top of it. Olham waded in, and at that moment a loud crack sounded, like a detonation.

Reynald had removed the stones from their base.

The horsemen understood at once and angry, they turned around to go after the real culprit. Olham watched them go, hoping that Reynald would have enough time to escape them. The old druid plunged into the water. Taking a deep breath, he opened his eyes. Only a small amount of light was visible under the surface of the lake. He still had his walking stick which lit up and created a sphere which he was able to breathe inside of. He knew he needed to find the exit and quickly. He moved slowly and watched as his shadow passed along the walls making him look twice his own size.

He could see a wall above him made out of rectangular stones and as he swam further he came across the remains of an old drowned city. Olham knew the story but he'd never imagined he would find the city in this cave.

It was straight and pyramidal, with a flat dome.

Meanwhile, Olham penetrated the hole and entered a long corridor. On the walls he noticed the drawings and the inscriptions in Sumerian, the original language of the Ancients.

This was where they used to live when they arrived in the Earth. Since then, their cities had become flooded. Human legend of the Mu continent was in fact a reference to these submerged cities of the Ancients.

SEASONS OF HEAVEN

Olham exited the corridor. He turned his head to see that in fact he was inside of a pyramid. From there he went inside of another small cave. The particles of phosphorescent dust moved through the water and the light beams blasted through the surface of the lake. It was an awe-inspiring sight.

Hundreds of stalactites looked like an underwater rock cemetery. When he dived in between them he could see bubbles coming from underwater channels to other caves and remnants of stone buildings that had gone to their watery graves during the floods. He swam alongside the fishs mostly in the darkness but every so often shards of light would break through the trees that surrounded the surface of the lake and illuminate the rough cold rock walls as he made his way towards the exit and put more space between him and the horsemen. At the bottom, the sand became more and more delicate and the plants appeared fluorescent green.

SEASONS OF HEAVEN

The trees became more frequent than the rocks and it started to look like an underwater forest. Olham touched the plants with his hands and left a luminous trace behind him. All of the plants began slowly waving in rhythm with Olham's moves. His stick shone irregularly as the lake became shallow.

Olham kept his head out of the water then, his feet were still in a sort of lagoon. Outside, the rocks and the air dust are sparkling.

In front of him a unique landscape was laid out and from the ceiling grew an apple tree. Olham seemed to not even notice the abnormality of it. It was because the old druid knew where he was going all along…and what he would find when he got there.

He made his way to the center of the space and looked up at the tree, and then down at his feet. There was a stone there that looked like a grave, covered with white, fine sand. Underneath it rested the bodies of the Ancients. It was a sacred place…a sacred tomb. The cave was cut into the mountainside and was a cross between jagged outcroppings and smooth brown rocks. The rocks were piled deep on the ground underneath Olham's feet and a tree grew out of them not far from where he stood. The rays of the sun penetrated down into the crevice, striking the rocks and the tree and encouraging the growth of moss across the moist ground. Olham stood on a high, flat rock and opened his right hand. A shower of fiery, dancing sparks shot out. They swirled around above Olham's head, lighting up the walls of the cave like a beacon. The old druid's eyes sparkled underneath the intensity of it all and his silver beard looked almost luminescent in its wake. A long, dark shadow stretched out behind him and seemed to move independently as if casting its own incantations. Then suddenly the sparks began to come together just above the palm of the hand Olham still held open. Little by little they joined and at last they formed a circle of light that seemed to capture him within it. The light spun around him quickly, shooting off sparks again in every direction and when it came to rest once more, Olham was left with a weapon in his hand. The weapon was an axe that had been used by Olham's descendants. It was strong with Ki, spiritual energy and Olham knew this was the only way to destroy the Banished and be rid of the evil ones once and for all.

****

CHAPTER TWENTY-NINE

2047 Present time somewhere...

"Dad, how do you know so much?" Nina asked him. "Who is in the tomb in Heaven?"

"How do you know all of this detail?" Ana asked. The girls were intrigued by the story, but confused about how their father knew it so intimately.

"I have spent a very long time trying to protect the precious elements of the world. I have learned a lot, and I want you to know the whole story so that someday you can help to change the world too."

"There is a lot to remember," Ana said, "How do we save the world? Our world is a mess Dad, all we have to do is look around to know that."

Her father gave her a gentle smile and said, "I promise that you will understand at the end of the story. We can change it and make it

Preventing the world from becoming terrible basically

right this time. It's just going to take a lot of heart and a lot of love."

To be continued...

SEASONS OF HEAVEN

THANK YOU SO MUCH FOR READING MY BOOK

« Lorsque vous êtes dehors et que les arbres bougent au grès du vent, rappelez vous toujours qu'ils dansent pour nous »

N.A

SEASONS OF HEAVEN

Any RIP April 8th 2012

SEASONS OF HEAVEN

Thanks

Mariana Augusto

Anthony Augusto, Denise Augusto, Manuel Augusto, Laura Augusto, Julien Fiocco, Mamie Claude, Mickael Garin, Grant Wilson, Julie Tirard, Gregory Delfosse, Scott, Benoit Iles, Ru Weerasuriya, Ben Mottier, Julien Chièze, Céline Tran, David Hallyday, Kris Zimmerman, Laurent Quessi, Johann Blais, Tom Crago Najib Zighed, Margot Malgorzata, Nassim Redjem, Gregory Benazech, Brian Flemming, James Helssen, Ariko Kimoto, Abe Masamichi, John Melchior, David Stelzer, Carrie Stelzer, Oscar Araujo, Gilles Lartigot, David Fréscinaux, Mylène Baradel, Alex Dracott, Ian Wittaker, Javier Garcia, Austin Farris, Sam, Gino, Kevin, my frirends, all the Rippers and every readers around the universe.

SEASONS OF HEAVEN

29° 58' 33.8"   31° 07' 49.5"

Made in the USA
Lexington, KY
22 May 2017